CAN'T WE JUST PRETEND?

E.M.MAVIS

CONTENT WARNING

This book contains depictions of:

Harassment

Grief

Anxiety

Other Books by E.M.Mavis

<u>Contemporary</u>

Always Back To You

<u>Fantasy</u>

Sophia's Requiem

To Kyle,

I love you

Chapter One

The last thing I want to do is go to a nightclub on my twenty-first birthday. Originally, I had planned a meal with my best friend Jeremy before he left me for his month-long vacation to Hawaii, the traitor. I'm not at all jealous of his vacation *or* the fact he is leaving me for an entire month to soak up the sun, whilst I wither away in my office.

Tonight we were supposed eat a lot of food, gain about ten pounds, and legally get drunk until I forgot why we were celebrating.

Those plans are now out of the window, all thanks to my selfish boyfriend Simon. He pestered me all the way up until last night, begging that we visit a local nightclub in town. Insisting that it will be the greatest night of our relationship, which I refuse to comment on, now that he can actually take me to bars to drink.

It's just another example of him knowing very little about his girlfriend, after five years of being in a relationship it's like he's meeting me for the first time. It's not like I haven't told him that big crowds, and blaring music, really isn't my thing. Every time we talk about my interests and dislikes it is in one ear and straight out the other.

I would much rather be with Jeremy tonight, giggling about which celebrity has the best ass. The answer is *always*

Zac Efron, to which Jeremy would respond with a glare.

But because I am weak and can't stand for an argument to last more than I day, I caved. I got so fed up with Simon's constant nagging about this nightclub that I agreed to it. It was very clear that if we didn't go, he would sulk for months and make me feel like shit about it. I didn't feel like having his glooming ghost over my shoulder on my birthday.

Jeremy was understanding, albeit disappointed, when I had to cancel plans with him. I was eager to have him to myself before he gets on his flight tomorrow, but I promised to make it up to him when he gets back.

A month without Jeremy, I might actually go insane.

"Are you excited for tonight?" My mother clears away my plate the second the last piece of bacon enters my mouth. It's hard to get excited when it wasn't my plan in the first place. Tonight was supposed to be *my* night, celebrate *my* birthday, but once again Simon had to make it about himself.

Eating breakfast at my parents house seemed like a better option than spending the morning of my birthday alone and dreading tonight. Mom always cooks the best breakfast, there has to be some secret technique that she uses to make the bacon extra crisp because I can't seem to replicate it in my apartment.

More of my thoughts are plagued by anger because of Simon. I didn't think he liked drinking, not in a nightclub, anyway. I can't remember the last time he mentioned going out for a meal in a restaurant never mind a bar, god knows he's never taken me.

"I guess," I position my long chestnut hair out the way of my chest so it sits over my back.

"I think you should let your hair down for once," Mom says from the sink, as she scrubs the dirty dishes clean. "You've been so focused on work I bet all you see is computer screens!"

She's not wrong. For a moment I thought the crest on Dad's shirt was the Photoshop logo.

"And you only turn twenty-one once."

"Please do not encourage her to misbehave," Dad drops his newspaper and slumps down his shoulders in defeat. "We have a son for that already."

Mom removes her rubber gloves and places them over the tap, moving to kiss Dad lightly on the cheek before wrapping her arms around his neck. "Lucy is a smart girl — " I hate how they talk as if I am not right in front of them. They might have actually forgotten, as Mom keeps planting small kisses over Dad's cheek. "Besides, Simon will be with her."

"Mmm," Dad makes a disapproving sound. I knew I was too hasty to introduce Simon to my parents, mostly my dad. We've been dating for five years and I still think *now* would have been too soon. They were polite enough, but I know both of my parents. They grew to dislike Simon more and more, and they still aren't happy that I am dating a guy who hasn't worked a day in his life. It didn't help that he dropped out of high school the week I introduced them.

Simon dropped out to pursue a career in streaming video games. I try to be supportive of it, but when he can only accumulate three viewers after five years? Then maybe it's time for him to be realistic, accept that's not the career destined for him. As a hobby, he could stream to his heart's content. But as a job...

I will never forget the day we all got together for a meal at a nice restaurant. Mom and Dad had met Simon previously, as he was Harry's (my older brother) best friend. That was already a strike against him, although there were many that night. The final, and knock out of the park, was when he grabbed my ass as we were leaving the restaurant. Certainly not something a father would want to catch happening to his (at the time) sixteen year old daughter.

When Harry found out Simon and I were dating, and we kept it secret for almost a year...let's just say that Simon's nose didn't have a crook in the centre when we started dating.

Over the years my brother hasn't fully accepted that we are together. He pretends like the other doesn't exist when we see each other separately. Harry will actively avoid any situation, any social gathering, if we're together as a couple. I've tried to make amends with him, tried to talk to him, but I receive the same answer every time.

It's fine.

I don't care.

Do what you want.

I oddly want my brother to be mad about it, I want him to show me how he really feels. I know he is lying when he says 'it's fine.' It's as clear as the sky in summer that he hates it, that he's angry with me. I just hope I can repair the relationship between my brother and I, one day.

The rest of my birthday goes by in a blur. I get some wonderful gifts from Mom and Dad, most noticeably a silver necklace with a heart-shape locket that I was eyeing up at the local jewellery store. Nothing can slip past Mom, she must have caught me staring at it when we went shopping a few weeks ago. Even if you think you have snuck something past her advances she is somehow always one step ahead.

Nothing from Simon, not that I am surprised. Maybe he will take my breath away with a gift from my dreams.

Doubtful.

I get dressed for my night out at my small apartment. I wear my new necklace with my blue silk dress, that cuts straight above my knee. It has a slight reveal of cleavage that I'm not used to, but I want to try and feel a little bit more confident on my birthday. Maybe I will actually get a compliment from Simon, and not have to force one out of him.

I curl my hair and pin a few pieces back to reveal my square jaw. I couldn't decide between having my hair up or down, so I went with half and half.

I only apply a small bit of make-up, anything more than mascara and eyeliner gives me a headache.

I take a cab to the nightclub, no point in driving, and wait for Simon outside. It's freezing tonight, I knew I should have put on a jacket. All I can do is pray that Simon doesn't keep me waiting too long. He did promise that he would be here before me because he knows that I hate waiting, especially outside of places like this. Ten minutes pass without a single sign of him. I check my phone every few minutes and not even a text to say he is running late. I'm still pissed he hasn't wished me a happy birthday. Not a call, not a text, nothing.

I should wait for him to make the move, wait for him to call to prove a point. However, the rational side of me knows that it will achieve nothing but satisfy my pettiness, and that has won in too many situations. I knock my head back and release a loud grunt. I dial his number and he finally picks up after the fifth ring.

"Hello."

"Do you even realise what day it is?" I snap, feeling tired of his excuses already.

"Friday?"

If I wasn't in public I would shove my phone into my mouth and bite it in half. "Try again."

"I don't know, Lulu."

I cringe at the nickname. A name that had me swooning at sixteen during his flirtatious winks, and sneaking around to see me behind my brother's back. Now I want to rip out his tongue whenever he refers to me as it.

I shouldn't be surprised that he's forgotten. What did I expect from a twenty-three year old man that still acts like he is eighteen?

"Don't *Lulu* me. I'm waiting outside of The Phoenix, where you were *supposed* to meet me for birthday drinks. Remember that? The place that *I* didn't even want to go to but you begged me, and *yesterday* I agreed."

"Oh shit!" I can imagine him scrambling, maybe even falling out of bed. I hope he lands on a piece of *LEGO* and is in pain for the rest of the night. "Lulu, I'm — "

"You knew that I had plans with Jeremy!" I yell down the phone, not caring that I'm in public and people are eyeing me up as they pass by. "You knew I was looking forward to it, and *still* you begged me to go to this fucking nightclub with you, and you don't even bother to show up!"

"Lulu…"

If he says 'Lulu' one more time I will scream.

"You know what," rage has interlaced with my blood. It finally clicks into place, the missing piece of the puzzle, I realise now that things aren't going to change. That selfishness that was present since the very beginning of our relationship hasn't gone away. Over the past five years he is still the same eighteen year old that finds farts funny. But I'm not sixteen anymore, I'm not the same girl who fell in love with him then. I'm twenty-one, a different woman who knows she deserves more than this. He's never going to grow up, and why should I settle for some guy who can't even be bothered to remember his girlfriend's birthday.

"Simon," his name is one big sigh. "I can't do this anymore. We're over."

I hang up before he gets the chance to say anything.

Tears threaten to spill from my eyes, but I refuse to break down in front of a nightclub. There are plenty of guys here who would be willing to take advantage of that.

I am single now, for the first time in five years I am a free woman. I can do whatever I want tonight without the shackles of a partner bringing me down. It's my twenty-first birthday and I am going to enjoy myself for once. I can have a fun alone, drink alone and still have a good time…right?

Drinking alone isn't as fun as I thought it would be. In movies there is always a sexy woman sitting at the bar, owning the room with her full hips and devilishly red lips, not wanting company. When I try to exude that same confidence, I look stiff and uncomfortable, and I feel like I am about to fall right off the stool I am sitting on.

It's not very sexy when I am constantly checking that my breasts haven't spilled from my dress, and tugging at the hem of the silk so I don't accidentally flash someone.

I've been here for an hour and I've spent more time rejecting drunken offers for a quickie in the bathroom than I have actually drinking.

I wish Jeremy were here, he would have been the only one that could save this dreadful night and turn it into something fun. I could text him and ask him to meet me here, but I'd feel bad because I cancelled our plans for nothing. Instead of standing my ground with my boyfriend, I let my best friend down.

If Jeremy were here he would pick my lounging body off this bar and he would dance with me until my spirits passed the stars.

He's not here. I have to somehow find a way to make the most of this dreadful night. How can I possibly do that with a broken heart stabbing against my chest? I complain about Simon every day, to Jeremy and myself, but that doesn't mean it softens the blow of a break up. That was five years of my life that I wasted.

We were supposed to grow as a couple, grow as people, but he refused to. I gave him everything. He was my first kiss, my first and only sexual partner, and first love. That's not something he could confidently say to me. I'm not even sure if I know the real him.

This break up has been a long time coming. I knew when I would confess to Jeremy that I *loved* Simon, I couldn't say it in the present tense. I don't love him anymore. It's not just today that I am realising that, I've known for quite some time now.

I'm sitting at the bar and swirling my vodka and coke around in my glass. I'm tipsy, and not in the fun way. I want to be so drunk that I forget about the pain in my heart. Maybe I overreacted, perhaps I should call him to try and hash things out. Those five years can't have been a waste.

I'm about to fish into my purse for my phone, when a man settles into the seat beside me. He looks as dishevelled as I feel. "A whisky on the rocks!" He calls to the bartender, slamming his green dollar bills on the counter. His short black hair is sticking up in multiple different directions, probably as a result of him shoving his hand into it so many times. He's already done it twice since sitting down. He's wearing a creased white shirt with a loose black tie and matching black pants.

It's as though he can feel me staring, this stranger looks over his shoulder to me. I am almost thrust off my chair at just how handsome his face is. His jaw is so sharp that it slice off my arm with a single graze, his eyes are as green as an emerald that can pierce through my soul.

"Sorry, is this seat taken?"

He's polite too.

"No, you're good." I force an awkward smile.

The bartender arrives with this stranger's drink and I knock back the rest of mine.

"Rough night?" He asks me, with a quirk to his lips. Oh god, he even has dimples! What I wouldn't give to reach out and trace them with my fingers.

Maybe I've too much to drink, I have a sudden urge to

climb onto his lap and run my fingers through his hair.

"Well, I broke up with my boyfriend of five years about an hour ago, and I am drinking alone on my twenty-first birthday." I purse out my lips and drop my shoulders. "So, a successful night I would say."

The stranger nods and takes a sip from his whisky.

I turn back to my own empty glass, awkward and embarrassed to be sitting next to such a hot guy.

"Happy birthday" he says.

"Thanks," I roll my eyes and order another drink.

The emerald of his iris is focused intently on his glass as he purses his lips, swirling the brown liquid around as he ponders something.

"Are you…here alone?" I'm not sure why my stomach knots at the thought of him here with another girl. How gorgeous he is, he could have any girl he wanted.

A smirk threatens the corner of his mouth. I wonder how he would taste, I bet his lips are softer than a cloud. "What if I am?"

It's probably because of the alcohol, and he is hot as hell, but my cheeks flush a crimson red. My fingers grip onto my glass tight enough that I could shatter it.

This stranger takes note of my demeanour and that ghost of a smirk has resurrected, flashing his perfect white teeth. He leans into me until his lips are inches away from my ear, and whispers. "Why don't we get a booth? So we can have some privacy?"

I swallow past the lump in my throat, my body suddenly yearning for this man to touch me in the most inappropriate ways. This is reckless, outlandish, and certainly not something I would normally do.

When I pull back and lock my gaze to his, I am completely under his spell. I part my lips and let out a rough sigh.

I could walk away right now. Tell him I am not interested

in having 'privacy' with him. There is a larger part inside of me that *wants* this. I've had a crappy night. I'm newly single, for the first time in years. What could be the harm in having a one off fling? People do this kind of thing all the time, heck, there are even apps for this sort of thing. I can have sex with a guy and never see him again, I assume that's what a lot of guys come here for.

"I have alcohol at my place."

His green eyes drop to my lips, and I find myself inching closer. It should be illegal for a man this attractive to sit so close to someone without kissing them. "Your place it is."

Chapter Two

Oh God, am I really doing this?

Inviting a stranger into my apartment so isn't me! This guy could be anybody. Just because he's handsome as hell doesn't mean he's not a serial killer. I have known him for less than an hour and he is inside of my apartment!

My anxiety now decides to make its appearance *after* I have invited him inside.

A thousand thoughts pop into my mind to argue and contradict one another. Mostly to argue my stupid decision against how handsome this guy is.

I really wish I cleaned up a little bit. I wasn't expecting to bring anyone home tonight, I was planning on staying at Simon's but that's obviously not happening.

I kick a few of my clothes out of my path as I make my way to the kitchen. Every so often I will look over my shoulder and see him looking around my apartment, he hands buried deep into his pockets. There is a distance between us at the moment, I wonder if he can sense my nervousness?

My hands are shaking as I pull out a bottle of wine from the cabinet. I am very aware of this man's movements. Even the way he walks is sexy, like he has no care in the world.

I start to pour the red wine into two glasses when I feel

him stop directly behind me. His warm hands move my chestnut curls away from my neck, so they tumbles down my left shoulder. I become as still as a statue, the rough caress of his fingers against the back of my neck makes my breath hitch. I want to melt on the spot when the softest, feather-like lips brush against the back of my neck, making my body yearn for more.

"You've got a nice place," he murmurs against my skin, his hands slipping around my waist and pressing my behind against his erection. This simple action is enough to drive me wild.

"Thanks, I moved here not too long ago so there's still a few boxes — " I can't finish my sentence because his hands slip up over my breasts and cups them in a firm grasp.

I gasp in more of a choked sound, knocking my head back and leaning against his shoulder. He crashes his mouth over mine. This devilishly handsome man's tongue slips into my mouth, my body in a frenzied state of yearning, to be touched in every available spot. He squeezes my breasts, causing me to whimper out sounds that are foreign to even me.

One hand drops down from my breast and slides down my stomach. I wait in anticipation as he slowly positions his hand under my dress and moves my panties to the side. Every moment that he is not inside of me is like torture.

"You're not a murderer, are you?"

This causes him to pause, then followed by a dark chuckle. "If I was I wouldn't tell you." Then he clarifies. "But no, I'm not a murderer."

After what feels like a lifetime he dips two of his large fingers inside of me.

Instant gratification consumes my body as this man makes slow circular motions, resulting in me pressing my ass firmly against his crotch. I've never done anything like this before, only by my own hand. Simon would use terms like 'gross' or 'not interested' whenever I brought up foreplay for *me*. Yet, he didn't complain a single time when he'd pressure me into pleasuring him.

"That boyfriend of yours was an idiot," he's groans into my ear, as though he can read my thoughts, taking a little bite of my earlobe. "Why would anyone give up someone who feels this good?"

I can't stand it, his fingers aren't enough, I need more of him. I spin myself around, almost knocking over the glasses of wine, and kiss him firmly on the mouth. My body automatically responds by wrapping my arms around his neck and pushing my breasts firmly against his chest. I open my mouth and welcome his tongue inside. He tastes so sweet with an intoxicating burn of whisky. He kisses me so desperately like his life depends on it, pushing his face hard against mine. Neither of us can seemingly get enough, like the end of the world will kick start if we stop for just a moment.

This is intense, and so sudden. I have never been so bold, so forward with a guy but this feels right. For once I can shut off my brain and enjoy the sweet taste of his lips.

Our kisses are wet and deep. He grabs my thighs and positions my legs to hook around his waist. When I secure myself in place, he carries me to my couch and drops down so I'm straddling him. I have never been so turned on by a guy before, and it happens to be someone I met only an hour ago.

"Can I at least know your name?" I pant as his lips trail down my jaw and throat.

"Will." He answers as his fingers graze against my thigh and slip around my ass. "And yours?"

"Lucy." It comes out as a strangled gasp, when he moves his hands to clutch both of my breasts, and I grind against his hard excitement beneath me. This is so erotic. Sex has never felt so passionate before, and we haven't even done it yet. With Simon he would just climb on top of me and fuck me until he was done. But this, the way Will's hands search my body, fuelling my senses with pleasure is something I want to kick myself for not trying sooner.

"Nice to meet you," he groans against my skin. "Lucy."

I roll my eyes at the sound of my name coming from his lips. How can he make that so sexy? Countless people have said my name, it's very common, but he somehow makes it sound unique.

His large hands explore my back, and my hips buck in response to his hard bulge beneath me. I grind against him, his arousal causing me to spiral deeper.

Will pushes his face against mine, and a hum vibrates my throat.

His strong, muscled arms wrap around my back and he starts pulling down the zip to my dress. When his large hands are pressed flat against my skin, he ignites an even bigger flame in my core. I pull back and swiftly undo the tie hanging loosely around his neck and throw it to the ground. I go to work and unbutton his shirt, and when I see the firm lines of his muscles that have been concealed up until now, I want to kiss every inch of him.

I notice a long protruding scar down the left side of his chest. It looks like it's only recently healed, I wonder how he got something so deep?

I don't have time to think about it. Will shakes off the shirt and drops it down with his tie, now beneath me is a very attractive shirtless man, with muscles as firm as boulders.

I feel shy about my own body, Will lowers my dress down so it gathers in a pool around my waist. With no bra on to conceal my perky nipples, I feel Will's cock twitch at the sight of them. He wastes no time in popping one into his mouth and sucking on it with desperate flicks of his tongue.

I'm so close to the edge already, and we have barely done anything.

I pull away only so I can unbuckle the belt to his pants. I need him, *now*. I can't possibly last much longer with the way his touch is scorching my skin. He first pulls out a square foil from his pocket before dropping his pants, along with his black boxers. He's really going for the black and white theme today.

I drop my dress entirely. Now we are both completely naked and making out on my couch. Need I remind you that I am making out with a guy I met only an hour ago.

Will positions me with my back against the couch cushions, and my head against the armrest. He towers over me, his vibrant green eyes lighting his entire face with desire. I open my legs wider for him, and watch as he slips on the condom over his huge length. I have to swallow at the sight of it, suddenly feeling nervous.

All of those nerves vanish, as though they never existed, when he enters me. I have to bite my tongue to prevent from screaming, and alerting my neighbours that I am having the best sex of my life. With each thrust, a whimper escapes from me and I wrap my arms around his firm back and hold on for my life.

Will grunts and groans in my ear as he fills me entirely, ensuring my satisfaction with every pump.

It's only when my hands stroke his back do I feel raised textures to his tan skin. Are these more scars?

All thoughts evaporate into bliss when I roll my eyes to the back of my head, feeling so satisfied that I never want this to end. I become undone in his arms, and Will follows shortly after with a shudder and a harsh groan. He collapses on top of me, burying his face into the curve of my neck as he pants with his hot breath against my skin.

My chest rises and falls like I have just run a marathon.

The hand at my waist is clutched tightly by him, and neither one of us moves until we eventually fall asleep together in this position.

Chapter Three

I wake up the next morning with a pounding head. I didn't even drink that much last night and I still managed to get a hangover. Maybe it was from all the...

I shoot up from the couch, memories of last night flooding into my mind. Did I seriously have a one night stand only hours after breaking up with Simon? How long is an appropriate amount of time to sleep with someone else after a breakup? I have a terrible feeling that it's more than a few hours.

I look around my apartment and find it empty, not a trace of Will anywhere. He must be used to this kind of thing, meeting girls at nightclubs and going home to sleep with them. I bet he mastered the art of sneaking out without-

Flush.

I lose my train of thought at the sound of the toilet flushing in my bathroom. I scramble to put on my dress from the night before as I see the door slowly start to open. I manage to get it on in time for Will to exit, completely dressed in yesterday's clothes.

"Morning."

My face flushes at the memory of his hands all over my body. I really didn't give him enough credit last night, in sunlight he looks more like a model. With high cheekbones that force my gaze to trail up to his eyes. Those green eyes that I certainly did not waste any time in memorising the details.

"Well," he rubs the back of his head so nonchalantly, like we didn't have sex last night. He has certainly done this before. "I'm going to head out. Thanks for last night."

Why does it feel as though he just slapped me across the face? *Thanks for last night.* As if it was nothing more than a business transaction between two people. I should not care so much, but the way he said it sparked a rage in my blood.

"Listen," he looks over his shoulder as he reaches for the door. "I don't make a habit of sleeping with guys I just met."

Will rolls his eyes, it seems he has picked up on my anger and it has spiked his own bloodstream. "I don't care what you do — or who you do — in your free time. This was just a one night stand, not some start to an epic romance."

"Did I say it was?" I cross my arms over my chest.

He opened his mouth to fight back, I can tell it took a lot of restraint for him to bite his tongue. Instead he rolled his eyes and left my apartment, leaving me only with a "Whatever."

When my own front door slammed to a close I felt ridiculous standing here in last night's dress. Do all one night stands end so clumsily, or am I just bad at it?

I run my hands through my hair and let out a long sigh to expel this anger from my body. I'm pretty sure one night stands aren't meant to mean anything, they are just meant for a quick night of fun and that's the end of it.

Why did the guy have to be so good looking? I won't be able to stop thinking of his muscled body for years to come.

Before I can divulge in more memories of Will's body, the firm grip he had on my hips and the symphony of noises he made, my phone vibrates. I unlock my screen and notice I have a few missed calls from Simon. This is probably the most he has tried to contact me in the past five years.

I delete all of the notifications from him and move to my text conversation with Jeremy. He has sent me an obnoxious amount of pictures of him at the airport, waiting for his flight with his boyfriend, Josh. Selfies with his bright smile, sipping coffee and sticking out his tongue at me. I already can't wait for him to get back so I can tell him about my one night stand, he will be so proud and so appalled.

Me: I miss you already! Is it too late for you to cancel your trip entirely?

Jeremy: I love you, but not that much ;)

Me: Enjoy yourself, you deserve a holiday and I'm sorry about last night

Jeremy: Don't worry about it. Did you at least enjoy your night with Simon?

Me: Ugh. Last night was…interesting

Jeremy: Interesting? What happened? Did he propose? :O

Me: The opposite, actually. I'm now officially single

I see him attempting to write a message as the three dots appear to signify he's typing.

Jeremy: You have no idea how much I want to run out of this airport and eat ice cream with you.

Me: Make sure you eat an ice cream for me in Hawaii!

I love Jeremy. I don't know where I would be without him.

He's been my best friend ever since high school. Even when friendships came and went, we always stuck by one another no matter what. I was there for him when he worried about coming out, mostly to his dad, and he was there for me when my grandmother died. I know he will be there for me now with my break up with Simon. It will be the best excuse for us both to pig out on ice cream, and watch terrible romcoms when he gets back. Not that we've ever needed an excuse for that.

I couldn't get that jerk out of my head all weekend. I was a mixture of angry and horny throughout all of it. Work will provide some welcomed distraction to my day. I've needed it ever since Friday, even if I hadn't have slept with Will.

Simon keeps blowing up my phone with calls and texts, begging for us to get back together. Funny how he only shows signs of care when I decide I no longer want to be with him. I have been tempted a few times to cave in, even if it's just to get him to stop with the constant texts. Then I remind myself that we broke up for a reason. He will just settle right back into his ways after a week and it will become a never ending cycle of misery. For both of us.

I settle into my work easily, designing a logo that will never get used. I try to add some creative flare to the logos my company wants. Every time I hand them one of my designs, my manager and boss complains that they aren't suitable for our clients. Nope, everyone wants a sterile boring bold font, as if that will make any of them stick out from one another.

Today in particular is dragging, I've been at my desk for an hour and it shows no signs of speeding up. I decide to make myself a coffee in the kitchen. I grab my polkadot mug from the cupboard, and pour myself a cup from the pot.

People from marketing are filling the room with an

obnoxious laughter, and I keep my head down to avoid interacting with them. Everyone tends to stick to their groups. Marketing, design, sales, it's rare we mingle apart from the dreaded Christmas party.

With my fresh coffee I settle back down on my desk and stare at my screen, willing the creative juices to flow. It's hard to create something I'm passionate about, when my manager tries to put a lid on anything remotely fun.

"Lucy?" I didn't hear my manager, Sally, approach my desk. She has a habit of sneaking up on me whenever I am engrossed in my work. Her hair has been chopped into a short straight bob, highlighting the deep curves of her jaw. She's nice enough to work with, but get on her bad side and you will wish you were never born.

"Hi Sally," I continue the framework on the giant S for a finance company called *Strong Hold.* "I've got some really good ideas for this logo, I really think they are going to-"

"That's all right," she puts up her hand to silence me. "Could you join me and Mr Jefferson in his office, please?"

My throat suddenly feels dry. I can feel the eyes of other employees on me, and their pity is almost blinding. It's like they're all in on some joke that I am yet to be told, but I have a feeling I'm walking right into it now.

I follow Sally into Mr Jefferson's office, and immediately my senses are bombarded with the overwhelming stench of cologne. It's like he poured an entire bottle over the carpet, my eyes are starting to water.

Sally sits down beside the head of the company, and a lady from HR at his right. I already know this is not going to be good news, the only time a member of HR is present is when an employee has broken a company policy or is going to get fired. And I've followed the rules to a T at this place.

"Take a seat, Lucy."

I do so, my back as stiff as a board.

Mr Jefferson leans forward, his grey moustache is the perfect mask to hide any sort of emotion in his face, which only makes my anticipation much worse. "Lucy, you have been at our company for almost a year now. It is no secret that we took a risk hiring someone so inexperienced in the field of graphic design."

He's not wrong. I didn't go to college for design, instead I applied for an internship at eighteen to try and figure out if graphic design was what I wanted to do with my life. I like art, and drawing, so I thought having a career in that sort of field would be perfect for me. Mr Jefferson took me on as a full time employee almost a year ago, and I'm not blind to the struggles I have faced in this job.

"Unfortunately, although we appreciate everything you have done for us." Mr Jefferson looks me dead in the eye with his brown eyes. "I'm afraid we are unsatisfied with the work you have provided for us, and we can no longer justify keeping you in this employment."

My heart sinks like a ship, plummeting down into the depths of devastation.

"You show promise for a future in graphic design," he continued to twist the knife in further. "We just do not feel you are the right fit for our company."

In non-corporate terms, I am shit at design and they can't stand to have me here one more day. I can't say I am too surprised, but it still hurts none-the-less. I put my heart and soul into every logo design I created, and the more I got rejected the more uncertain I would feel in my own ability.

"I understand," I bite back the tears, forcing them to wait until I am alone in my car. I don't think I can hold it in until I get home. I could kick off, scream in their face that I tried to provide creative flare only to be shot down, but it's clear that nothing will change their decision and it will reflect poorly on me. I can only hope that they will give me a good reference for future jobs.

"Thank you for the opportunity."

"We wish you luck on your future endeavours." Mr Jefferson shakes my hand, and all three of them look at me and expect me to leave now that they have said their piece.

I don't want to be here much longer anyway. I get up and leave his office and pack up my things with as little drama necessary. I'm not sure how much dignity I can maintain whilst doing so, but I clamp my mouth shut to prevent from making any sort of scene in front of these people.

No one says anything to me on my way out, what can they say? Sorry you suck at design?

I prefer the silence in all honesty.

Tears are already threatening to leak down my cheeks as I stand and wait to reach the ground floor in the elevator. I manage to swallow the burning lump in my throat.

I take a brisk walk to my car, throwing my things on the back seat. I grip my hands tightly around the steering wheel until my knuckles turn white, and cry.

Chapter Four

If I read one more email that starts with, *Thank you for applying for our Graphic Design role, unfortunately...* I am going to scream this apartment building down.

Two weeks ago I was on a path to building my career, I had a boyfriend and now I am unemployed and single. I swear that nightclub put a hex on me the moment I walked through the door. Or Will did, with his frustratingly handsome face that I cannot wash away from my memory.

I bury my face into my couch cushion, in an attempt to suffocate all of these nauseating feelings from my chest.

Although my skill is all my own, I can't help but feel like I am letting so many other people down. My parents always encouraged me with my art growing up, my granddad back in England would always ask for a drawing to frame whenever I visited him. He has a section on his living room wall dedicated to my art, and just thinking of that spikes more tears.

My phone starts to vibrate, I don't check the caller ID before answering.

"I'm outside," I'm so grateful my mom has a British accent in times like these. It certainly saves a lot of time with asking who it is. "Buzz me in."

"Fine," she probably didn't hear me from speaking into a

24

pillow.

I hang up and walk like a zombie to my front door to buzz her in.

Mom walks through my door holding a bag of groceries. Instead of offering me a sympathetic gaze, she rolls her eyes at me. I can't blame her, I am still in my fluffy pink pyjamas on a Wednesday afternoon.

"I picked you up a few things from the store," she starts emptying a plastic bag on my kitchen counter and putting away various groceries.

"I have savings Mom," I meet her at the kitchen counter and rest my head against her shoulder. "I can afford food."

"I know, I just thought I would drop you off a few things." She turns to me and pinches my cheek. "Can't a mother do nice things for her daughter?"

When I don't respond, Mom pulls me at arms length and looks me dead in the eye. She used to do this on days I was feeling the most insecure at high school. I always felt I wasn't the prettiest in comparison to others, a trait that has followed me into adulthood.

"Get dressed, I am going to treat you to some new clothes."

I knock my head back. Shopping is the last thing I want to do. I want to sit around and be depressed over the countless rejections I have received for entry level design jobs.

"Go," she turns me in the direction of my bedroom and marches me inside.

There is no use in fighting with Mom. In one way or another she comes out the victor.

I'm not wearing anything nice. I slip on some black skinny jeans and a plain white t-shirt. I pull my hair back into a ponytail and apply a small bit of mascara. When I step out of my room, Mom is already waiting at the door for me. She's holding her phone out in front of her, and it doesn't take long for me to figure out she is on a FaceTime call with someone.

"You can probably cheer her up," mom says, then hands me her phone like it is as delicate as a diamond.

I hate how Mom is always right, because when I see my grandad's face take up the entire screen of her phone, my heart fills with warmth. He smiles at me like he has just met his idol in a supermarket. "How's my favourite granddaughter?"

As much as I want to pout and whine about losing my job, my grandad somehow coaxes a smile out of me. Even on my darkest of days, when I am feeling so lost, his smile sparks a light for me to follow. I just wish he didn't live in England, then I could be a ball of sunshine every day.

"I don't think Jennifer would be happy to know you still call me that, Grandpa."

He chuckles, in a husky way that sounds like he needs to clear his throat. "My favourite granddaughter in *America.*"

I can't help but laugh at that, especially with the little wink that accompanies it.

He's looking a lot older than the last time I saw him, and it was only a couple of months ago. He looks thinner, with a couple more wrinkles creased at the side of his eyes. At least his hair is still the same, an envious thick layer of white snow combed over to the left.

We visit England every year, it sucks that I won't be able to see him again for a couple of months. It's comforting to know that my Aunt Tamara and cousin Jennifer still take care of him. He's got to be pretty lonely in that house ever since my grandma passed away two years ago.

"How's your boyfriend?"

"We broke up."

"You deserve better than him anyway, honey."

"Thanks grandpa," I start to hand the phone over to Mom, until grandad's voice calls me to halt.

"Make sure you make me one of those pretty drawings.

You forgot this last visit, and I want two." Grandad has been my number one fan ever since I picked up a pencil and began drawing. My passion started as a kid, where I would draw my favourite cartoon characters before I realised I wanted a career in this sort of field. When I was a kid, I would draw a picture for my grandad upon every visit, and no matter how old I got, he still posted them up on his wall. Even now I keep this tradition with him, it helps keep me motivated. If my artwork can make at least one person happy, then it makes the climb worth it.

"I promise I will bring two next time."

"Good, now hand me over to your mother so I can use up more of her minutes."

I hand it over to Mom and she rolls her eyes, "It's the internet not — " she cuts herself off, realising it would take her a while to explain it to him. "Anyway, I'll call you tomorrow, Dad. Love you."

"Love you too," I hear him say. "And you Lucy!"

I don't get a chance to respond before they hang up, and now we are officially ready to go shopping.

I have a horrid sense of déjà vu standing by my front door waiting to go, she would stand like this when she would drop me off at school. If there is anyone to uplift me after feeling down, it's my mom. In high school if someone said my best friend would be my mom I probably would have died on the spot. Now that I'm twenty-one I can say with confidence that she *is* my best friend. Her and Jeremy often battle it out over the top spot, currently I'd say they're on equal footing.

We shop for almost two hours and I am exhausted. Mom has somehow gained more energy as she has gotten older to withstand long shopping trips. When my brother and I were kids she couldn't get home fast enough. I suppose it's less exhausting to stop every ten minutes so your kid can have a tantrum about having a household item in the shape of a cat.

Mom abruptly halts in her spot, and I panic for a moment as her blue eyes bulge out of her head.

"What? What is it?"

"That new flower store has opened!"

I glower at her, one of these days she is going to give me a heart attack over the most insignificant thing, probably a slice of cheese.

"Mom, I'm done with shopping for today — "

"It won't take long," she insists and somehow manages to open the door without dropping her bags of shopping. "I have been waiting for this store to open *forever.*"

I can't help but smile at her enthusiasm, she only gets a glint like this in her eyes when she is sitting at a piano, or when dad sneaks up to give her tender kisses. I hope I can have a relationship like theirs someday.

I step inside of the shop and immediately I am greeted by a lush aroma. All of my worries seem to have melted away at the sight of so many gorgeous flower arrangements outlining the counters. One that catches my eye is a soft pastel arrangement, made up of mostly pink roses, peach germini and a few lilac roses.

"Welcome!" A beautiful middle-aged woman calls from behind the counter. She has a smile that could light up an entire ocean. She could be the same age as my mother, perhaps a few years older. She's adorned with a bright green apron and a simple white blouse underneath. The woman meets us at the bouquet and her glossy lips stretch into an even wider smile. "These are perfect for loved ones, especially if a special someone gifts them to you."

I gathered that with the card that reads, *Especially For You* in a cursive font. I wish someone would buy me flowers, no one ever has before.

"I'm so glad you've finally opened," Mom said. "I saw the

sign a few weeks ago and I've been dying on getting some flowers for my dining room table."

The woman beams, considering how empty the store is I wonder if we are her first customers. "Did you have anything in mind?"

"Our kitchen is mostly blue, but I'd prefer to break it up with a bit of colour."

The woman immediately gets to work in arranging a bouquet of flowers. She pulls out three white roses, some wildflowers and daffodils and ties them together with a cream bow. With only a selection of three flowers she's made something quite pretty.

"That's perfect!" Mom gushes as she takes the flowers from the lady. "I'll buy them."

"I'm so glad you like it!" She says, and makes her way to the till and punches in a few numbers.

As Mom waits for the retailer to work out the change, she nudges my arm and points to a sign hanging on the back wall:

Help Wanted
Part Time
Immediate Start, No Experience Necessary

"Why don't you apply?" She drops her voice into a whisper, but I am pretty sure I saw the retailer's ears prick.

"Working at a flower shop won't exactly look good on a resume for *graphic design.*" I hiss back, feeling embarrassed that this employee can most likely hear everything I am saying.

She confirms it by saying, "You can always spin the truth on a resume." She says with a laugh, tucking a piece of her caramel coloured hair behind her ear. "We are in desperate need for a part time employee. I'd be happy to give you a job."

I stare at her, waiting for the catch. "Just like that? You wouldn't want to interview me?"

"Well, you will have the kind of passion for creativity we need if you eventually want to be a graphic designer."

That's true. Maybe I could at least keep my creative juices going working in a flower shop. I will be around vibrant colours, and working out what looks best for an arrangement, and what flowers will work for different occasions. It will certainly be better than being unemployed. Maybe when I get my confidence back I can start applying for jobs again.

"Would you like the job?"

I can't nod fast enough, "Yes please."

"Wonderful!" She reaches out her hand and I take it. We seemingly shake on it, and I can't help but smile. After being rejected so many times, it's refreshing to be wanted by someone, even if it is only part time.

"What's your name?"

"Lucy," I retreat my hand and offer a lame smile. "Lucy Wilson."

"I'm Rosie Dawson." She turns to my mother and takes her hand also.

"I'm Emma, her mother."

We start discussing my available dates that I can work. Since I am unemployed I am free every day of the week at anytime, which seems to be perfect for Rosie. My first day will be tomorrow morning at nine o'clock sharp. It doesn't give me a whole lot of time to prepare myself, but it's probably best I get thrust into it instead of allowing an entire week for me to panic and stress over the smallest of details.

"Mom, what have you done with — "

My smile fades when a tall young man steps out from the back room. He goes quiet when he sees me standing here, equally as shocked as I must look right now. Those emerald eyes, the sharp cut of his jaw, the thick raven black hair that my fingers got lost in…

Will.

"What are you doing here?" I can't seem to stop the question from passing my lips.

"My mom owns the store…" he says as if it is something I should already know, like it wasn't an obvious fact.

"You two know each other?" asks Rosie, as her green eyes — that are the complete copy of her son's — look between the two of us. I can feel my own mother looking at me with a raised eyebrow. "That will make the induction a lot easier."

"Induction?" Will asks his mother.

"Yes, Lucy will be working here. Starting tomorrow."

"What?" He snaps, he's about as happy as I would expect a man to be after hearing a girl he had a one night stand with was going to be working with his mother.

My cheeks flush and I can't get out of this situation fast enough. I grab my mom's hand and start pulling her out of the store, almost knocking her new flowers out of her hand in the process.

"See you tomorrow!" Rosie calls as I exit through the door.

I can't get back to Mom's car fast enough. I throw my bags into the back seat and stare out the front window. My heart is beating so fast against my ribcage I feel like it is going to burst out of me at any moment.

Why? *Why* did it have to be him?

Not once had I ever had a one night stand before. I always worried it would be more trouble than it was worth, and I was right. Because of all the people that had to be associated with my next job, it had to be the man that gave me pity sex.

I could always walk in and change my mind about the job. But then I would be back to square one, with no job and no idea when my next opportunity with arise.

"Who was he?" Mom asks with a knowing smile as she

fastens her seatbelt.

"No one," I lean back in my chair and lower my eyelids into a glare.

Mom makes a *hmph* sound and turns on the engine. "Didn't seem like no one to me."

Chapter Five

Rosie didn't mention anything about a dress code for the shop. I rushed out the door before I could ask any questions.

For my first day I decided to wear something similar to her homely outfit yesterday. I'm wearing an open white blouse with a black vest underneath, and my trusty black skinny jeans. I've tied my hair back into a high ponytail, allowing a few loose strands to veil my face.

When I enter the shop, of course the universe can't get enough of throwing me under buses, Will is standing at the cash register with his back to me.

I look around for any sign of Rosie, hopefully she can save me from this awkward encounter that I know is coming up. Nope, it seems like the universe would rather crush me with a boat today, because Rosie is nowhere in sight.

Will turns to glance over this shoulder at me, and regards me with a raise of his brow. "I've never had a stalker before."

"Excuse me?"

He eventually turns to fully face me, leaning against the counter in an effortlessly sexy way. Folding his arms like a pretzel he regards me with that same smirk that filled my body with fire the first night we met. If I knew he was an asshole I would have picked a nicer guy to take home that night, maybe then I wouldn't be haunted by my actions.

"Normally, when I have a fling with a girl I don't see her again," he appears to be frustrated by my very presence. Him and me both.

I'm not going to just stand here and allow him to speak to me like I am a nuisance for simply showing up for my job. He must think so highly of himself that I would waste my energy to track him down, find out where he works and apply for a job. When all I knew about him was his first name and the size of his cock.

I sputter a laugh to myself at the thought and walk to the counter so I am standing beside him. "Will you be conducting my induction?" I keep my gaze to the back wall, admiring all of the posters that have a fifties vibe to them.

"Unfortunately, yes." Will is now holding a clipboard and scribbling something down on the sheet of paper. "I will go over everything once, should you have any questions you can ask my mother."

I shoot him a glare and follow him around the store as he points around to the different displays and explains that they need changing every four days, the window display needs a new arrangement every day and when I am not busy I should clean around the store.

He takes me into the back, it's quite a cramped space that is mostly for storage. It somehow can fit a small desk and a laptop against the furthest wall.

"This is where everything is," he points to a box labelled, *cleaning*. "I'm sure you can guess."

He sounds so bored with this entire induction, why did he agree to do it if he hates it so much? It's hard to believe this man is the same person who gave me my first orgasm during sex, and it *not* requiring my own hand to do so.

"You will be expected to work every Monday, Wednesday and Sunday."

"Can't your mom go through this with me instead?"

"Why?" Will's eyes darken as he places the clipboard down onto the desk. His hands slip over my waist as if he has been comfortably doing so for years. "Are you struggling to contain yourself around me?"

I should not be doing this, and on my first day working in a flower shop of all places. I can't help but feel drawn to him, when he tugs at my hips I want nothing more than to kiss him again.

"I can have you screaming my name again."

This knocks me out of his trance. I shove him back with flaming red cheeks. "I did *not* scream your name."

Will's seductive expression turned into amusement. "Oh, you did. Multiple times." He moves his lips to my ear and I gasp when he bites my earlobe. "You begged me not to ever stop." If I was a sensible woman I would push him away and slap him across the face. I can't deny that sensation that fills by body at the closeness of him, the thought of his body on mine.

He takes a wide step back, giving me enough space to breathe. "I'm flattered that you would track me down, find a job where my mother works, just to see me again." He picks up the clipboard again, holding it in his fingers. Those exact fingers were grazing my entire back, melting my skin from a decade of being frozen in ice. "I should tell you that I'm not looking for a relationship."

"Please spare my heart," I roll my eyes at him. "I don't want a relationship either, I've only *just* got out of one. I especially don't want one with someone as pompous and arrogant as you."

I've clearly struck a nerve when he flicks up an eyebrow. "Pretty brave for you to talk to the son of your boss that way."

A snort of laughter exhales from my nostrils because of the way he is acting. It reminds me of a toddler that can't get his

35

own way, and resorts to threatening to call their parent to get them into trouble.

That snort of laughter bubbles into a giggle, then I double over laughing. It's not even that funny, but the reaction I am getting from him is priceless.

"What's so funny?" He demands, as his knuckles turn white from clutching the clipboard.

I drag my thumb under my eye to catch any tears that might spill. "It's just funny that you think this job is my life." Any amusement vanishes from my face and voice, and I stick out my chin to square him up. "Go ahead, have me fired. It's hard to get attached to something that's been in my life for less than an hour."

A thick fog has settled around us, and my only beacon is his bright green eyes that somehow provide my heart with an additional beat to its already erratic rhythm. I watch his every movement, the deep rise and fall of his chest, and how his eyes have trailed down to my lips. Keeping his gaze firmly in place, my mind can't help but think back to when those lips were kissing my jaw, down my neck and my own lips. It takes a lot of strength not to bite down, to give away exactly what I am thinking. Based on the hungry look in his eyes, I wonder if he is thinking the same thing.

"Good morning," a voice that could only belong to Rosie sings from the front of the store.

I push myself out of the backroom and meet Will's mother at the door. My heart is drumming in my ears from my encounter with Will, is he like that with most girls?

"Morning," I tuck a loose strand of my hair behind my ear, and wait with my hands clasped firmly in front of me.

"Did William go over everything with you?"

He showed me where everything is, the flowers, the ribbons, and the cleaning supplies but he never actually said what it is I will be doing on my shifts. "I'm not entirely sure what I'm supposed to do."

Rosie rolls her eyes. For a moment I feared she was frustrated at me, that I couldn't pick up the simple tasks that came along with a flower shop, but when she storms past me I can tell she has her sights set on her son.

"William Dawson, I told you to go through *everything* on that list!"

"It's almost eight pages long!"

It's awkward to be standing on the shop floor and listening to a mother and son argue over me. I wish I lied, and figured it out as I went. It was my first day after all, Rosie doesn't seem the type to expect greatness from me on my first day. Her original sign even said *no experience necessary.*

After a while of just standing around and awkwardly admiring the flowers, Will storms out from the back room and throws the clipboard down onto the front desk. He walks straight past me like a breeze of frost and exits the shop.

"Don't mind him, sweetie." Rosie grabs a green apron from the hook and hands it to me. "He's just..." she lets out a deep sigh, and a wash of sadness crosses her face. It's like I can see a piece of her heart get chipped away in this very moment.

"So, do you have a guide for how to put together a bouquet flowers?"

Rosie snaps out of her sad state so suddenly it almost gives me whiplash. "We have pre-made bouquets and gift sets already made up." She gestures to the right wall, hosting a whole garden full of flowers that overload my senses with colour. "But if a customer would like their own custom bouquet then that's where the fun part happens." Rosie winks at me and takes me around the store to show me where each individual flower has its own section. An entire row of roses in a variety of colours are on one shelf, lilies on another and so much more.

"Allow your creativity to flow through you," she picks out

a selection of flowers. "What colours compliment each other. Think of the occasion, the tone the flowers should convey."

I'm actually excited to put together my first bouquet. I can already feel my creative juices being called into action.

"Do you want to do a practice run?"

"Sure."

Rosie claps her hands together, "Pretend I am a picky bride, I want flowers for my wedding but I can't find an arrangement I like."

"All right," I think about my options for a moment. A wedding is a sign of love and union, I will have to research into the meaning of most of these flowers. I don't want to accidentally offend someone by giving a bride a flower of death. "What is the theme of this wedding?"

"Vampires."

I can't swallow my laughter fast enough. "Vampires?"

"You will get all kinds of people come through here, best to start off with something a bit out of the ordinary."

She has a point. Okay, so vampires it is. I look around the store for what could be best suited for a wedding themed around vampires. My immediate thought is coffins and blood, and roses are a symbol of love. That's about the only flower I know anything about. I pick thirteen roses, six red, five white and two black. I mix the white and red roses so there isn't a block of a single colour, and I add a black rose to the left and right side. I tie them together clumsily with a black silk ribbon — well, it's more of a knot than a ribbon — and I hand them to Rosie.

She smiles as she examines what I have put together. "I like it. Don't be afraid to use different types of flowers. Perhaps take out a few of the white roses, and add an orchid or sweet peas."

I take note of her suggestion, and keep it in mind to not rely on one set of flowers. I appreciate her advice, I feel like she is giving me tips to actually help me improve instead of focusing solely on what I did wrong.

Rosie is such a kind and gentle woman, it's remarkable that she raised a spoilt brat like Will. Yet, I can't help but shake the sadness in her eyes when he stormed out. She was going to open up about Will, I could tell it was difficult for her so I decided to offer a distraction.

I shake the thought off. Whatever is Will's problem is *his* problem. I just want to get on with my life and work until I have the confidence to apply for graphic design jobs again.

Later that night I try to distract myself by working on my portfolio, adding a few new pieces of work and personal project to the mix. I try to show off all aspects that my creativity can offer, from concept to final product.

I turned my phone onto silent, Simon has been pinging my phone constantly since we broke up. I've been avoiding his calls and not reading his messages. I can't even respond to Jeremy because I'm too scared to see what the last text Simon sent was.

What bothers me the most about what happened on my birthday, after everything, Simon didn't bother trying to make it up to me. He didn't fight for me to stay with him, he didn't show up and beg for me to forgive him, he just let me be. Simon expected me to forgive him, blow off steam and come crawling back to him.

Only now has it sunk in that I meant what I said, that we're over.

I eventually give in, since I can see my phone light up ever few minutes.

Simon: Lulu, can you answer me? I just want to talk xxx

Simon: Please, I need to talk to you xxx

* * *

Simon: I'm sorry I missed your birthday, please just talk to me so we can work this out. I miss you Lulu xxx

Simon: Wtf Lucy?? You won't even talk to me when I am trying my best!!

Simon: Just answer your fucking phone

Simon: FFS LUCY!!!

Simon: Answer your fucking phone. We need to sort this shit out NOW!!!!

Simon: I will call the fucking police if you don't answer, you're clearly unstable if you're willing to ignore me like this

I read that last message a few times. I want to laugh at how ridiculous it sounds, that he would call the police because... what? I'm not answering his texts? He thinks that would warrant wasting police time? I know it is just a threat, to scare me into replying to him and beg him not to do so, but it does scare me. I will never admit that to him, reading his texts fills my blood with an anxiety that's more intense than I am used to. It makes me fear what he would be willing to do to talk to me again. I'm just grateful that I never got around to giving him a key to my apartment.

Was he always like this? Thinking back, there must have been red flags for his behaviour but I don't really want to waste my energy thinking of them, and regretting not leaving sooner. I do the only thing I can do right now.

I block him.

Chapter Six

I've been working at the *Flowers Over Thoughts* shop for two weeks now, and so far all I have achieved is selling pre-made bouquets. The customers don't seem eager to stay and shop, they usually point at a display and they buy it.

It has been pretty much silent today, and with my free time I decided to pick up a notepad and doodle a few logo designs for this place. The one out front is too bold, too plain, for something as delicate as a flower shop. It looks as though someone picked a random font from a selection and wrote out the name. No care, or consideration went into it. Working on these doodles is just a way for me to kill time whilst I wait for customers to enter the store.

The bell above the door rings, signalling someone has just walked in. My eyes snap up to see Will standing there, looking as frustratingly handsome as ever. His black hair is slightly more ruffled today, I wonder if that's from a weekend of taking home girls from bars. He's dressed in a simple black t-shirt that hugs against his slender frame, and jeans.

"Just you?" He asks as he approaches the counter.

"Yep." I keep my head down and resume scribbling on my notepad.

My entire body tenses when I see his tan arms fold over the counter, and I make the mistake in looking up to meet his gaze. A stupid smirk on those soft lips that I just want to slap off. "I'm actually glad you're here."

"Oh really?" I raise a suspicious brow to him, waiting to hear what the catch is.

His smirk grows into a smile. "I wanted to apologise to you, for being an asshole."

"Wow, you're actually apologising?" I pinch my wrist. "And I'm not dreaming."

Will rumbles a chuckle. "I forgive you too."

I bark a laugh that actually resembles a squawking parrot. When I wait for him to laugh that moment never comes. "Excuse me?"

"You know," that smirk pisses me off, and he knows it. "For calling me pompous and arrogant."

"I don't see why I would need to apologise for stating facts."

Will straightens his posture, his arms still folded like pretzels over his chest. "We're stating facts, are we?"

"No..." he ignores me and continues speaking anyway, like the pompous and arrogant man he is.

"I have to state the fact that the way you screamed my name was probably the sexiest thing I have ever heard." His eyes darken with desire, like he is picturing it right now.

I look into his eyes, and it's a wonder he hasn't gone into a career as a magician, his eyes could hypnotise me into doing whatever stunt he wanted.

"You have to admit, our night together was fun."

I curl up my nose and let out a sound of disgust as I pick up my notepad and clutch it to my chest. "You can add 'asshole' to the list. You're really a triple threat."

"I never said I wasn't," Will said. "It was supposed to be a compliment."

"Can we just...never talk about it again?" I let out a defeated breath. "Pretend like it never happened? I'm embarrassed enough as it is."

"Why are you embarrassed?" He seems genuinely confused.

I drop my voice into a whisper, even though there is no one but the two of us in the entire store. "I've never had a one night stand before. Well, I *didn't* until..."

He shrugs so nonchalantly. Why is it that every movement he makes my blood boil. There is something so frustrating about his presence that I can't put my finger on.

"I'm not talking about this anymore. It never happened."

Will found my response amusing.

"Don't you have somewhere to be?"

Will meets me behind the counter and pulls out a laptop hidden deep within one of the shelves. "I've got my own work to do," he waves the silver case in my face. "I'll be in the back should you need me."

"I won't." I call before he shuts the door behind him.

Will hasn't come back out since he hid himself away in the backroom. I've been tempted a few times to check up on him, even if it's just to make the day go faster. I have fifteen minutes until the store closes, and I am eager to waste my evening watching some cheesy romance movie.

Just my luck, the bell dings to signify a customer. When I look up I see Simon standing in the doorway. His sandy blonde hair is drastically shorter since the last time I saw him. He's got a look on his face that reminds me of a lost puppy wandering the streets alone. Standing there, I'm reminded of just how tall he is, it was hard to comprehend when he would spend most of his days slouched down in a beanbag chair playing video games.

"Hi," it comes out hoarse, like it was difficult to speak just looking at me.

"Hi," I look around for any form of distraction. Something

to take me away from this moment, who wants to run into their ex that they broke up with over the phone? What good could possibly come from this?

As he approaches the counter the palms of my hands begin to sweat.

"It's really good to see you," his thin lips are anchored into a frown, I'm not in the mood to try and lift his spirits.

"How did you know I was here?"

"I was just shopping and saw you in the window." Simon abruptly reaches for my hand but I snatch it back before he can have the chance to make contact. The air changes suddenly, and I am grateful to have an entire counter to separate us.

"I miss you, Lulu. I want us to get back together, give me another chance?"

I knew he would do this. I really can't catch a break recently, I have to fight out of every single situation recently.

Did he forget about the string of texts messages he sent me? Demanding that we talk, and threatening to call the cops on me for simply not answering him? Does he think that I just *forgot?*

"No, Simon. I just want us to walk away from each other and move on with our lives. We both deserve that."

That soft expression he was clearly forcing over his face had melted away faster than a block of ice over a fire. "What the fuck, Lucy? We're together for five years and you can't even give me a chance?"

"I gave you a chance every day for the past five years and nothing changed." I snap. "Please, leave Simon."

"Why the *fuck* have you blocked me, Lucy?" He yells so loud that I actually flinch back. "This is fucking bullshit. I gave you *everything* and you can't even fucking talk to me? After five fucking years?!"

"Just leave…" I can barely speak, I feel like my throat is

being trampled.

"No," he reaches for my wrist, but this time I don't pull away fast enough. He grabs me in a tight fist and I pull back to no avail. "I'm not done here — "

"But *she* is."

Suddenly, Will appears from behind me, I didn't even hear him enter, and somehow manages to release Simon's grip from around my wrist. He pushes him back, almost knocking over a flower display in the process.

"Who the fuck are you?" Simon spits out every word, looking between us as though I had betrayed his trust. As if I have cheated on him. "Fucking slut — "

"I don't care who you are," Will's neck rises in red as he steps around the counter and grabs Simon by the collar of his shirt. "You do not lay a hand, or speak, to a member of staff like that again. You are banned from entering here." Will releases him with a long shove to the door. "And if I catch you sniffing around anywhere near here, I'll break your fucking arm."

Simon doesn't get a chance to say a single word, as Will shoves him out of the door and slams it behind him. He proceeds to lock it to prevent Simon from storming back inside.

I am so overwhelmed right now, my wrist hurts from where Simon grabbed me and my stomach is in knots. Too much has happened in such a short amount of time. I got fired from a job that was supposed to be the start of my career, I slept with a stranger who is now my co-worker, and broke up with my boyfriend of five years, only for him to turn up at my new job and put his hands on me.

If Will wasn't here what would have…

No. I can't dive into the *what if's* because it will drive me insane, and I will fall down a rabbit hole too deep to claw me way out of.

"You okay?" Will is now in front of me, a tender expression on his face.

I go to wave my wrist, but a sharp pain shoots up my arm. "Ow, he must have grabbed hard." I'm calm when I speak, but the emotions start pooling out as tears slip down my cheeks. I do my best to hide my face with my palms, expecting Will to just leave me in my current state. He's done enough as it is, he shouldn't stick around to comfort a girl having a breakdown.

"Come with me," he leads me into the back room and shuts the door behind us.

"I'm sorry," I say, still not raising my head from my palms.

"Don't apologise, it's *him* that's in the wrong," his voice is softer than I've ever heard it. His finger make contact with my sore wrist, and he unveils my face to get a good look at it. "I can't see any marks. Do you think you need to go to the hospital?"

"No," I sniffle. "It's just a little sore."

Will keeps his hand over my wrist, his large thumb idly tracing invisible circles over my skin. It's helped me to calm down immensely, in this moment it helps to focus on Will. When did he start standing so close? I can feel his warm breath hitting against my face, and get lost in the deep pattern of his chest rising and falling.

I suddenly forget to breathe, all I can think of is how his hands felt against my skin. How his touch managed to ignite a flame that had been dormant for my entire life. I want to feel that spark again, I want to be touched I want...

"Kiss me." The words come out as a breathless whisper.

For a moment I think he is going to back away, laugh in my face and tell me our one night stand was all there would be. Just one night.

Instead, he crashes his lips over mine and I immediately lose myself to the taste of his mouth, his tongue. Will pushes me up against the wall as I circle my arms around his back, his arms surround my body and hold me in such a tight embrace that I never want him to let go.

I don't care what this is, or if it even means anything to him. I just enjoy the feeling of his hands over my body, and the pleasure it brings to my core.

One of his hands graze over my hips and slips over my tummy until he reaches the edge of my jeans. He pauses for a long time, and I buck my hips in response giving him permission to go further.

Just when I think he is about to give me what I want, Will rips his lips away and looks down on me with a fierce gaze. "I meant what I said. I don't want a relationship."

I'm too turned on to care about any of that. I respond by unbuttoning his trousers and sticking my hand down his pants, under his underwear. I grab the length of him, he's so warm in my palm. Will releases a grunt at my actions and proceeds to do the same for me. He unbuttons my jeans and digs his hand beneath my underwear.

He dips his large fingers inside of me. Both of us stand like this for a short amount of time, and I can't help but grind my hips to rub against his fingers. When I start moving my hand up and down the length of him, in a tight grip, Will grunts and starts stroking me until I am already nearing release.

We keep our movements in time with one another. When one of us picks up in pace so does the other. If Rosie were to walk in on us like this I would surely lose my job, but I don't care. This feels too good for it not to be worth it.

We become undone together, my entire body convulses from such an intense climax.

Will presses his forehead against mine as he tries to regain his breath. I look up at him through my lashes and slowly remove my hand from his pants.

"Lucy…"

"It never happened." I offer a meek smile, and Will raises his head only to look down on me. A coy smile tickles his lips. "Right."

Chapter Seven

I haven't seen Will since our intense moment in the backroom. I try to subtly ask Rosie what he's up to and she usually says he's working. Not that any of it should matter. What happened in the back room never happened, and what happened the night we met also never happened. There is absolutely no way I am picturing how his hands knew exactly what to do to make me feel the most erotic sensations.

It's Friday, which means I don't have work for another two days. I spend my free time either working on logos for imaginary clients or watching movies. Right now I'm curled up on my couch with a pot of chocolate ice cream. It's not exactly a meal fit for lunch, my mother would scold me until the cows came home if she saw me right now. It's just one simple bliss I have right now, considering my savings are going towards paying my rent. I've calculated, I only have enough money to pay for another two months, and since my salary has been cut drastically from working in the flower shop, I may have to consider moving back in with my parents.

It's not like that would be the end of the world. I didn't move out because I was tired of living with them and their rules. I just wanted my independence, and now that I have it I feel like it is going to be ripped out from under me again.

I've tried applying for more graphic design jobs in hopes someone will hire me. I am still faced with nothing but rejection.

My buzzer rings, which startles me enough to spill a drop of ice cream over my pyjama bottoms. "Oh no," I huff as I try to quickly wipe it off, only smudging it further into the material.

It's a wasted effort, so I jump up and scurry over to the intercom. "Who is it?"

It's probably Mom, here to drop off more groceries that she 'happened' to pick up.

"It's Will."

My entire body freezes.

What is he doing here?

"What do you want?"

"Can you buzz me in? I need to talk to you."

I don't have to, I can just walk away and leave him to stand outside. It's satisfying to think of him out there, alone on a day that is particularly cold. He's probably here to tease me about getting off to his fingers down my...

I roll my eyes at myself and buzz him in. I can stand here and debate to myself all day, wonder what he wants, when I know I'm going to see him at work at some point.

I buzz him in and pace around my living room, nervously taking giant spoonfuls of ice cream. I eat it so fast that I give myself a brain freeze.

My front door knocks and I almost trip over my own slippers to answer it. Opening it up, my breath catches in my throat at the sight of Will standing before me, with his hands tucked into his trouser pockets and a ghost of a smile tickling his lips.

"Can I come in?"

I nod and step aside, watching his every movement as he elegantly walks into my apartment.

"It's funny," he scratches the back of his head. "I feel like I have been here before."

I can't help the small laugh that escapes as I shut the door behind me. "Not sure why, since *nothing* happened here and this is the first time you are visiting."

He walks to the couch, thrumming his fingers over the arm. "Hmm, this couch certainly seems familiar."

"Nope."

Will chuckles, he stands and stares at me for a while. His green eyes dancing over my face as he takes in my appearance. I must look like a sight. My hair is pulled up into a messy bun, and my pyjamas are two sizes too big for me with cartoon cats scattered around. "What did you want to talk to me about?"

"I need a favour from you," he says. "At the same time, I need you to not get mad."

I scowl. "Why would I get mad?"

"I'll cut to the chase," he helps himself to a seat at my small dining room table. Why do I feel like he is about proposition a new business idea?

"My father has been trying to set me up with someone for about two years," the confession makes my stomach contort for some reason. "It's purely for business. So much so that he has started to insist I marry her. It started off as a playful joke but recently he has gotten really serious about it."

I put my tub of ice cream down on my kitchen counter, confused what any of this has to do with me.

"Not only that but he would lie to me," Will continues. "He would invite me to dinner with him only to not show up and his associates daughter be in his place."

"Well, the other night he kept pushing and pushing about why I won't give it a chance. He set up another date with this woman, even started making arrangements about a wedding. I ended up snapping and I said…" he stares at me with an intense focus, like I should be able to pick up on what he is saying but I am as lost as an inexperienced traveller in the dessert.

Will drops his head and releases a long sigh. "I said that I'm already seeing someone."

"When my mother asked who, I..."

When he doesn't remove his gaze from mine, my heart starts to flutter in my chest. No. He can't possibly mean me? I must have my signals crossed because why on earth would he say that to his parents? "What did you tell them?"

"That we're dating."

"*We* as in...you and me?" I gawk at him, waiting for him to slap his knee and laugh at my expense. He can't be serious, why would he do that? "What - I - then tell them we broke up!"

"No!" He gets to his feet and meets me at the kitchen counter. "If I do they will keep trying to set me up with his associate's daughter."

It's hard to believe that Rosie would be okay with something like this, by the sound of Will's story they are both eager for him to marry.

"Just tell them you don't want a relationship right now."

He shakes his head, the ends of his black hair brushing against his forehead. "My father doesn't care about that. Please, Lucy..." he places a delicate hand over my shoulder.

"Please *what*?" I gawk at him. "I fail to see what any of this has to do with me."

"Can you just pretend to be my girlfriend until they forget this ridiculous idea of me marrying?"

"What do I get out of this?"

"What do you want?"

Why did my cheeks have to flush in this exact moment? Ever since Will and I slept together I can't get my mind out of the gutter, and he doesn't miss a thing.

"I can give you all of the benefits of *being* a fake girlfriend? Just without the actual relationship part."

I shove his chest. "Why me? Can't you find some other girl to do it?"

"If I make up a girl they will want to meet her, and I don't want to be a creep asking girls if they want to fake date me." He takes a large step forward. "If it's you, and you play along, my mother will ensure to my father that this is real. You can talk about how amazing I am as a boyfriend whilst you work together."

"So, you want me to lie to the woman who gave me a job? My *boss*?"

"I promise if they somehow find out you will not lose your job."

What would be the harm in helping him out? It wouldn't be forever, just until his parents lay off him about becoming engaged. It does seem like an unfair situation to be in, and he must be desperate to want my help of all people.

I'm not ashamed to admit that I might even enjoy having said benefits if I feel like it.

Do I want the complication of a fake relationship? How far would this lie go? I'm not sure I can manage this along with all of the other pressure I have been put under recently. I don't know if I could cope with being responsible for Will's future. How could I possibly make it believable that this man, who drives me insane by his mere presence, is someone I want a romantic relationship with? Plus I like Rosie, and I don't feel comfortable lying to her.

"As tempting as your offer is, I'm afraid I'm going to have to decline."

The gems of his eyes dim, the single ray of hope he was holding onto vanished. He didn't seriously think I would say yes to that? "Come on, Lucy. I am *begging* you."

"That's your idea of begging?" I can't contain the hysterical laugh. "Regardless, my answer is no."

Will says nothing more and doesn't miss out on an opportunity to send me one last glare before he leaves my apartment in a storm of fury.

All I wanted was for my life to be stress-free. A smooth road with no crossroads or speed bumps. Why do I feel as though I have just thrown myself head first into a road block?

Chapter Eight

Will is such an asshole. I can't believe I ever slept with that guy, *and* I let him get in my pants for a second time in the backroom of this flower shop. This is supposed to be a place that I can focus on expanding my creative flare, and not partaking in promiscuous acts with the son of my boss.

I need to clear my mind, rinse it out completely and focus on my designs. That is exactly what I am doing today. I can't just stand and wait for the rare sign of a customer to appear behind the counter. I have to *do* something, because with all of this stagnant creativity I might as well be curled up at home watching movies all day, and achieving nothing.

I set up a few new displays, arranging a variety of pastel bouquets by the door so customers are greeted with a calming colour, not to overwhelm them with bright yellow sunflowers or deep red roses.

I spend most of my morning cleaning, and arranging the flowers. Once I am done I realise that I am happy with the few flower arrangements I have created. The anxiety starts to kick in when I realise Rosie should be here any moment, and she might not like the changes I have made. Maybe that will be my sign that I am not destined to be a designer?

Like clockwork, Rosie enters through the front of the store holding a seemingly endless about of shopping bags.

Considering how little customers we get I do wonder how she can afford to have so many frequent shopping trips?

"Let me help you," I take some of the bags that are seconds away from falling from her grasp.

"Thank you, sweetheart." We put the bags down behind the counter and Rosie immediately starts finishing through to find one of the items she brought. When Rosie remerges she is holding a sleek black sketchbook and a pack of pencils. She holds them out for me to take and I just look at her.

"These are for you," she chuckles and puts them into my hands. "Will says he caught you drawing out a few logos for the store, and I want to see what you can come up with."

He saw that? I thought I snagged the notebook away in time to avoid him snooping. I guess nothing can really get past him, it would be endearing if he wasn't such a prick.

Rosie takes note of our surroundings, for a moment I think she is angry when her face slips into a blank expression as she takes in the displays. "I like what you've done in here," and just like that, I feel my shoulders relax. "It feels more inviting."

"That's what I was going for," I smile.

Rosie brings my attention back to the sketchbook by tapping one of her long crimson nails on the cover. "If you could come up with a few logo designs we can use it for the store. Don't worry, I'll pay you extra, and if I choose one of your designs I will give you a raise."

The way she said it, like she has confidence in my ability to create something, design something that will suit the store has given me a sense of reassurance. Not only did she like the layout of the store and the flowers I arranged, but now she is giving me a task that is more suited to my actual skills. I feel like Rosie believes in me, and I am determined not to let her down.

Before I can open my mouth to thank her, the bell to the

shop door rings.

Rosie and I turn to greet the customer at the same time, but any ounce of joy I felt in that moment washed away like chalk in the rain.

Simon steps through the door, clearly Will's threat — and banning — meant nothing to him. I do notice he takes a scope around the store to check Will isn't around, and this is the only time that I will ever admit that I wish he was here. At least I'm not alone, it's comforting to have a mother figure by my side. I haven't known Rosie very long, but I trust her to have my back.

Simon already knows what I am going to say, raising his hands in surrender as he approaches the counter. "I won't take up too much of your time."

I can feel Rosie's eyes shift between the two of us, her shoulders tighten like I imagine she would if Will was about to get into a dangerous situation. It's then I realise she believes that I am dating her son, because Will is a moron who blurted it out to save his own ass. Simon could unknowingly put Will into hot water if he says anything that might require further explanation. Simon could imply that we deserve another chance of being together, and what would I say to that? I just hope Will told his parents that he misspoke when he said I was the girl he'd been 'dating.'

"I'm sorry about the other day," Simon tries his hardest to find my eyes but I keep my head down, the faster he says what he has to say the faster he will be leaving. "I was just so surprised to see you and I've missed you like crazy."

Out of the corner of my eye I see Rosie pretending to keep herself busy, but she makes her actions as quiet as possible to listen in on our conversation. I know it's not to be nosey, it's to be prepared in case she needs to jump in.

"I already told you, Simon. I'm not interested."

"Just give me one last chance, please." His begging makes

me cringe, even more so that he's not afraid to do it in front of a stranger. "I will do anything to get you back, my life feels so empty without you."

It's a shame he didn't figure that out years before.

"No. I can't."

"Why not?"

Clearly an answer as simple as: *because I don't want you, I don't like you or we aren't right for each other* aren't going to be enough. As long as there isn't a reason for him *not* to come back he will. I sometimes forget how pushy he can be, it's easy to remember him as a slob but at the times when we would be together he made my skin crawl. God, why did I *wait* for an excuse to break up with him? Why did I stay with him for so long?

"Because I'm seeing someone." I blurt out, and the moment the words fly past my lips I wish I could take them back.

Even Rosie doesn't hide her shock as she whirls her head around to stare at me. Maybe she was sceptical of Will's admission to us becoming a couple? Anyone would think this was news to her based on her reaction.

It's not her reaction I am concerned about at the moment, it's Simon's. The pity party has departed from his system, and the uncomfortable rage is rising up his neck. "You're seeing someone?" He bites out.

"Y-yes." I keep my chin up but my trembling voice gives away that I feel no confidence at all.

"Who is he?"

I drop my head then. This would be so much easier if Rosie wasn't here. I could say Will; what if he has already found a fake girlfriend for his scheme with his dad? Do I really want to collaborate further lies just to get out of this one situation with Simon?

The way his hands are balled into tight fists, I feel like I don't have a choice.

"Is it that asshole who threw me out the last time I was in here?" He demands.

Fear rises in my throat as he leans his upper body over the counter.

I feel trapped, with Rosie's eyes still on me waiting for me to confirm it. She knows he means Will, no other guys come in here and even if they did they wouldn't be throwing customers out. I didn't even know if company policy allowed for co-workers to date. It might be seen as a conflict of interest.

"Yes," I hiss, feeling more uncomfortable in each passing second. "So if you could leave..."

"After five fucking years it takes you weeks to move on with someone else?"

"Excuse me," Rosie steps to my side, protective mother mode engaged. Her hands are pressed down onto the counter, her eyes glaring at Simon with an intense fire. "You cannot speak to a member of my staff that way. Whatever personal issues you have, take it outside of my store."

Simon ignores her, his frightening glare unwavering from my trembling face. He starts to shake his head from side to side, baffled that I could possibly move on from him. Technically, I haven't moved on *with* anybody, but I moved on from Simon years before our relationship came to an end. Without another word he turns on his heel and heads towards the exit. Just when I am about to release a sigh of relief, Simon picks up one of the displays I had created this morning and slams it against the wall next to him.

I hear Rosie protest but still he ignores her, continuing to the exit and slamming the door behind him so hard I feared the glass might shatter.

My hands are shaking after that experience. I like to think that is the end of it, that Simon will take the hint and never step foot into my life again. That feels like a lie.

I'm not given enough time to compose myself, as Will enters the store. He must not have seen Simon leaving, thank god, as he has a nonchalant look on his face. It's only when he notices the mangled flowers on the floor does his expression shift into confusion. When he meets my wide stare his mouth falls open slightly, "Are you okay?"

Do I look as bad as I feel? I know my eyes are wide, I can't seem to blink them back to normal. When I look down, my fingers are violently shaking.

Then Will realises what could have shaken me up so much, "Did your ex come back?"

I manage a nod, the tears blurring my vision but I *refuse* to let a single tear fall.

Luckily, Rosie is here to distract from my almost breakdown. "So, you two *are* dating." She said with a bright smile on her face, the way I would expect her to react if he had just presented her with a million dollars.

"What?"

Really? He's not catching up on his *own* scheme. When Will looks my way I manage to pull a face to signal for him to play along. It takes him a few seconds to catch my drift.

"Oh!" Will scratches behind his head. "Yeah, I told you it's a fairly new thing so..."

I hope Will's job outside of this flower shop isn't acting, he would win a *Razzie* for sure.

Rosie doesn't pick up on his poor attempt of acting, she is radiating a joyful energy that is almost blinding. "And you complained about hiring her," she scolds Will, who glares at his mother. "Sometimes mother knows best."

"Wait until Raven hears about this." Rosie chuckles to herself.

Who's Raven?

I am supposedly Will's 'girlfriend' and I don't know

anything about his life. I don't know what he does outside of this flower shop. Does he have any siblings? Where did he grow up? Does he have any hobbies? How old is he? His birthday?

I am very much on edge, and when Rosie places a hand over my shoulder so suddenly I can't help but flinch. It's a jarring jump which brought down Rosie's current mood, she seemingly forgot that my ex-boyfriend was in the store moments ago and demanding we get back together.

I keep my gaze down and point towards the backroom. "I just…I need a minute."

When I steal a glance, Rosie realises she must have come on too strong considering the events that occurred. I feel guilty lying to her, when she has been nothing but kind to me, which doesn't help my shaking hands. "Of course, take as long as you need, sweetheart."

The moment the door shuts behind me I sink to the floor and bury my face into the palms of my hands. I cry, causing a small pond to form in the centre of my palms.

When did everything start feeling like too much?

Maybe it's because decisions for my life are being made by other people. I didn't decide to quit my job, they fired me. The only decisions I have made have consequences to them. Breaking up with Simon should have given me freedom, but now I am afraid of the next time he will show up unannounced. Will he become some sort of stalker? Start following me home?

God, he knows where I live. He knows my routine and he knows where I work now.

Then there is Will. Lying to his mother made me feel so dirty. I should tell her the truth, that it was just a lie to get Simon out of the store. But Will confirmed it, he said it was true. Would that mean I would be causing a wedge between them? I don't want to hurt anyone, I just want to build a life for myself but my own life — future — feels so out of my hands.

"Hey," a deep voice that I recognise at Will's suddenly says from behind me.

I get up from my crouched position, only to keep my back to him. I'm already embarrassed for him to find me like this. I hug my arms over my chest as I try my best to stop the waterfall of tears from falling down my cheeks. It's no use, the dam has broke and my tears will spill until I am dry.

I hear the *click* of the door shutting, and I have a moment of hope that he has realised I want to be left alone. Of course not, he comes into view and I look away. He is trying so hard to meet my gaze but I keep my head to the side, annoyance sparking my blood.

"Did he hurt you?"

"No."

"What did he want?"

I scrape the curve of my hand under my eye, in hopes of catching some of these stupid tears. "The same thing he wanted last time."

"Did he touch you?"

I curl my lip, "Why would it matter, Will?" I snap my head up to look at him, giving him exactly what he wants. I bet he loves to see me like this, completely broken and stressed beyond belief. "You should be thanking him, really."

"Thanking him?" He looks disgusted at the mere suggestion.

"If it wasn't for the uncomfortable situation he put me in you wouldn't have gotten your own way," I poke his chest. "I wouldn't have felt the need to lie about being in a relationship with you." I don't care if Rosie is outside of this door, I kind of want her to hear the truth and I can play it off as an accident.

I can't read Will's face, he could be feeling anything and

masking it so well with a blank expression. When his eyebrows pinch together I get the sense that he is annoyed, when he has no right to be. This whole ordeal was his idea.

"Are you scared of him?"

"What?"

"Are.You.Scared.Of.Him?"

No, of course I'm not. Or…am I? Having time away from Simon these past few weeks has been an eye opener. I never realised how uncomfortable he makes me feel, and how I feel as though I need to walk on eggshells in his presence. He's never hit me, but a part of me wouldn't put it past him. He didn't even flinch when trying to grab my wrist the other day because he couldn't get what he wanted. Today, although they were only flowers he threw across the room, it's only a matter of time before the soft objects start to become purposely heavy.

I realise now he's never put a hand on me before because I actively tried to give him anything he wanted, because I was scared of what his reaction would be.

"Yeah." I feel so small, so pathetic admitting that to Will.

He runs a hand over his jaw, scratching up and down as he clearly thinks something through in that beautiful fat head of his.

"What if I were to become a sort of fake-boyfriend-bodyguard?"

I sniffle. "What?"

"I'm sure your loser of an ex will move on eventually," Will reasons. "If I'm your 'boyfriend' he will be more likely to keep away from you if I'm around."

That would make it less frightening if Will were to do things a normal boyfriend would do. He could take me home, check in on me, and do what a normal guy would do dating a girl who is being harassed by her ex.

It would be better for me than feeling alone.

"Okay."

The emeralds in his eyes sparkle. "Really?"

"Yes, but on one condition."

"What's that?"

I may regret this, but it will save any confusion about feelings in the future. "No sex."

Chapter Nine

Will and I have been "dating" for a week now and nothing has really changed. I don't know what I expected. That every day he would bestow gifts upon me, wake me up with a morning call to tell me he's thinking of me, *kiss me.*

If anything, I have seen him a lot less since I agreed to this ridiculous arrangement of his. If it wasn't for Simon I don't think I would have changed my mind. My stomach did knot at the idea of Will being forced into a marriage with a stranger, so having a fake relationship with a girl he had a one night stand with holds a little less commitment.

My parents and I met up for a coffee at the local cafe. They plan on meeting with my Aunt Sam and Uncle Lucas for lunch later, so I thought I would hog their time until my shift starts at the flower shop.

"How's things going at your job?" Dad asks as he pours half of the jar of sugar into his cup of coffee. He has such a sweet tooth, just looking at his drink makes my teeth rot.

"Fine, there's nothing else to really add. Unless you want me to talk about the different types of flowers?" And that I have a fake boyfriend, who happens to be my boss' son.

"No, thank you," Dad smiles against his mug.

"Have you seen that tall chap?"

I freeze mid-bite of my chicken salad wrap and stare at her.

There is that blasted knowing smile on her lips. Why would she ask about him after the last time she saw me with him?

I don't want to involve my family into my lie. It will only add more confusion, more people to ask questions and more people to get involved. I need this to be as hassle free as possible until I am certain Simon will leave me alone, and Will's family are satisfied he doesn't need an arranged marriage.

"Who?" Dad asks, looking so lost in a matter of seconds.

"Nobody," the colour rises to my cheeks. "Just someone at work."

"A handsome somebody," Mom mumbles into her tea, causing Dad to shoot her a look that screams: *seriously?*

I roll my eyes, and direct what I'm about to say to my dad. "He's just somebody I work with."

"Your brother mentioned something about helping him pick up some new furniture for his apartment," Dad is the expert of changing the subject, especially if the topic involves his daughter and boys.

"Did Harry ask for my help?" Not sure why I am asking, I'm pretty sure I know the answer already.

"No," Dad answered, flatly. "It would be good if you two got together and talked things out though. We're not blind that there has been...an edge between you both ever since you started dating Simon."

I know Dad doesn't mean that as a jive, he merely wants a peaceful family life. I don't disagree with him, but it's not like I haven't tried to talk to Harry. It's him who won't return my calls and brings the conversations to a halt whenever I talk to him.

Mom checks the time on her phone, "Speaking of work, you're going to be late aren't you?"

I check the time for myself and realise she's right. The flower shop is only around the corner from this cafe so I'm not too worried about being late. We all get up, Dad sorts the bill and leaves a tip, and we exit the store in single file. Mom forgets to hold the door open for Dad and the glass door almost smashes against his face.

"It's like you want me to lose my nose," he grumbles to himself.

Mom and Dad decide to walk me to work before splitting off to meet my aunt and uncle.

As we approach I notice Will is standing outside of the shop, casually leaning against the window with his hands deep into his front jeans pockets. I actively slow down my pace, hopefully whoever he is waiting for will show up to lead him away from the shop, that my parents are also approaching.

If I go any slower I will be coming to a standstill.

"I don't know how old you think we are," Dad says. "But you don't need to walk so slow for us to keep up."

I can't think of anything to say. Why is Will waiting outside of the store? I'm trying to send internal shockwaves into his mind to command he disappears into the store. It's no use. If anything my mental mind trick does the opposite effect of what I want. He turns and sees me, and my parents, approaching.

The moment he catches my eye a wide, shit-eating-grin appears on his face. He lifts himself off the wall and opens his arms to me. I don't even have time to react when he wraps his arms around me and pulls me in for a tight hug. Will squeezes me hard on purpose, making it difficult for me to inhale a breath, and I want to claw his face off right about now.

The awkwardness and confusion from my parents is immense, and I can't even see them right now.

"There you are!" Will enthusiastically proclaims, like we are in front a live studio audience.

Just as abruptly as he pulled me in for the hug, he pushed me back at arms length. If these motions continue I am going to get whiplash. "Aren't you going to introduce me?"

"Uh..."

Again, another motion that I am not prepared for in the slightest, Will slips his hand around my waist and pulls me to his hip.

I want to shrivel up and die right now. I make the mistake of looking up at both of my parents. Mom has an electrified smile on her face, like she couldn't be happier to see me in the arms of — let's face it — a handsome stranger. My dad...well, let's just say he looks about as sceptical as when Harry claimed he got an A in math back in high school.

"Well...since you have given me no choice." I shoot daggers up to him, which only widens Will's grin. "Mom, Dad, this is Will...my..." the moment I say the word it will be a lie. I hate lying to them, they haven't done anything to deserve it. If this is going to be a seemingly 'real' relationship, I need to make it appear as though that is what it is. "My... boyfriend."

If Will wasn't standing right next to me, his hand literally over my hip, my mom would be bouncing up and down on her heels. Dad's eyebrows flick upward, like that was the last thing he was expecting.

"I'm Emma," Mom waves, her cheeks blushing like Will's very presence means he is flirting with her. The kind of reaction I would expect if he used the line: *are you her mother? I thought you were her sister.*

"Caleb," Dad sticks out his hand for a firm handshake. Will smiles as he accepts it, those blasted dimples on display that would win over anyone.

"Nice to meet you both."

"Yes, wonderful." I cannot stand to be in this situation for more than a second. I push Will into the flower shop before any more words can be exchanged. If this were *The Sims*, I would have died from embarrassment by now, the Grim Reaper would be on time to steal my soul away for eternity. And honestly? I would welcome it.

I say a swift goodbye to my parents and shut them out before Will can humiliate me any further. Not only am I embarrassed but I am furious.

"Why would you do that?"

"What?" He asks as a laugh. Will is so proud of himself, he knows exactly how mad I am right now and it seems to be fuelling his energy for the day.

"You made me tell my parents about us!"

Will takes small steps towards me and plants a quick kiss on my cheek. "That's what girlfriends do."

I hate myself for blushing at that simple action. I wipe it off with the back of my hand and let out a throaty groan. "I don't want them involved in this, Will!" I move around him and grab my green apron from behind the counter. "You may be comfortable lying to your parents, but I'm not."

"I'm not *comfortable* with it," all the playfulness is lost now. "I'm just doing what I need to in order to get out of an arranged marriage."

"Yeah, well," I tie the back of my apron into a knot, almost suffocating myself in the process. "I'm sure your parents wouldn't *actually* make you go through with it. Rosie seems like — "

"You don't know my family."

I freeze entirely, turning as cold as a statue. I've struck a nerve, sliced into it, based on the look on Will's face. There must be something more to his family's story that he is not telling me. The hurt I saw in Rosie's eyes the first time I met her are present in Will's right now. I might be wrong, but his looks all the more painful.

"I'm still mad at you," I announce. "And as my *boyfriend,*

you need to make it up to me."

That gets a small chuckle out of him. "What would you like?"

I grab my sketchbook and pencil from under the counter and turn my back on him, grinning like a madwomen. "Surprise me."

Chapter Ten

When I told Will to 'surprise me' I was hoping for something like a gift, or even something as simple as a night out at a fancy restaurant.

But no.

I have come to realise that Will is a man of inconvenience. I should have known that from the moment we met. Ever since our one night stand my life has turned completely upside down. It's so off track that I can't see the road anymore, instead a giant brick wall has been placed in front of my feet, and Will's name is scribbled on it in a giant graffiti graphic.

It's two o'clock in the morning, and my phone is vibrating at my bedside. It has been doing that for a few minutes; I refuse to answer because it's Will. The moment I saw his name pop up in my phone is the moment I regret giving him my number, heck, even *meeting* him.

On the fourth attempted call I finally decide to answer with a, "What?"

"Oh, sweet girlfriend of mine!" Will yells down the phone, making me keep my phone a distance away from my ear. In the background I can hear a lot of commotion, like music and a crowed cheering.

"What do you want?"

"I want *you* to come here and give me a kiss," he starts

laughing.

I should hang up, he's clearly wasted. I can't help but feel somewhat responsible for him, as his fake girlfriend if anything happened to him I would be the one catching heat because he's the idiot calling me.

"You're so drunk, where are you?"

"Be still my heart," every single word in that sentence slurred. "Where our love story began, darling mine."

I roll my eyes. It doesn't take a genius to figure out he is at The Phoenix, nightclub where we first met.

Removing my blanket, the cold immediately settles over my body. "I'll come and get you."

"I *knew* you wanted me."

I could easily climb back into bed, put the covers on and sleep soundly without helping that moron. I know I won't do that, I would worry about his safety. It's not because I have any feelings for him, it's just because people can get into dangerous situations when they are so blindingly drunk. I'm assuming he is alone, I didn't hear anyone with him and why would he call me if he had someone else to distract him?

I know I will only beat myself up if something happened to him.

Begrudgingly, I change out of my pyjamas and into simple black sweat pants and a long sleeved white shirt. Probably not one would expect to be wearing when going to a nightclub, but I'm not going for fun. I'm simply going to drag my drunk fake boyfriend, out by his ear if I have to, and drive him to my apartment so he can sleep in the safety of somewhere that isn't surrounded by a busy street.

When I pull up, I can feel the bass of the music beneath my feet. I park on the road, praying Will makes this quick enough that I don't get a ticket. Once inside I find him at the bar, the only person who has drank so much that he can barely stand.

Looks like I got here just in time, as the security is now

beside Will and telling him he's had enough. I can see Will getting frustrated, pleading for just one more drink but the bartender and the security refuse him.

I can imagine this going very wrong if I don't step in and take him away. I hurry over and drape my arm over Will's shoulder. "I'll take him home," I explain. "I'm his girlfriend."

I internally cringe at myself.

The security seems satisfied with any reason to get him out of here.

"He does this shit too often," the tallest of the security guards says. "Once he's sober, make sure he understands he's banned for a month."

Will slumps against my shoulder, and is somehow walking with me. I'm pretty sure he has fallen asleep whilst walking. It should make it easier for me to get him in the car and drive back with little disturbance.

We make it to my car, not without almost dislocating my shoulder, and as I am about to open the door Will suddenly snaps up his head. It's like he was suddenly possessed by a demon that had a bucket of cold water thrown over him.

"Lulululu," he laughs. "That's what your ex called you, wasn't it? Lululululu…"

"Uh-huh," I'm too tired for this. I try a second time to open up my door, but Will turns his body so he's pressed against the handle of the passenger side, his butt completely blocking my hand from opening it.

With his chest in my face I can do nothing but stand and wait for him to be done with this. "I can just leave you here."

"You won't do that," his hands slip over my waist, and he buries his face into the curve of my neck. His hot breath colliding with my skin. "Lulu," he whispers. "I prefer Lucy."

"So do I," my voice comes out hoarse. I shouldn't enjoy the feeling he is giving me right now, how his lips feel against my neck, but I do. I have to focus on getting him to my place, even if it's just so I can go back to sleep. "If you get in the car we can..."

Suddenly, his hands tighten around my hips. In a sort of possessive way, like letting go would mean losing his life. It's an action I don't quite understand, it's not to be annoying but like he is genuinely terrified.

"You're not drunk?" He asks.

"Of course not," I sigh. "I came here to get you."

Will presses my body firmly against his, his lips trailing kisses over my shoulder. "You promise you haven't drank?"

"I've had water?"

Will finally raises his head, a drunken glaze in his eyes that seems to be masking his annoyance. Even when he is in a complete state he is the most handsome man I have ever seen. "Don't be like Greg." He suddenly says, and then turns and reaches for the handle of the door. He struggles for a few minutes and eventually opens it, then crawls inside.

I still stand in my position for a while, confused by what he could possibly mean.

Don't be like Greg.

Who is Greg? And why did Will look so angry at just the mention of his name. Yet, there was something else in his eyes, a hurt of some kind.

I'm too tired to try and piece together what all of this means. I just want to go to bed and not think about it, at least until I have a full nights rest.

I climb in the car and Will has fallen asleep in the passenger side. I could just leave him like that and drive home, but I'd rather be safe than sorry. I pull his seatbelt over his unconscious body and strap him in like a grown toddler that tired themselves out at the park. As I am about to pull away, Will grabs my hand and intertwines our fingers.

I look up at him through tired lashes, and in this moment in the light of the streetlamp, he doesn't look drunk. He looks as sincere as he ever has before. "I'll be your bodyguard, I'll protect you. I promise I won't let him hurt you."

A lump forms in my throat, and it hurts to swallow. Why does he sound like he's in pain? Not physically, but there is damage within his heart that he is trying to repair. Alcohol clearly didn't work for him, and based on what the security guard said, it's not the first time he has gotten himself in this state. It makes me worry how many times he has done this and had no one to help him get home. It's a miracle he's not dead.

Rolling the window down on the drive home seemed to help Will sober up, even if it was only a little. He still can't seem to keep his head still as I turn off the engine and take a moment to just look at him.

My car now reeks of booze. It's clear this wasn't a night of fun that got out of control, there is something remarkably sad swirling around him. It's like he wants to drink to forget something.

I can't focus on that right now, I have to figure out to get him into my apartment by making the least amount of noise. I would leave him out here, but it's a particularly cold night tonight and I know I'd feel guilty leaving him alone. I have a feeling in my gut that he wouldn't want to be left alone.

I get out of the car and I walk around to the passenger side. I open up the door and find Will with his head slumped down, his black hair veiling the upper half of his face. Looking at how strong he is, and the weight of him when he was somewhat conscious, there is no way I can carry him upstairs.

"Will?" I try to shake him, which causes his head to roll back. "Will?"

"Mmm," the slits of his eyes opens just enough that I can see the green of his iris. At least he is somewhat awake.

"Can you get out of the car for me?"

Will tilts his head, now fully facing me. A grin tickles his mouth as his veiled eyes stare at me. "You're gorgeous."

"You're drunk."

A frown has now anchored down his entire face.

I grab a firm hold of his arm and drag him out of the car. Will helps as much as he can by not going completely limp on me. Draping his arm around my shoulder, I use my ass to close the door behind me and ensure to lock it before heading upstairs.

It's awkward to grab my key and hold Will up at the same time. Once inside I haul him up the stairs and into my apartment.

If only the elevator wasn't out of order, then this would have been so much easier.

I can't get him off me fast enough when I walk to the bedroom, not because I want him to be comfortable, because it is the closest room to the front door.

I lay him down on my bed, propping up his head on my pillow and turning him onto his side. Before I manage to fully roll him over, Will grabs my arm and pulls me down so I smack my face against his firm chest. He captures my body with his arms and holds me tightly against him. There is something oddly soothing about being in his arms, and the pounding rhythm of his heart against my ear.

"Will..." as much as I'd love to fall asleep here, it wouldn't exactly be appropriate. "Will I need..."

"Stay," he mumbles.

I hate how fast I concede. "Only if you roll onto your side."

I help him turn over, both of us now on our sides and facing one another. His fingers tangle in the ends of my hair, spilling the strands within his fingers. This action lulls me to drift into the beginning of a slumber. "If you get sick on me in the night, I will kill you."

I feel him rumble a chuckle, his hand now cradling to back of my head firmly against his chest. "I'm sure I can find a way to make it up to you."

"You already have something to make up for," referring to embarrassing me in front of my parents.

Will plants a kiss on the top of my head, "I haven't forgotten. I'm sure I can come up with something... satisfactory."

I blush, thinking of his hands all over me in my living room and the back room of the flower shop. I settle in his arms and fall asleep with a smile on my face.

Chapter Eleven

I wake up earlier than I expected, considering I was rudely awakened in the middle of the night by a drunken Will. If I'm so mad then why am I standing at my stove and making him a buffet of a breakfast?

Have I gone insane?

I can't help but feel a bit bad for him. Last night it was obvious there is something he is trying to wash away, like there is something that he wants to erase from existence. I'm oddly intrigued to find out what it is. Maybe finding out who Greg is might be a starting point.

The door to my bedroom creeps open, and out walks a very hung over Will still in his clothes from last night. I'm not going to lie, waking up in his arms was the most comfortable I have felt in years. I can't explain it, even though he was pretty much blackout drunk I felt safer in his arms than I ever did with Simon. It's like my head was designed to fit the curve of his neck.

I shake off all ridiculous thoughts and dish up breakfast, "Morning."

"Ah," he winces when he heads further into the room, the sun almost blinding him.

"I made you breakfast."

It takes a few seconds to take in what I just said. He slides into one of the stools at the island and props his head up with his hand. "Aren't you a sweet fake girlfriend."

I roll my eyes and shove the plate in front of him.

"What's this?"

"Breakfast…"

He glowers at me, "I know that. It looks so greasy."

I'm going to pretend he isn't insulting the dish I made for *him* so he can feel a bit better. I'm tempted to take it back since he is being so ungrateful.

"It's a full English breakfast. My mom made one for me when I had a really bad hangover one time. I promise it works." I bring my shoulder up to my ear. "Well, it helps at least."

"I thought you turned twenty-one a few weeks ago?"

"We visit England every year to see my grandpa," I explain. "The drinking age there is eighteen, so I made the most of it two years ago and decided never to drink that much again."

"Your mom's from England?" Will asks after shovelling a strip of bacon into his mouth. "I thought her accent was Australian."

I shake my head, and he actually gets a small smile out of me. It could be because he is inhaling the meal I prepared.

He points at me with a fork, after I pour us both a cup of coffee. "You not eating?"

"I already ate," it's sweet that he thinks I would put his hunger before my own.

Something has been bothering me for a while with Will, aside from his general attitude and *being*. I swirl my coffee around in my cup and take a small sip before saying, "You know, I don't really feel like we have done much to prove to your mom and dad that we are together."

Will finishes his plate and takes a gulp of his coffee, "Yeah, I've been meaning to talk to you about that." He gets up from

79

his seat and runs his fingers through his thick black hair. "My mom has told my dad about you, and he's asked to meet you. He's booked a table for this Saturday at some restaurant."

I suddenly regret asking. Why am I nervous? It's not like I am actually meeting his father for real. If his father doesn't like me then it will make zero difference to my life because this is just pretend.

This might be over sooner than I was expecting. His dad is the main man we need to convince that our relationship is real. Rosie seemed over the moon because of it, but that's not saying his father will be easy to win over.

"So, once I meet him do we say that we broke up shortly after?"

"I wouldn't end it too quickly, then he'll know it was fake. Maybe we could pretend for another month? Hug and kiss at the store, or anywhere else we'll be seen together."

I nod, a sudden anxiety bubbling in my chest. I want this to be over so I can go back to having a normal life, maybe find someone who will like me for me and not some strange arrangement.

Simon suddenly appears in my mind. I can't help but be afraid of him, the unknown of what he is willing to do to try and get me back. He could still come back after a month, I don't think something like that simply goes away in a short amount of time.

"What's wrong?"

Will is now right next to me, his emerald eyes scanning my face. I must be wearing my troubles on my sleeve, so I decide to be honest. "I'm just…not sure when to expect Simon to go away. It's scary."

"Even if we 'break up' in a month, I'll still look after you. If you need me, I'll be there."

I meet his eyes. The sincerity from last night is there, only clearer thanks to the drunken fog no longer taking shape.

"Really?"

"Of course," he grins. "You were there for me last night." His voice dips into a thick whisper, and I find my body being drawn to him. I know I said no sex as apart of our agreement but with him here, looking as handsome as he is, how can I possibly follow through with that?

"Speaking of last night," I say. "You are banned from The Phoenix for a month."

Will doesn't seem to react, or even care about it. "Is that coming from you? Are you banning me from there?"

I shoot him another glare. "As if. One of the security guards told me to tell you once you are sober. Apparently it happens too often, you getting so drunk you can't walk."

The frustration I was expecting is now painted over Will's face. He runs a firm hand through his hair and discards a sigh. "Long time coming, I suppose."

"You drink a lot?"

"I'm not an alcoholic," he snaps at me. "I just want to forget sometimes."

I'm about to ask what exactly it is he wants to forget. Then I remember it's not exactly my place. Besides, he seems to be very much on edge now, so I decide to change the subject. "So, what do you do for a living?"

I turn my back on him and place the dirty dishes into the sink. "You're rarely at the flower shop these days."

"I'm a writer," when I look over my shoulder, he is leaning the curve of his back against the island with his arms crossed. "An unpublished author."

"Wow, what do you write? Let me guess, romance?"

He shakes his head and fights a smile. "You'll find out when it's published."

"Can I read it?"

"Nope." He didn't even need a second to think about it, and I can't help but pout. "Suddenly when you say you are a writer everyone becomes interested in reading. That, or they insist on being a character."

"That's good, isn't it? Maybe not everyone wanting to be a character, but people taking an interest in your book? Or can only snobs appreciate your work?" I put on a fake snooty accent, somewhat mimicking ones I heard in England, and raise my chin high.

"Oh yeah? What was the last book you read?"

My cheeks flush as I pretend to be very interested in washing up my empty mug. *"Twilight."*

Will laughs, "And when was that?"

I am grinning, I try not to but I can't help it. "Back in high school."

Will suddenly steps to my side and places a firm hand over my shoulder. He removes it just as quickly as he placed it there and whispers, "Exactly."

"You know, if you were to self-publish I could design the cover for you?" I turn to face him, and flick the end of his nose. "I'm somewhat experienced with design."

He looks like he's considering it, and a small bit of hope swells in my heart. "I'll tell you what, if my mom chooses one of your designs for the flower shop logo, you can design my cover."

I beam a bright smile. It's not because of the conditions he has set for me to achieve, to work toward something as a reward for my craft, but it's the way he said it. Like he already knows that I am going to be the one to design it.

"That means I'll have to read it, to grasp what you like."

Will sticks out his bottom lip, "Nope, I tell you what I want and you deliver. No reading necessary."

Damn it, I am just too interested to know what he writes about. I am hoping it's a romance, anything else bores me.

"Can I at least know the genre? It's not a biography, is it? The Great Tales of William Dawson."

"I'm afraid I haven't lived enough to write an entire book about my life."

"So, what's the genre?"

I swear Will blushes at that question, and now I am almost certain he writes romance. I have no idea why he would be embarrassed about that, but it's cute. "Get the logo approved, and you will have the details."

I purse my lips, struggling to contain my smile. I'm not used to seeing Will so flustered, and over something like his work. I would have never pinned Will as the creative type, I just thought he floated through life and caused as much trouble as he possibly could. I'm a little relieved that's not the case. There is certainly a depth to Will that I am yet to discover, and a part of me wants to dig down to his core and find out every single detail of him. It might provide more of an understanding into why his parents insist he needs a wife.

I'll just have to stop myself when this fake relationship starts to feel real.

Chapter Twelve

I don't think I've worked so hard on a logo before. I wanted to impress Rosie, but now I have even more of an incentive. After Will left my apartment I have spent the last two nights in the same spot on my couch. My cushions will be forever be moulded to the shape of my ass, that would be embarrassing for visitors to witness.

My phone suddenly vibrates, when I pick it up I half expect it to be Will. When I see that it's not I can't help but feel disappointed. Instead it is my friend, Melissa. It's strange that I now feel a scepticism whenever she messages me. We used to be best friends, where an hour would seem like a lifetime for us not to text. She was practically my conjoined twin throughout high school, still not as close as Jeremy and I, but we still loved each other like we were the sisters we never had. That all changed this past year and I have no idea why. Maybe I became too busy trying to further my career that we lost touch. Yet, I can't help the sinking feeling that followed me, that she was purposely avoiding me.

We would have a weekly sleepover, watching movies and eating ice cream every Friday since we were fourteen. Only once had it been missed, when I got the flu and couldn't get out of bed for an entire week.

Then, last year when I had planned to visit her house, she

suddenly texted me saying she had plans that night. Then she had plans every Friday night until I stopped bothering to try and show up. Eventually, we both just stopped talking all together. It saddens me to think of now, that there was a point where I thought we would be BFF's until we were old and in rocking chairs.

Melissa used to tell me everything, then one day I felt like she was keeping secrets from me. I never found out what, but there was a guilt surrounding her whenever I was around. Almost as though she was embarrassed to be in my company.

Now if I see her in the street I hate to admit that I will often avoid her, because I don't want the awkward conversation. Where once it would spill off our tongues, when we had so much to talk about that there was never enough time in the day. Instead we can barely think of anything more of 'how are you?' Then followed by a 'good thanks, you?'

I open up our messages, reading that our last conversation was over six months ago and she was asking if I had borrowed one of her favourite dresses, to which I replied with a simple 'no.'

Melissa: Hey, long time no speak!

My thumbs do a little dance as I think of what to respond with. I type and erase so many options. I hate how strange this feels to me now, when talking with her was as easy as breathing. Now it's like I've just received a message from a stranger.

Me: Hi, how have you been?

Melissa: I've been good, busy with work! I was wondering if you were free for a coffee? It's been too long since we've had a catch up.

* * *

I can't help but smile at my screen. I have missed her like crazy, she and Jeremy were the only two people I trusted with my deepest thoughts. I'm grateful that Jeremy is still his over the top self, I don't know where I would be without him. Just one more week and he will be back from his month long vacation.

It will be a good thing to reconnect with Melissa. I hope.

Me: I'm free tomorrow? Shall we meet at *Starbucks* around 11?

Melissa: Sounds perfect :)

Anxiety is becoming way too comfortable in my chest recently. Even now, waiting for Melissa to show up, I can't help looking around and keeping my hands busy with my napkins. I have shredded three now and soon I will need a forth.

Finally I spot Melissa looking for me. I almost didn't recognise her. Her once brunette hair is now a platinum blonde and trimmed short so it hangs just above her shoulders. Her make-up is flawless, with a smoky eye to really bring out the dazzling blue. She's always looked like a fashion queen, today is no acceptation. Melissa is wearing a fitted red dress with a sharp black blazer, and glossy black heals to match.

When she spots me, a smile beams on her lips but if I blinked in that moment I would have missed that reoccurring guilt I felt before we disconnected.

I get up and greet her for a hug, I can feel in this embrace that she has missed me so I hug her a little tighter.

We both sit down and order our coffees. I have a caramel latte whilst she goes for a standard black coffee.

"How have you been?" I start off, unsure of what else to

say.

"Great! I've been super busy at work, but what's new?"

"Are you still a manager at that marketing company?"

The waiter arrives quickly with our coffees and we both take a sip before continuing out conversation. "Yeah," she answers simply.

The air suddenly feels colder, like someone left the door open on the peak of a winter storm. I can't help but feel like Melissa asked me here for a reason. That she didn't actually want to catch up, because all of the questions have been about her and not once has she asked how I am doing.

"Is there...something you wanted to talk about?"

She can't look at me, her painted black nails start tapping against her mug as she contemplates telling me whatever it is she has to say. "I've just...I..." she lets out a sigh before meeting my gaze. "There has been something that I've needed to get off of my chest for a year now. I can't move forward if I don't."

"Okay?" I take a small sip from my latte, pretending that I'm not as nervous as I feel.

Melissa sighs and sinks back into her chair. "Look, I'm just going to come out and say it. Simon and I are seeing each other. And...we have been for a year now."

I visibly freeze, staring at her and trying to take in her words. Everything from the past year suddenly makes sense. Why she had avoided me, when she was busy she was probably visiting my boyfriend and fucking him. This is why she felt guilty about even talking to me, because she was seeing my boyfriend behind my back.

I am angry, I shouldn't care because I don't want Simon anymore. I would be so happy if I never saw him again, but it doesn't make this betrayal hurt any less.

"I'm sorry, Lucy."

I can tell she means it, but then I suddenly feel a tidal wave of confusion. Regardless of how I feel right now, if Melissa and Simon are a couple now, why is he trying so hard to get me back?

Why does he care?

Why is he so set on harassing me if he's wanted my ex best friend this entire time?

"I really don't know what to say..." I confess the truth.

"I understand if you hate me," she said. "We never planned on it happening, he was there for me after my break up with Scott. When you guys broke up, it gave us a chance to be together like we've always wanted."

I can't tell if she said that final part to twist the dagger into my heart further.

Should I tell her about what he has been doing? The texts begging for another chance, storming into my work demanding that we talk? I know if I was in her shoes I would want to know.

"Melissa, Simon has been trying to get me back. He's been coming into my work, he even *grabbed* me..."

"I know that you are mad," Melissa has a venom of spite in her tone. Tears are now pricking her eyes but she easily fights them back. "I get it. But Simon and I are good together, we want this to finally be real. You need to let him go and stop harassing him."

"Excuse me?"

Harassing *him?* She cannot be serious, but the look on her face implies that's all she is.

"You don't need to make up lies about him to try and turn me against him," Melissa gets to her feet, leaving her coffee cup half full. "I wanted to be nice about this, but you need to leave him alone and let him move on."

I am rendered speechless and even more confused. I'm not even sure if any of this really happened. I don't get a chance to ask more about it, as Melissa leaves without looking back.

Leaving me with two cups of half drank coffees, and the tab. I wouldn't mind paying, I was planning on offering, but when someone says they've been having an affair with your boyfriend for the past year, paying for anything for them isn't at the top of my priority list.

I can't believe what Melissa had said. To truly believe her words as they left her mouth. I knew Simon was a liar but I never knew to what extent he could be so manipulative. Clearly spinning his actions and making them mine. Implying that I am coming into his work and begging for a second chance, when I would be happy to never cross paths with him.

I am knocked out of my thoughts when the door to the shop bursts open, almost ripping the bell from the wall. When I look up, my heart blooms with a joy that I haven't felt in a while, as Jeremy stands in the doorway with a grin almost as big as mine on his face.

I run to him and practically leap into his chest. His strong arms circle around me, and he lifts me into a spin. "I have missed you!"

"You are not allowed to go on such a long vacation again," I tease as he sets me down. "Not without me, at least."

He agrees with a nod, planting a kiss on my forehead. "Agreed."

I lead him into the shop and he takes a seat at the counter. His skin has got a warm tan, just showing off how relaxing his vacation must have been. His brown hair has been neatly trimmed, with faded sides and a gorgeous blowout of hair on top. Jeremy crosses his arms over his red t-shirt and looks at me with a raised eyebrow. "So, a hell of a lot has changed for *you*." He gestures around the shop I now work in.

I knock my head back and groan, "I know, my life feels like it's in shambles."

"I go away for a month and *this* is what happens."

Jeremy takes my hands in his and brushes his large thumb across my knuckles. "Talk to me about it. Tell me what I need to do to fix it."

I explain everything that happened with my job, how I got fired for simply being shit at it. To which Jeremy responds with a roll of his eyes. I then tell him everything that happened with Simon, including my little meeting with Melissa.

"I want to hate her, but I'm more mad at Simon." I confess. "He's obviously manipulating her. I really wasn't trying to make her jealous — or whatever it is she thought — when I told her about him coming into the store and demanding we get back together."

"I know," he sighs. "I'd say you've tried to warn her and it's up to her to see the signs. Maybe she will realise that he's a sleaze when he cheats on her."

"You think he will cheat on her?"

Jeremy gives me a poignant look. "He's begging for you back, isn't he? He's clearly already willing to. Besides, once a cheater *always* a cheater."

"Hmm."

"Is that all of the depressing news?" He asks with a quirk of his mouth. "Or is there any exciting news?"

I'm yet to even mention Will to him. I wasn't sure how to fit our entire ordeal into one text without it being an incoherent mess. I'm about to find somewhere to start, when the door to the shop goes again, and of course, it's Will.

It's like he knows the exact worst time to walk in on me. Just like every other time, I know he is going to cause more awkward questions for the person in my presence.

"Hey," he greets me with a smile, but that soon falters when he spots my hands in Jeremy's.

Will steps behind the counter and greets me like any other

boyfriend would, with a quick kiss to my cheek. I can feel Jeremy's shock radiating from him, and that's only confirmed when I steal a glance at his slack jaw.

"I'm Will," he introduces himself to Jeremy by shaking his hand.

"I'm Jeremy…nice to meet you."

Will offers his most charming smile before slipping into the backroom.

I can't help the red flush that my cheeks become, and Jeremy does nothing to help my embarrassment. He presses his entire body into the counter and tries to force my gaze to his, I am far too flustered to do that right now.

"Excuse me?" He's laughing like this is the funniest skit he's ever seen. "What was that? You didn't tell me you had a boyfriend — pardon me — a *hot* boyfriend."

"He's not my boyfriend," I hiss.

"No?" He raises a brow like he doesn't believe me. "Then what was that kiss, hmm?"

"It's not what it looks like…"

Jeremy knocks his head back and laughs like an evil kid. When he brown eyes meet mine again, they are filled with amusement. He's a lot like Will, in which they both like to watch me squirm. "You have to the count of three to give me the details, otherwise we are no longer friends."

He starts counting down, and I finally confess after two, "We had a one night stand on my birthday."

"Lucy!" He reacted just as I expected him to, with complete shock.

"I just wanted a simple night of fun after all the shit with Simon, and he happened to be there." I go on to explain the events leading up to now. I trust Jeremy with my life, and I admit that this entire relationship is fake. I don't even need to ask him to keep it a secret because I know he will. I'm pretty sure if I murdered someone Jeremy would be there to help bury the body, I'd go so far as to say he would pick the burial spot.

When I explain to him what Simon has being doing recently, the harassment, all of the playfulness vanishes from his face.

"I can't stand him," he snarls. "It's nice of Will to look out for you, but know you have me too. I'll always be there for you, in a heartbeat."

I bring his knuckles up to my lips and kiss them. "I know. Same goes for you."

Jeremy and I go onto lighter topics. He gushes about his holiday, and how romantic it was for him and his boyfriend. He does confess that he was expecting a proposal, there were times at dinners that he was sure he was going to leave with a ring, but he's sitting here without a single piece of jewellery. Regardless, Jeremy had a great time in the sun. I just demand that next time he takes me with him, so maybe I can catch a break.

Chapter Thirteen

I'm smiling in the shower, the moment I realise I clamp my mouth shut. The reason why I can't stop smiling is because I am thinking of Will and his stupid smile. The way he finds any inconvenience to my life amusing. If his grin is wide enough I can make out the groove of his sweet dimples.

Standing in the shower, rinsing the soap from my body I can't help but picture what it would be like for Will to be in here with me. It's so inappropriate. I can't help it, just remembering how it felt to have his hands on me, worshiping my body like I am goddess is divine.

Before I realise it, my hands are slipping slower and lower. I stop myself when I realise where my fingers are drawn to.

I am alone in my apartment. I have touched myself many times, before Will it was the only way I experienced any sort of relief. Yet, apart of me feels wrong to do it when I am actively thinking of a man I am not in a relationship with. It feels…intrusive, but I can't help the yearning between my legs. The ache that I feel at the memory of his own large fingers rapidly touching me in the backroom, how his mouth tasted, the way his tongue sucked on my nipple, how his…

"Ah," I dipped a finger inside, chasing an orgasm that is so close yet so out of reach. I replay that night in my head, the one night stand. How his cock felt, how he pumped inside of me makes my fingers frantically move trying to recreate that feeling.

I'm sure I can come up with something…satisfactory.

His voice takes over my mind, his deep and rumbled words make my clamp down on my bottom lip.

I grab my breast and squeeze, pretending it is Will. Does he think of me when he is alone? Does he crave one more night with me as much as I do? Does he touch himself at the memory of us together?

I press my back against the cold tile wall, the climax is so close I can taste it. My moans out weigh the hissing shower spritzing water all over my body. If I asked Will to join me? Fuck me against my shower door, would he do it? I hope so.

Just picturing it…

Release consumes me, my body convulsing from such an intense orgasm.

I take my time to step out of the shower. When I do, I feel like the floor is spinning beneath my feet. Wrapping a towel around my frame, I rub the condensation from my bathroom mirror and stare at my reflection. My cheeks are a rose red, my chestnut hair is slicked back, the ends of my hair dripping water onto the floor.

Even though I am all alone, the only witness to what I just did being these four walls. I feel a little embarrassed. Maybe I took it too far, maybe doing things like this will confuse my heart about what Will is to me.

I slap my cheeks firmly and lock eyes with myself through the mirror. With a fierce glare, and pouting lip I promise myself. "I will *not* fall in love with Will Dawson. I will not."

I haven't been able to look at Will the entire time he's been in the store. I'm embarrassed to have touched myself at the thought of him, and that I orgasmed imagining it was by his hands. I was never this horny with Simon, I honestly hated sex before. Ever since Will it's all my mind can think about. I have the most inappropriate thoughts of him at the most inappropriate moments.

For example, I was working out my finances for upcoming bills at the apartment, and that spiralled into some weird scenario. I pictured sitting in Will's lap as I worked out the math. I imagined him throwing my papers and calculator to the ground, bending me over my coffee table and taking me right there.

It's like he's awoken some sexual demon within me, one that won't be satisfied by anyone else.

When Rosie enters the store, Will ensures to take a position right next to me, slipping his hand around my waist and tugging me close to his hip. Now really isn't the best time to be in a close proximity as him, since my mind was in the gutter just seconds ago.

Rosie eyes us and greets us both with a charming smile, "Hello, lovebirds."

"I didn't think you were here today?" Will asks.

"I'm just picking up a few things before your father gets back from his trip."

I am blushing a crimson red, and Rosie notices the second she looks at my face. Her smile only widens, revealing her perfectly polished teeth beneath her pink lips. "You are adorable, Lucy. You're making her blush."

When Will looks down at me I can feel his shit-eating-grin. It's not his hands around me that's making me this way, it's my own dirty thoughts *of* him.

"What can I say," he says, and plants a long — over the top — kiss to my temple. "She can't resist me."

That makes me roll my eyes and step out of his hands, busying myself with till roll.

Rosie seems to buy our fake relationship, no doubt she reports back to her husband how 'happy and in love' I seem.

When she disappears around the back, I shove Will by the chest. I so desperately want to kick him in the shin. "Fuck you," I say, my heated cheeks still giving me away.

Will only finds my reaction even more amusing. "You blushing over me? Aren't you a cutie."

I turn my back on him, demanding that my face cool down. The more I plead with myself, the hotter my face becomes. Any make-up I am wearing has melted off at this point.

"What is it, Lucy?" He teases. "My devilish good looks?"

"Ha!" I knock my head back and laugh as loud as possible.

"My irresistible charm?"

"Hmm, not quite." I huff.

My entire body freezes when his hands slip around my waist, connecting at my stomach and pressing my backside against his crotch. Similar to the night at my apartment, the night that kickstarted this entire headache. "Or is it how I made you come?" His words are dipped low and whispered directly into my ear.

I gasp but make no move to get out of his embrace.

Does he know? Did my bathroom walls betray me and reveal my secrets?

"Ah," Will growls. "So, that's what it is."

I want to punch myself, and him, in the face. I step out of his arms and he releases me instantly. "Do not hold me when there could be customers." I start polishing the front desk with a cloth, just to keep my hands busy. "If they wanted to watch porn they can do so at home."

"You must watch very boring porn if *that's* what you would class as it."

I'm about to retort, when Rosie exits from the back and Will immediately shifts into wholesome boyfriend mode. I swear, he must have a switch on him to make that change seem so effortless.

This man is infuriating.

"I was thinking of grabbing a coffee," Will said.

"Why don't you go with him, Lucy?" Rosie offers, and I want to shrivel up and die right here. "I can look after the store whilst you're gone."

There is no reason for me to decline. I have to make it seem like I want to spend every waking moment with Will, which couldn't be further from the truth in this very moment.

"Sure."

"Make sure you bring me a chai latte back."

Will gives his mom a thumbs up before escorting me from the store.

This is awkward.

I knew I shouldn't have let my mind have its own way in the shower. I'm pretty sure I am now cursed with Will's presence, ever since my unholy actions he has been hanging around me a lot more.

"What are you having?" Will asks me as we approach the counter.

I fumble a few words before finding my footing. "A caramel frappuccino."

"One of those, and an Americano please."

I fish for my purse but Will doesn't even hesitate to pay, he doesn't even ask. Does he think I am not capable of paying for my own drinks? I don't want him to be nice to me, it will only make me feel worse about being a creep.

"Drinking in or taking away?"

"Drinking in…"

"Taking away…"

Will and I answer at the same time. I don't get a chance to demand a take out cup when Will taps his fingers on the counter and says, "Ignore her, drinking in please."

The tips of my ears are hot with rage. "For your

information I am currently *supposed* to be at work."

"Does my mother not give you a lunch break?"

"Yes but…"

"But?"

"Coffee isn't food."

Will makes a surprised face, as if that is news to him. Instead of dignifying him with a response, which will lead to more sarcastic comebacks, I fold my arms over my chest and sulk.

We wait for our drinks to be prepared, and I keep my gaze anywhere but in Will's direction. My back is to him as I take in the scenery of this cafe, as if this isn't a place I visit regularly with my parents. I pretend to admire the black and white poster of celebrities drinking coffee, looking like they are having the time of their lives.

"Americano and caramel frappuccino!" The barista calls.

I swing around, still avoiding looking in Will's direction, when I can feel his green eyes drilling into the top of my head.

I grab my drink and lick off a trail of cream that is skating down the side.

"What the hell is that?" Will asks, disgust lacing his tone as he examines my drink. "Is there any coffee in that cup of sugar?"

If looks could kill, Will's head would have exploded from the lasers I am shooting.

I take a long, satisfying sip of my drink and exhale a deep moan as the cold coffee trickles down my throat.

Of course Will picks a seat by the window, where I have to climb a mountain before finding the seat. I settle my coffee down before attempting to climb on, it's like mounting a horse (which I have never successfully done in my many attempts growing up). My ass slips off the chair at least three times. The simplest of motions I can't do and Will is loving every second of witnessing this from his high chair.

"Having fun?"

I respond with something of a grumble as I finally hoist myself up, breaking a sweat in the process.

"I know you're short but I think a child could have sat down with more grace."

"If you are going to sit here and make fun of me, I will leave."

"I would *love* to see you attempt to get down."

I go to do so, until Will's hand grips lightly around my wrist, the action completely halting me. I can feel his eyes on me, they are burning a hole into the side of my face. My body is fighting an almighty urge to look up, steal a glance at his eyes but I am still so embarrassed about what I did. I know it makes no sense, I shouldn't be. Will and I have had sex, he's touched me like that, but there was something so intimate about my thoughts. The way that he consumed my mind, made me feel things I never have before, is scary.

"Are you okay?"

"I'm fine," I hold my coffee in a firm grip, my hands becoming wet from the melting ice.

I can feel Will's eyes study my face. "Are you sure? You seem particularly mad at me today."

"In case you haven't noticed, you are insufferable."

He really is insufferable. I can't help this brick that has planted itself in my stomach whenever I am in his presence. I should not feel as awkward as I do right now. We have had sex for crying out loud, and me touching myself at the memory should not be this huge of a deal. He doesn't even know that I did it.

"I need to talk to you about something by the way," Will's voice is dipped low. "Something important."

This doesn't sound good.

"Okay."

Will's quiet for a while, taking a small sip from his own coffee. "I need you to promise, whilst we're 'dating' — " he uses air quotes on the word *dating*. " — that you won't fall in love with me."

My stomach dips. I have a weird combination of wanting to laugh and cry at the same time. That would certainly make an interesting sight if I let my emotions fully take over.

"I need you to promise me."

"I promise I won't." I hiss without really thinking it through. It comes out harsher than I intended, rushed. There is something about the way he said it, as if the idea of either one of us falling in love would be a disaster. Am I that undesirable that he has to tell me not to fall in love with him?

Not that I plan on it. I have already made this promise to myself in the bathroom mirror.

I can't explain the irrational thoughts that take up most of the space in my brain. A lot of the time I don't make sense to myself. Right now, I'm feeling a level of insecurity I haven't felt before. I've always been hard on myself for my looks, comparing myself to others, and when I am next to Will it's hard not to feel inferior.

I am like a gremlin compared to him. With his strong, sharp jaw, his green eyes that would break even the coldest of hearts, and a smile that ripples me to my knees with a single quirk.

Sitting in this coffee shop right now, I bet people are looking at us and wondering why he is sitting with someone as plain as me. When he could get any girl he wanted, any supermodel with successful ambitions.

Why do I care what Will wants? I don't — do I?

There is something thrumming against my ribs, demanding to be released from its prison. The thought of Will with someone else, giving them a real relationship, isn't anything I like the thought of.

I am startled out of my thoughts when something flicks my nose. I turn to see the culprit, and of course it's Will. He's leaning his entire body forward, his mouth a firm pressed line and a single eyebrow raised. "What's going on in that head of yours?"

My cheeks flush, and I take another long sip of my coffee. "Nothing."

Will makes a humming sound, like he doesn't believe me. Not that I can blame him, I'm not exactly hiding my feelings well. "You can talk to me, you know?"

I shoot him a glare, unable to keep my eyes on him for longer than a few minutes I stare out of the window. "It's nothing."

Will releases a deep sigh, and turns his body to face me fully. "Don't you think a girlfriend should be able to confide in her boyfriend?"

The words 'girlfriend' and 'boyfriend' set me back for a moment. Suddenly I forget about our little arrangement. The way he said it, as if it was real, made my heart pick up in pace.

Stupid heart.

This is fake, you hear that heart? *Fake, fake, fake.*

My heart actively protests in my chest, thumping louder in my ears. *Real, real, real* it seems to respond with. I will excuse it with the caffeine I am practically inhaling.

Just to make matters worse, Will places his large hand over mine, engulfing my fingers. It's just a show, in case anyone he knows walks past and spots us. Is it so wrong that this feels right?

"Talk to me, Lucy."

The way he said my name, like it is the most beautiful name in existence spoken from his tongue sends my boiling blood into a frenzy.

"I just don't see how anyone expects us to truly be a

couple," I admit, feeling a little less weight on my chest. Only to be replaced by a crippling sadness at the admission.

"What do you mean?"

Is he really going to make me spell it out? Can he truly not *see* the difference between us?

Why am I getting emotional? I can feel the tears pricking behind my eyes. I try to swallow it down with another long sip of coffee, but that only makes it worse. I don't want Will to see me cry again. There have been enough times already. It's embarrassing.

"You know what I mean."

Will's fingers squeeze my hands, asking me to elaborate. I oblige, "You really think people will believe that someone who looks like me could get a guy like you?"

Will doesn't answer right away, but I can tell he is trying to figure out what I mean. Like what I said didn't make the slightest bit of sense to him.

"You mean someone as beautiful as you with a handsome guy like me?" Will's face shows no sign of amusement. "I'm not sure I see the scandal?"

Beautiful.

Will called me beautiful. He thinks *I'm* beautiful? And how effortlessly he said it, no force behind it but like he truly sees me that way. It's just a word, but to me it holds so much weight.

I don't know how to answer, so I just look away and pretend to be interested in the pile of napkins on the table next to us.

"Lucy?"

I swipe away a tear before it gets a chance to fall down my cheek.

I'm clearly under a lot of stress. I know I must look ridiculous. I'm allowing my stupid insecurities to take a hold of my body, all logic pushed to one side. It doesn't matter what Will thinks of me, why would it? As soon as I meet his father we will fake break up and I can get my life back on track.

When I don't turn to face Will I can imagine he's got the hint that I don't want to talk about it anymore. I'd rather just bury it down and try and move forward.

"We should get back to the shop," Will says in a weighted breath. "My mom will be mad if I return without her coffee."

Chapter Fourteen

My spells of insecurity have become frequent, but the one thing I have exuded all of my confidence into is my designs. The entire process of creating something new has been a therapeutic. From creating the skeleton, to trying out different styles of lettering, and drawing out patterns. Now that I have a few ideas and concepts drafted, I'm not so sure Rosie will like any of these.

I can still hear my old colleagues telling me everything I do wrong, and not in a constructive way. They would say they can't use any of my work because it is too *frilly*. Whatever that means. On some occasions they would ignore my emails with design suggestions, and the dirty looks they would give me across the office didn't go unnoticed either.

"How's the shop today?" Rosie asks as she appears from the back room.

I shrug, "Same as usual. Quiet."

I figure saying *quiet* is more polite than saying *completely dead*.

Rosie doesn't seem to bat an eye. I've come to assume that this shop is more of a passion project than something to provide real income. We rarely get customers, and when we do they tend to buy the cheapest bouquets. It makes me wonder how much money Rosie and Will actually have. I wouldn't dare ask because it is none of my business, and as long as they make money to pay my wages then that's all that matters.

I close my sketchbook before she can take a peak inside. I know I will show her eventually, I'm just not ready for criticism right now.

"How's things with you and my William?" Rosie's grin is from ear to ear. "I can't tell you how happy it makes me to know he's found someone as sweet as you."

I can't help but snort a small laugh at that. "I don't know about that."

Rosie reaches out and touches my hair, like my grandmother used to. That flick of sadness is back in her eyes, her smile is struggling to stay up and I can see the sorrow trying to consume her. "You'll look after my William, won't you? He's been hurting for a long time, ever since…well, you know."

No, I don't know. Maybe this could be my chance to find out more about him, why he wanted to drink to excess at the nightclub.

"Is this about Greg?" I ask.

Rosie clamps her mouth together, her lips forming a firm thin line. Just the mention of his name has made her eyes glassy with tears. Perhaps I should have kept my mouth shut, I didn't mean to upset her. Whoever this Greg person is has a clear connection to both Rosie and Will.

"Did he not tell you about him?" Rosie asks.

I shake my head, "He only mentioned his name," I chose to leave out the circumstances, I'm sure she would be worried to find out how wasted her son was. "Who is he?"

Rosie blinks to the ceiling, silently commanding that her tears remain in her eyes. When she drops her head again, a single tear had managed to escape and trickle down her cheek. "Greg is —" she winces, like she has been struck in the heart. " — *was* my youngest son."

I regret bringing this up, it feels far too personal to be talking about. I'm not even Will's real girlfriend, and this seems like it should be saved for someone who is. At the same time, I can tell Rosie has bottled this up for a while, and she needs someone to confide in. What kind of person would I be if I just simply ignored her?

"I'm so sorry," I rub her back gently. I'm not the best at offering comfort but sometimes saying nothing is the better option, and allowing her to get her distress off her chest helps.

"He was in a car accident a year ago," she blots her eyes with a tissue that she pulled out from her purse. "He was only twenty-one, and he..." her sobs come out in chokes now.

It really hits you when hearing about someone dying so young, and when they were your age when it happened. I can't help but reflect on my own life, if I were to die today would I be proud of my accomplishments?

I shake the thought off. That is a whole rabbit hole that I do not want to go down right now. I will spend more time thinking about my regrets than thinking of my future.

"A-and he...he..."

"It's okay, Rosie." I can tell this is still an open wound for her. The icy tears streak down her cheeks. "If it's too much right now you don't have to talk about it. If you ever need to though, you know where I am."

Rosie looks at me with a sad smile, and pulls me in for a tight hug. I do my best to comfort her, rubbing her back and not letting go until she does.

She inhales a gargled breath whilst attempting to busy her hands by fixing her hair. "Would you like to join me and my daughter Raven for lunch sometime? She has been dying to meet you."

I remember them mentioning a Raven before. I had no idea

Will has a sister, or any siblings for that matter. I don't really know much about his life, only that he must be wild enough that his parents thinks he needs a wife to settle down.

"Sure."

"Oh brilliant!" Rosie chimes. "William's father is eager to meet you, too. I am looking forward to Saturday."

I gulp. That will be the big night, the man I have to impress and convince that I am madly in love with his arrogant son. "Looking forward to it." I lie.

"You're good for my William," she mutters. "With you I feel he will finally stop blaming himself."

Blaming himself? For what? His brother's death?

I appreciate that Rosie has a lot of confidence in me. I feel sick that Will's plan is working so well, in that Rosie truly believes we are together. I feel dirty right now, and with every passing moment that I am in Rosie's arms is just another layer of betrayal I am sticking on her. Will promised I wouldn't lose my job if they found out this was all an act; how could I possibly face her after this moment. After she confided in me about her son? After Rosie had put all of her trust in me to take care of her son.

Today is the day I am meeting Will's father. The sooner I get this out of the way, the sooner I can go back to normal.

I went with an elegant look for the meal. A pink dress with a long shimmering skirt. A basic dress would not cut it for the restaurant his father had picked. I Googled it after Will forwarded me the address and it looks like a place where the highest earning celebrities would go for a birthday meal. It's far too extravagant for my taste.

I said I would drive myself, I'd rather have this meal and go straight home afterwards.

I check my reflection in the bathroom mirror, my chestnut hair is curled at the ends and sitting perfectly over my shoulders, hiding the straps to my dress. I've applied more make-up than I usually would but nothing too out there. Just a shimmering eyeshadow, black winged eyeliner and pink lipgloss.

Everything should be ready, I just need to show up and act like I am madly in love with Will.

My stomach is in knots. Why am I so nervous? I could actually throw up right now, the toilet looks tempting.

I shouldn't be anxious. This isn't *real*. Their opinion will change nothing about my life because in a month's time this will all be one weird dream. But why are my hands sweating?

I shake my hands, and then my entire body to try and calm my unwarranted nerves. I'm about to head out of the door when my phone starts vibrating in my purse. It's probably Will telling me he's at the restaurant.

When I pull out my phone, it's my dad.

It's usually mom who calls me if she needs to drop me a message. I have a really bad feeling in the pit of my stomach. I almost don't want to answer but I know I have to.

"Hi Dad," I try to sound normal, like I am not terrified to know why he is calling.

"Hey sweetheart," there is a sadness in his voice, and I don't think I'm ready to hear this. "Sorry to do this over the phone, but I thought I'd call to let you know that your grandfather has just passed away."

Chapter Fifteen

Numb.

My entire body feels empty. I'm silent for a while as dad tries to offer some comforting words. Words aren't really going to cut it right now.

I sink down to the floor of my apartment with my back against the wall. A rush of memories of my grandad flood my mind. We would visit him every year, and he would always be so happy to see us. He would be the one to meet us at the airport and drop us back. He would pick me up and shower me with kisses, even when I was too big to be picked up he would be willing to break his back to try.

"His funeral will be next week in England," Dad sighs. "We can't afford for all of us to go. Since we visited them a few months ago, we only have enough for one ticket. I hope you understand we decided it's best for your mother to go. If you have enough to buy a plane ticket then that would be great."

I shake my head as if he can see me. I have spent most of my savings making up the difference in rent ever since I lost my job. My money is running out. I'm hurt at the decision but of course it should be mom. It was her dad, I just wish there was a way to say goodbye to him.

"Do you want me to come get you? You can stay with us if

you don't want to be alone."

I haven't said anything since Dad announced it, and I honestly don't think I can move from this spot on the floor. All of the times I promised I would call my grandad, just for more regular updates. How I didn't get around to drawing either of those pictures for him. I had planned a sketch of a boat on a dock and something else when it got closer to our visit. That's all he wanted, and I let him down the last time I saw him in person. I've had nothing but time recently and I couldn't even take a few minutes to FaceTime him. I know it takes him a while to understand how to set it up, but I should have called. I should have done more. I didn't even know he was ill.

"Um...I'll probably come down tomorrow," my voice trembles the entire time. "I think I need time to process it."

"Of course," Dad says. "Call me if you need anything."

"Before you go," I cut in before he hangs up. "How's Mom?"

"I'll be honest," just from the tone of his voice I already know the answer. "She's devastated. I think because it came out of nowhere."

"So, he hasn't been secretly ill?"

"No," Dad said. "We would have told you and your brother. Your Aunt Tamara called her about an hour ago, we still don't know what the cause was but he was found in bed so we think he went in his sleep."

The tears fall freely down my face now. I can picture everything he is saying perfectly. I have to swallow the sobs as Dad and I hang up. He insists that I'm not alone at a time like this but I don't think I can physically get up even if I wanted to. I curl myself into a ball and sob as more memories fill my mind of my grandad. The more I think of his face the more my heart shatters like glass. It breaks even more when I realise I won't even get a chance to say goodbye to him. I'll have to wait until our next yearly trip to England to visit his grave.

I'm not sure how much my heart can take.

It could have been hours that I have been crying, sitting in my pretty dress and wallowing in self pity. I'm knocked out of my state in a jolt when the buzzer goes off multiple times, whoever it is sounds like they might break the button, pressing it so fast and repeatedly like the apocalypse is upon us.

With the little shred of strength I possess I get to my feet and push the buzzer, "Hello?"

"Hello? So you are still alive?!" Will's voice booms through the speaker. His choice of words right now really isn't helping. "Where the *hell* were you? My family and I were waiting for over an hour and you just didn't bother to show up! Not a text or a call! What the fuck, Lucy?"

I grit my teeth as my finger digs into the button of the speaker. I can do nothing but sob uncontrollably, the very last thing I need right now is for Will to yell at me. Over something that is so insignificant like a meal, when I feel like I have just had my heart ripped out from my chest.

"Lucy?" All rage vanished in a second when he heard my sobs through the speaker. "What's wrong? What happened?"

"I-I'm sorry," I can barely speak without feeling like my lungs are on fire.

"Buzz me in," there is guilt in his voice.

I should turn him away, let him feel guilty for yelling at me before knowing the full story. But I don't. I buzz him in and wait for him to come upstairs.

My door knocks and I take a few seconds to compose myself before answering. When I do, I find Will standing in a powder blue shirt and navy dress trousers. He looks so smart, like I have just opened the door to a scene from a romance movie. But I'm not the girl that is blushing and excited to go out on a date, I'm a mess with tears staining my cheeks with a boy who looks like his world has crumbled beneath him.

"Lucy, what happened?" He invites himself inside, delicately placing his hands over my shoulders. His eyes scan over my entire body, checking for any marks or possible bruises. He must think that Simon had shown up or that I have physically been hurt.

I'm not sure why, but the moment his fingers touched the skin of my shoulders, an overwhelming emotion electrified my veins. I can't fight back the tears as my face creases into sorrow. "I just found out my grandad died."

Will's shoulders drop in defeat. He takes his hands away from my shoulders and for a moment I think he is turning to leave. Instead he closes my apartment door, and opens up his arms to me. Right now I need that comfort, I need this. I wrap my arms around his back and hide my face into his shirt. I do nothing but cry, loudly. The sound is only muffled by his shirt, that I have probably stained with my smeared make-up.

"I'm so sorry, Lucy." His large hand smooths down the back of my head, as he rocks me from side to side.

I'm not sure how long we stand in my apartment holding each other. I should be embarrassed to be crying as hard as I am to Will, but I don't. I feel safe to cry to him. Maybe it's because I know he understands grief, after what Rosie told me of his brother's death, I can only imagine how much pain he must have endured — what he still endures. A loss of a grandparent is somewhat expected the older you get, but a sibling is worse. You expect to grow up together, share in the joys of milestones at a similar time if you are close enough in age like I imagine Will and Greg were. To have that suddenly ripped away, and in an accident, must be world shattering.

"I can't even say goodbye," my sobs get caught in my throat, my eyes are stinging and my lungs are on fire.

"Why not?"

I fist his shirt in my hands, holding on like my life depends on it. "His funeral is in England. We already took our family trip a few months ago, and my parents can only afford one ticket." Just knowing I can't say goodbye to the man who inspired my creativity just shatters my happiness. "Of course my mom should be the one to go, it was her *dad*. But I…" I'm hysterical, my high pitched voice is only masked by Will's firm chest pressed firmly against my mouth. My mouth is slick with saliva and I feel like I lost a piece of my heart the moment my dad told me the news. "I can't even afford a plane ticket, I spent most of my savings and current wage on this fucking apartment that I don't even like!"

My fingers tremble as I try to hold onto Will, afraid if I let my fingers slip then I'll sink into darkness. "None of us earn enough to pay for flights. I know my brother would try but on his wage it's impossible."

"I could have travelled with my Mom if I had left this fucking apartment." I whimper like a pathetic dog. "Now my mom is going to be alone on a, God knows how long, flight. Just thinking of her all alone, then having to come back alone…it's too much."

The entire time I cry into Will's chest, not once does his firm grip waver. Not once does he pull me away and tell me to get my shit together, he just lets me grieve.

Once I've calmed down I pull myself out of Will's embrace, only to feel an instant chill when he drops his arms.

I have left water and mascara stains on the front of his shirt, "Sorry," I mutter, pointing them out.

Will looks down and smiles. "I hated this shirt anyway."

I force a smile of my own, but it's painful right now.

"I'm sorry I didn't call or text about not coming to the restaurant," I sigh, feeling another wave of tears forming. "I just wasn't thinking…I couldn't…."

"Don't worry about it," Will hooks his finger under my chin and pulls my gaze to his. "This is more important. I'm sorry I yelled at you before knowing."

I offer a meek smile. "It's okay. You didn't know."

He guides me into my living room and sits me down on the couch. Will makes his way to my kitchen and looks around my cupboards. When he finds the glasses he takes one out and pours me a glass of water.

Will kneels down in front of me and hands me the glass. "Thanks," I mutter and take a long drink. After a while I stare down at the water, and wonder how much of a sight I must appear to be. "I think your dad would have set up the arranged marriage if I showed up looking like this."

He drops his head and chuckles, only looking up to meet my eyes. For a while he just stares at my face, his eyes looking right through me as if I were sitting naked in front of him, making me feel vulnerable.

"You're still beautiful," he sends my heart into a weird flurry.

I drop my gaze to his lips, those addictive lips that I have had the privilege of kissing. Even in moments like these I can't deny that I am drawn to him, like a moth to a flame. I lean in and kiss him deeply on the mouth.

Will returns my kiss almost instantly, his hands slipping up my thighs until they settle over my waist. I place the glass down on the table, not caring if it tips over. I grab the cuff of his shirt and drag him to be on top of me. I position him so his entire body covers mine, kissing him with everything I have to heal my broken heart.

I sigh against his mouth as I open my mouth and welcome his tongue inside. He's like a forbidden dessert when on a diet, one I would happily cheat to indulge.

I pin him in place with my thighs. I slip my hand down the centre of his broad chest, when I reach his belt his firm grip suddenly startles me into a halt. Will rips his lips away from mine, and shakes his head at me. "I'm not having sex with you, Lucy."

The rejection stings, "Why not?"

Will leans down and presses a kiss to my temple. "You're upset, and I don't want to take advantage of you."

"I'm telling you it's okay," I slip my fingers in his hair and try to kiss him again but he pulls back from me completely.

"It's not, and you know it." Will sits on the opposite side of the couch. "What kind of man would that make me if I had sex with you when moments ago you were sobbing."

I look away, humiliation settling over my already confused feelings.

His hand cups my cheek, and for a while I refuse to look at him but what's the point? He's seen me at my absolute worst, wailing from crying, what's a few more tears that outline my eyes?

"You know you would regret it."

I bury my face in my hands. What am I thinking? He's right. As much as I want a distraction from my pain, it will only put it off for a few minutes. This kind of pain can't be buried to deal with later.

Before I can apologise, Will pulls me close to his chest and lies us down on my couch. With my back pressed against the cushions, and Will facing me, all it will take is a slight movement and he will fall to the ground. I remain as stiff and still as possible in his arms, but when he tightens his grip I can't help but melt into him.

"Talking is a good distraction," Will says into the silence.

"When's your birthday?" I ask the first thing that comes to mind.

"October 19th."

"My birthday is May 5th."

Will plants a soft kiss to my forehead. "I'll write it in my calendar."

"How old are you?" Asking questions is helping me get my mind away from the pain, even if it's just to wait for his answers.

"Fifteen."

A fleeting moment of panic fuels my veins at his answer. I know he is joking, but it still doesn't help with that sudden whoosh of anxiety. I playfully smack his chest, which gets a light laugh out of him.

"I'm twenty-four." He clarifies.

"I've nearly finished the logo for your mom," I say. "I hope she'll like it."

"I'm sure if you puked on a page she would call it art."

That makes me smile. I press my face into his shirt, inhaling his intoxicating scent and fluttering my eyes to a close as he encircles me with strength. "Why don't you want a relationship?" I blurt the question out before I can stop it. I should take it back, but I don't because want to know.

"It can be..." he trails off for a moment, trying to think of the right words. "When you invest your heart, your love, into someone it's too painful when it's taken away."

He's not simply talking about breaking up with someone. He is talking about his brother, Greg. I can see how something as traumatising as losing a brother can have that effect on someone. But surely, having people around you in your darkest of moments should be more comforting than pushing everyone away. Like right now, sitting in Will's arms feels a lot better than crying alone on my floor.

Maybe Will and I are just too different.

"Want to watch a movie?" Will asks, derailing my train of thought.

I lift my head and look at him with a smile, "That'd be nice. Thank you."

Will gets up to grab the remote from my coffee table. He

switches on my TV and starts scrolling through the options. When he gets to my *Watch It Again* section, I see a smile quirk his lips.

I get up and sit beside him, pretending that there aren't over a dozen romantic comedy movies on the screen, exposing my terrible film taste.

"A woman of taste," he laughs. "It's been a while since I've watched a rom-com, pick one and we'll watch it."

I take the remote from him with a small smile and we settle on *Love, Rosie.*

When the movie begins, Will opens up his arms to me and I settle comfortably into his chest. I cuddle him and he starts tracing invisible circles over my back, leaving heat in his wake.

I realise as I lie with him now, how real this feels. I have to keep reminding myself that this isn't a relationship between a boyfriend and a girlfriend. If Will asked to keep this charade for another year…another ten years, I wouldn't complain.

Chapter Sixteen

Will stayed the night last night. I fell asleep in his arms halfway through the movie. Waking up to the sight of his muscled chest, and his strong arms around me, is something I could get used to.

He's doing everything that a real boyfriend would do in a moment like this. Actually, I don't think Simon would have been this considerate. If I wanted to distract myself with sex, in the exact same scenario, he would have done it. Simon wouldn't have cared to comfort me like Will. Simon would have made it about himself, and he would somehow spin it into how hard *his* life is, making me feel guilty for feeling the way I do.

Not Will.

He was really there for me when he didn't need to be. He let me grieve, and held me close while I cried. Not just cry, but ugly cry.

Will offered to drop me off at my parent's house, insisted actually. He said he didn't want to worry about me driving whilst I'm still in an emotional state. It was just another thing I agreed with him on. I packed a bag because I plan to stay with them until Mom gets back from England. She leaves tomorrow, and will be staying with my Aunt Tamara for a few days to help prepare some loose ends for the funeral.

Will pulls up to my childhood home, and it feels strange to be coming back under these circumstances. This is a place I only have fond memories of, and to walk up those front porch steps with a hollow heart, it doesn't feel right.

"Just call me if you need me, for anything."

I look over at Will, his hand firmly over the steering wheel his eyes intently locked on mine. "Even if it's just to go for a drive. Let me know and I'll be here."

What is this uncomfortable rhythm he has set off in my heart? It's like a heavy metal drummer is playing a set over my heart, thrashing it with little thought of breaking it. My confusion is only amplified when Will reaches across and kisses me on the mouth, his warm fingers touching my cheek.

When he pulls away I look toward my parent's house and see no one is there. "There was no one looking." I say, breathless. "You didn't need to do that."

I small grin quirks half of his lips. "I know. I wanted to."

Before I can question what any of this means, Will kisses me one last time and I decided to exit the car. If I stay any longer I will probably end up making out with him, and now is probably not the best time to be doing so.

I watch as Will drives away, my heart somehow feeling heavier with a new sensation that Will has introduced.

Entering the house, there is a sadness that has coated the walls. Sorrow fills the cracks of the wooden floor. Grief paints over the picture frames.

"Hello?"

"We're in here." The voice belongs to my brother.

Entering the living room felt like walking into the funeral. It was silent. When I saw my mom I couldn't hold it in, I burst into tears and ran into her arms. She holds me tightly and strokes the back of my hair. I feel guilty for crying to her, she must be hurting the most out of all of us. Growing up I would hear her talk to Dad about how hard she found it to be away from her family. She moved her entire life to be with Dad. She's always assured him that she has never regretted her choice. Mom always said, how could she regret a decision that gave her the love of her life and two beautiful children. There must be so many conflicting emotions in her heart right now, that I can't even imagine.

"I'm sorry," I say as I pull away, wiping my eyes.

"We're all grieving," Mom tries her best to smile but there is so much pain forcing it down.

"When's your flight?"

"Tomorrow morning," she tries to exhale all of the grief out of her to no success, it only makes the tears fall harder.

"We're all going to drop her off at the airport," my brother, Harry says from the couch. I'm not surprised he's not crying, he's a lot like Dad - in looks and personality. They both grieve alone, they act as more of a rock for Mom and me. My brother can be a pain in the ass a lot of the time, but I don't doubt he would drop everything to support me.

"I'll come too."

I have seen a lot of people cry in my twenty-one years on this planet, but there is nothing more heartbreaking than the person being my mother. She always tries so hard to keep herself together, she tries not to burden us with anything she might be dealing with, but even the strongest of people need just a moment of weakness.

When the tears start spilling out of my mom, I reach out and hold her as tightly as I can, just like she would to me growing up. I know my mother would never expect to be repaid for all of the love and support she provided us with throughout the years, because she loved doing it, but I want to repay her. She deserves all of the happiness in the world for the type of mother she has been to me.

"What did I do to deserve such thoughtful children?" She tries to laugh into my shoulder.

"You raised us," I replied.

Mom steps out of my embrace with a roll of her eyes. "If I get compliments like that I should cry more often."

I laugh with her at that. We all sit as a family in the living room and watch movies for the rest of the night. It's a good distraction for all of us, especially Mom. She's snuggled tightly into Dad's chest, and I catch him planting soft kiss atop her head. Moments like these I forget that they are my parents, they seem to be a young couple in the honeymoon faze. Forever in a state of happiness, support and bliss.

I wonder if I will find someone to love me as much as Dad loves Mom?

My heart creates a static shock when Will's face appears in my mind. I blush profusely, like I have just admitted to the entire room how attractive I find my fake boyfriend. I can barely tolerate Will, and falling in love with him seems like something that could only exist in a fairytale.

If I am so certain that is true, why do I feel like I am lying to myself?

I internally shake it off, I shouldn't be thinking about him now. He was there for me the moment he realised something was wrong, not without being angry for not showing up to his family meal first. I wonder if his dad hates me? I wonder if Rosie is mad? Was his sister there too, what must she think?

If I was alone right now I would slap myself. Why can't I get him out of my head? His stupid grin that makes my heart swell to ten times the size, his gorgeous green eyes that I could get lost into like a forest, and his...

Stop.

Enough.

Focus on the movie. Focus on the actors playing characters that are happily in love.

It doesn't work. Even when focusing on the movie all I can think about is when is Will going to kiss me again?

* * *

I'm up later than I wanted to be. We are dropping Mom off at the airport at five a.m. tomorrow so I want to get as much sleep as I can. After showering, washing away the events of today, I'm more awake that I was before. I've changed into my pjs and sitting on my old bed, that still has my old pink and baby blue patterned sheets. This whole room screams pink and pastel, it's a lot more colourful than my beige apartment.

I've been distracting myself with the logo for Rosie. I've created a final sketch that I'm happy with and now outlining it on my very slow laptop in Photoshop.

There's a light knock on my door and I don't look up from my screen before inviting the person in.

"Hey," the low voice belongs to my brother. If it was just a pitch lighter I would have easily mistaken him for Dad. "Mom wanted me to tell you to pack a suitcase."

I look up at him with a cocked brow. "Why?"

He scratches the back of his head, an action that implies he's trying to think of a lie. "Apparently they found enough money to get us all a flight to England for tomorrow afternoon."

"What?"

That doesn't make sense to me. Dad seemed pretty sure over the phone yesterday that they couldn't afford for us all to go. Surely he would have checked every option available for something as important as grandad's funeral. Why *now* have they come up with a solution? And so close to when Mom was originally meant to fly out?

"So...Mom is going in the morning and we're going later?"

Harry shook his head, "No, we're all going on the flight tomorrow afternoon."

Why would they buy a ticket that is most likely non-refundable? None of this makes sense, I go to question it but

Harry swiftly changes the subject. "Mom also told me about Simon, sorry to hear that."

Not only did my break up effect me, but I didn't even stop to think about Harry. He and Simon were close friends for years, and when we announced we were dating a few years back my brother didn't speak to me for months. He thought I was doing it to get under his skin, a sort of sibling rivalry. Only when we were together for over a year did he 'accept' it. He didn't like it but he knew that nothing he said would have changed our minds.

It only makes my anxiety flare up thinking that Simon may never be fully out of my life. If he remains friends with my brother, then his harassment might continue. I'm not sure I want to burden Harry with that, he already felt betrayed by us being together in the first place, I don't want to risk falling out with him again.

"At least you have your friend back," I force a smile.

"You're also dating someone else now?"

I roll my eyes, "I'm guessing Mom - "

"It was actually Simon." Harry folds his arms like a pretzel over his chest. "All he's done is rant about this new guy you're with, how he's a thug and not good for you. But he seems like a decent guy to me."

I nod because Will *is* a decent guy, but then I freeze for a moment. Harry has never met Will, how would he know what he is like? Based on his phrasing, he has met him in person but *where?* Surely Will would have mentioned that?

"Anyway," Harry unfolds his arms and heads to my door. "Be packed and ready for tomorrow. We'll be staying in Derby for a week."

"With Aunt Tamara?" I can't imagine her small house being enough for us again with such little time to prepare.

"Hotel."

And we have enough money for a hotel?! Why do I feel like

everyone is lying to me? Why wouldn't they want me to know where our sudden rise in funds have come from?

There must be a reason for it.

Chapter Seventeen

Requesting a week off from Rosie was as easy as breathing. She even insisted that I take another week off once I am back to settle. She understands first hand how difficult funerals can be, especially for ones you hold closest to your heart. If I were at my old job, if I requested a week off on such short notice I would either be rejected and miss the funeral or fired for going anyway. As much as a corporate company would like to project that they are a 'family' when it comes down to moments of needing support, they are never there.

We got two rooms in the hotel, one for Dad and Harry and one for me and Mom. I didn't have a black dress that would fit me on the night I was told to pack. I had to go shopping the day after we arrived, it served as a good trip for Mom and me. It was as a good diversion of the days to come, where it will mostly be us consoling one another.

Today is the day where we all say our goodbyes to my grandfather. I've just finished changing into my high neck black dress with a layered skirt. I've kept my hair down but placed behind my back.

Jeremy has sent an assortment of texts and heart emojis every hour, reminding me how much he loves me and ensuring that I'm not alone in this.

Mom exits our bathroom wearing her knee-length black

dress, and her golden hair spun up into a bun behind her head. She's just finished applying her simple black headband and taking in her appearance at the mirror. "I was going to put on a little bit of make-up," she says as she blots her already tear coated eyes. "But we haven't even left yet and I'm already crying. I don't want to show up looking like a witch from a horror movie."

I offer a sad smile, "You look beautiful, Mom."

She meets my gaze in the mirror, doing her best to smile. I can see in her eyes the moment her heart contorts, that the grief wants to consume her entire body no matter how much she wants to fight it. Mom shakes her head at herself, dropping hear head. "It's so silly."

I take her hand and walk her to my bed, I sit her down and hug her. "It's not silly to cry, Mom."

"I know," she rubs my back and pulls away, our hands joined in her lap. "I mean…I know that people die, it happens every day but…" she drags her thumb under her eye to catch the tears. "I just thought he would always be here. I can't imagine my life without him being just a phone call away."

Her bottom lip trembles, causing me to squeeze her hand tighter.

"I'd expected it with my mother," she sighed. "When we found out she was ill it gave us time to emotionally prepare, in a way. It still hurts like hell, however it was an expected pain. But with my dad…" a whimper escapes from her. It breaks my heart to see her so vulnerable, looking so young as she grieves over her parents. "He was always so strong, he always did what was best for us. And…in a way, it's thanks to him that I met your father."

I suppose that's true. My grandad got a promotion from his work when my mom was around seventeen years old, causing them to move out from England to America. If it wasn't for grandad's job and promotion, my mom never would have met my dad and fallen head over heals in love.

"Oh," she tries to force a smile. I wish she would stop doing that, she doesn't need to try and be happy on a day like this. I squeeze her hand to let her know it's okay to be sad, she can cry to me because I'm not a kid anymore. However, no matter how old I get I know my mom will still try and protect me from this world. "I should be saving this for the speeches. I'm not sure if your Aunt and I will make any word of sense throughout."

"We'll see who lasts the longest."

Mom laughs, it's not forced or fake, but she genuinely chuckles which makes my heart swell in my chest.

Today is going to be difficult for all of us, but we'll get through it like we always do.

The funeral was intense, we all got a chance to say goodbye. Mom and I cried the entire time, whilst Harry and Dad patted our backs and squeezed our hands every so often. With every sudden change, every heartbreaking turn of events, I know I can always rely on my family to help pick up the pieces when I drop my heart.

Even Will has become somewhat of a person to hold the bandages that can help hold me together.

At the wake I stick with my parents, mostly for Mom as all of our relatives come up to her and offer condolences. My Aunt Tamara has finally managed to escape the crowed that formed around her, not much for giving space for the grieving, my mom's side of the family.

Tamara greets my mom with a tight hug, her pregnant stomach causing my mom to arch her back to fully wrap herself around her.

"How are you doing?" Tamara asks as she pulls away from my mother. They could be mistaken for twins, although they insist they look nothing alike, I can see it. Both have the bright blue eyes that I inherited, both as beautiful as the morning sun. Honestly, the only real difference is their hair colour. Mom has always been a sleek golden blonde, that she likes to pin up behind her head to hide any grey's coming through. Whereas Tamara has a dark chocolate box dye to hide her years of stress.

"As okay as I can be. It's good to see you, Tam." Mom tucks a strand of her sister's hair behind her ear before dropping it down to her thigh. "I can't believe how big you are now."

Tamara slips her hand over her baby bump and offers a small smile, "I know. We weren't planning on anymore so it came as a surprise."

"I bet."

"No more for you two?" She points between my parents, and they both go pail, mostly my dad.

"Diaper changing days are well and truly behind me," he said, pulling my mom by the hip and kissing her temple.

They laugh and lose themselves in conversation about the family, when we are visiting again, and how life is across the other side of the world.

After catching up with Tamara, I run into my cousins at the buffet. We exchange a few pleasantries and offer to call one another if they ever need anything. I doubt they will take me up on my offer, since I only see them on family occasions like this. They're usually too busy with friends to spend any time with us on our yearly visits. I sometimes forget I even have cousins.

I decide to take some fresh air, a little break from the sad cloud in the function room will be refreshing. I take a long inhale of the damp British air and exhale out my troubles as much as I can.

"Need a break?" My brother appears at my side, balancing a cigarette between his lips. He sparks a match and exhales smoke, the wind knocking it in my direction. "Sorry," he says, and steps around so he's on the other side of me.

"I thought you quit?"

"Not when I'm stressed."

I can't argue with that. I'm not a smoker but I'd be lying if I said a cigarette wouldn't sound heavenly right now.

Standing with my brother, I look out to the cars that pass by the venue. I can't help but wonder what I am doing with my life. I'm faking a relationship to avoid my ex causing me trouble, shouldn't I just be strong enough to handle him? Do I really need Will to fight all of my battles? Yet, when I think of the moments that Simon would confront me, I feel powerless. Like, no matter what I said to him, no matter what I action I took, it wouldn't matter. I can't change anyone's mind, I can't change what Simon wants, but I can control what I allow to get to me.

"Harry?" I abruptly say. "Can I ask you something?"

"Yeah?"

I look up at him through glassy eyes, "The other night, when you said that Will seems like a decent guy, what did you mean?"

Harry blows out a long cloud of smoke and drops the bud to the ground, stomping it out on the wet cobblestone floor. "He made us promise not to tell you," he sighed.

My heart leaped for a moment. "Tell me what?"

"He stopped by the house asking for you, but you were in the shower."

Why do I feel so nervous about what he is going to say?

"Mom and Dad answered, I happened to be going upstairs at the same time," my brother said. I wish he would just get to the point. "When we told him you were busy he gave Dad four plane tickets, and a reference number for the hotel we're staying at."

I must have misheard him. Will paid for our flight *and*

hotel stay? That must have cost him a fortune! Especially for how last minute the flight and accommodation were.

"Why didn't he want you to tell me?"

Harry shrugs, "He said he didn't think you would accept it. Which Dad nearly didn't, I don't even want to know how much that cost."

I feel like my heart has grown three sizes too large, now it's pushing against my ribcage and demanding to be set free. Why would he do this? Will was right about one thing, I would not have accepted it if he handed me the tickets. I'm not even his *real* girlfriend, so why would he do this?

Has the time we've spent together made him gain feelings for me? A little light of hope twinkled within me, I oddly don't hate the idea.

"He's more than a decent guy," Harry interrupts my inner thoughts of confusion. "He's good for you."

I smile at him. "Thanks Harry." I still can't help feeling guilty that I am technically lying to them. It's one continuous lie, and being at a funeral for my grandad isn't making me feel any better about it.

"Um," Harry dips his head, the ends of his sandy blonde hair shadowing the upper half of his face. "I know Simon didn't treat you the best," his voice is low, there was even a wobble at some of the words. "I guess I was mad that you took my best friend from me. Looking back, it's so dumb." He lifts his head, and it takes a lot of him to look over at me. "I could tell you were really unhappy for a while, and the stupid part of myself thought *that's what you get*. But...I'm sorry I didn't say anything — tell you to break up with him sooner."

I'm crying now, and not because of the funeral. I had no idea Harry felt this way, that he felt the need to apologise to me. Not once did I ever think he should step in and speak up for me, because I've only *now* realised how toxic Simon was. I was blind to it throughout our whole relationship. "Even if you did say something, I wouldn't have listened." I nudge him with my elbow. "Who would listen to their older brother for romance advice?"

Harry snorts a laugh, "Certainly not you." He chews on his bottom lip for a while and then says. "I've cut Simon out of my life now."

"You didn't do that because of me, did you?"

My brother tilts his head to the side and brings up his shoulder as a sort of shrug. "Your break up kickstarted it. He's really an asshole, and why would I care to keep someone in my life that was a dick to you?"

Apart of me feels like I should tell him about the times that Simon has come into my work, demanded we get back together, and even grabbed me. The words are on the tip of my tongue but I can't. I already feel like I took his friend away from him, I don't want him worrying about me when I have Will.

But I don't have Will.

He's not my boyfriend.

Maybe I should stop relying on people in my corner and try and looking out for myself. How would I even do that? Self defence classes, maybe?

"I meant what I said," Harry said. "Will's good for you."

"Yeah…he is." That didn't taste like a lie.

Chapter Eighteen

Today has been an emotional day. Saying goodbye to my grandad was the hardest thing I've had to do but I feel a sense of relief from coming out here. If I hadn't gotten the chance to say goodbye I know I would be wallowing in my grief for a long time. Of course I am not going to be healed instantly, I will still grieve for him, but at least I have a sense of closure.

And it wouldn't have been possible if it weren't for Will.

I'm ridiculously grateful for his gesture, that he went out of his way to spend — what I imagine — is a lot of money for my family when he will gain nothing from it.

I bite my bottom lip and pull out my phone, it's midnight here in the UK and I'm not sure on the time difference back home. I think we are six hours ahead, if I call Will now I shouldn't be disturbing him…I hope.

I roll onto my side, thankful that Mom isn't back yet, and dial Will's number. I feel anxious for some reason, I want him to answer but at the same time I don't. I want to talk to him, but I'm scared to face him. It doesn't really make sense, and right now my heart is bouncing all over the place.

I'm surprised when his face appears on my phone screen, in my moment of confusion I realise I pushed FaceTime instead of call. My heart catapults against my ribcage when I see him, greeting me with a small smile as he positions his phone on — what I assume is — his desk.

"Hey," he says softly.

"Hi." Why am I blushing? "Sorry, I didn't mean to FaceTime I pushed the wrong button."

His tooth-filled grin ignites my blood, "It's fine, I'm actually glad to see you."

I smile at him, nuzzling my cheek against my pillow and just enjoying watching him. I have a strange feeling in my chest, it's uncomfortable like someone is wrapping a piece of rope around my heart.

"It's dark," he says. "What time is it there?"

"Just past midnight."

"How did it go today?"

"As well as it could have," I lower my gaze to the mattress beneath me, picking at the material. "And…it sounds like I have you to thank for that."

When I look up I see Will has an unreadable expression, a blank canvas which makes it difficult for me to read what he thinks of that. "Why did you do that for me?"

He shrugs like it's nothing. Does he really not realise how huge of a gesture that was? How ridiculously kind it was?

"Why didn't you tell me you were going to do that?"

Will runs a hand through his hair, sinking his teeth into his bottom lip. "I'm sorry, I knew that if I gave you the tickets you wouldn't take them."

"The last thing you need to do is apologise, Will." I offer a smile to show I'm not mad, even a few grateful tears have decided to make themselves known.

"It wasn't like I planned on not telling you, your mom and dad answered the door and you were in the shower. I figured it was easier for you this way," he said. "Because when I got home I couldn't stop thinking about how distraught you were. I have money, and there was no reason for me *not* to do this for you." A sly grin appears on his mouth. "I do owe you, after all."

"You technically owe me one more favour," I giggle. "I may have to put a request in when I get back."

"Whatever you want you can have," he was joking but there was something behind it that felt real.

I don't know why my first instinct was to say: *I want you*.

I shake my head at myself, it's such an inappropriate thought to have on a day like today. I can't help it, as I sit here and talk with Will, I realise that I've missed him. He's such a pain in the ass, even when he is being kind he is somehow a bigger pain in the ass. Yet, I truly miss being with him and there is apart of me that is slowly forgetting that this is a fake relationship. Lying here talking to him, both of is in different countries, this is what it should feel like with a boyfriend. I should be catching up with him late at night, feeling excited to see him again.

"What if I asked for a million dollars?"

"I'd tell you to go to hell."

I sputter a laugh, "You did say *anything*." I deepen my voice at the word 'anything' to mimic him.

Will laughs too, but then it fades and my joy sinks with it. "I'm sorry about your grandad, Lucy." He says, sincerely. "I know it's hard, but you're strong and I'll be here if you need anything."

My heart, why is he doing this to me?

"Thank you, Will."

"I will send you something that might cheer you up, just a little." Will moves so he is slightly out of shot as he types something on his laptop that is beside his phone. He looks so sexy when he concentrates. He hits a button and says, "There you go."

A message from Will pings up on my phone. I open up his text and find a PDF attached, after a moment of confusion I read the title of the document. *IHYDMILY*

"Am I supposed to know what that stands for?"

Will snorts a laugh as I open up our call again, "It's an abbreviation for my book title."

A smile stretches over my mouth when I put the pieces together, "Is this your book?"

He nods, and a bit of colour comes to his cheeks. "Don't get too excited! It's only the first few chapters and I'm still editing them."

I feel like I have just been gifted an iPad with what he has sent me, like it's the holy grail of novels in my texts. "So, what does *IHYDMILY* stand for? Seems like a long title?"

His cheeks are definitely red now. "You'll find out when you read it."

"I'll let you get some sleep," he said before I could pester him more about it.

I chew on my bottom lip, feeling such a desire to talk to him all night until his words follow me into my dreams. "Will?"

"Mm-hmm."

"Can...Can I see you? When I get back? I'd like to request my second favour."

His bright green eyes pierce my soul as he watches my features intently. "Of course, just text me when you're back and you can come to my place."

We say goodnight — for me — and hang up, my heart suddenly feels like an anvil has attached to a rope, and I am about to be plunged into a messy spiral of confusion.

Before I fall asleep, I open up the PDF that he sent me. A gasp lodges in my throat when I am immediately greeted with the title of his book:

I Hope You Don't Mind, I Love You.

Chapter Nineteen

Will writes romance.

Not only does he write romance, but he's an amazing writer. His opening line had me hooked and I was devastated to find out he wasn't lying that he had only sent the first few chapters. I need more, I need to find out where this story is going.

I've been back home for about a week and only now have I decided to visit Will. He's texted me his address and I'm on my way. I didn't want to do this with the funeral fresh in my mind but now that I'm feeling more emotionally stable, I am ready now.

I pull up to his house, and I must have the wrong address because this is more like a *mansion*. It screams spoilt rich kid, with it being bigger than my apartment building. I feel like I do not belong here, especially with the run down piece of crap I am driving. When Will said he had money, I thought he meant a bit to spare, but *this*...this is ridiculous.

I park up and the path leading to his front porch, the winding path that is made of gravel. There is even a water fountain out front!

Making my way up to his front door, wearing nothing but jeans and a thin strap shirt I suddenly feel like I should just give up and go home. It's probably not the smartest thing to do, especially if it will make this fake relationship complicated.

I go to leave when the front door opens, and I am greeted by Will in a simple black t-shirt, that hugs at his biceps, and jeans. Not the look one would expect with a house that could rival Buckingham Palace...maybe an over-exaggeration.

"Hey you," he grins.

My stupid heart decides to skip a beat at the sight of him, trapping a breath in my throat. I somehow compose myself and pretend that my heart isn't racing a million miles an hour.

"Hello, Mr Millionaire," I mock.

Will gives me a poignant look and invites me inside. If I thought the outside screamed rich, it has nothing on his interior. I can see my own reflection in the black and white tile floor, golden spiral staircase that leads to the second floor and rooms upon rooms down a hall that seem never-ending.

"This is where you live!"

Will scoffs, "No, this is where my *parents* live. I thought it would be funny to see your reaction. I live in a condo across the street."

I glare at him, of course he lives in a condo. Even still, for Rosie to own a house like this is wild to me. This is why she never seems stressed about having barely any customers, with money like this she could throw dollars out the window without losing a moment of sleep.

"Come on," he said, lacing his fingers through mine and pulling me up the stairs. "Let's go to my room, I can see your jaw might fall off if you stand here any longer."

Will's room is surprisingly *regular* considering the rest of the house. It's very simplistic, with minimal furniture. With only an oak desk, a laptop and his bed taking up most of the room. Even his clothes are hung up on a wrack and not in a wardrobe made of gold, like I was expecting.

"So, what is your second favour?"

"Hmm?"

"You came here to request a second favour, how may I assist you?" Will leans back against his desk, folding his arms over his chest, waiting for my answer.

"Oh," my cheeks flush a crimson red. "I-it doesn't matter." I look everywhere but where Will is standing. Right now, every inanimate object is far more interesting than his intense stare. I knew I was too much of a coward to go through with this, how can I even ask such a thing. He would probably laugh in my face anyway.

"Lucy?" He drags out my name and steps toward me. Dipping his head, he tries to make contact with my eyes but I can't look at him. "Are you blushing?"

When his warm hand makes contact with my cheek, I react out of instinct and snap my gaze to lock with his. They are so enchanting, so inviting, I could spill all of my secrets to him without a moment of hesitation. "What was the favour you wanted, Lucy?"

My chest rises and falls in quick motions, I'm breathing so fast that I might pass out. I manage to drop my gaze but they land on his lips, making my intentions very clear. I know Will, he won't touch me unless I say so. Whether it's to be a gentleman, or to make me feel embarrassed, it doesn't matter.

"Will you have sex with me?"

Although Will knew what I wanted before I came up to his bedroom, it still didn't prevent the surprised shine to his eyes. He licks his bottom lip, dragging his top row of teeth over the surface, and smiles. "What about 'no sex' during our fake relationship." Will slips a hand over my waist, pressing our bodies firmly against one another.

I swallow, the desire to rip his clothes off and have him inside of me becoming overwhelming. "Well," I clear my throat to try and speak. "We do need to make it seem that we have a real relationship, don't we?"

A deep rumble rises up his chest, making my knees quake. "I couldn't agree more."

With little warning after that, Will crashes his mouth over mine and kisses me fiercely. I open my mouth for his tongue to find mine. I immediately slip my hands over his firm chest and grip the material of his shirt in my fists.

Will grabs each of my thighs and guides them to wrap around his waist. Moans are already fleeing from my mouth, just his touch is enough to send me into a swirling flurry. He carries me to his bed and lies us both down on the mattress. His entire body covers mine, and I slip my hands up into his hair, holding him in place as we kiss.

His lips make a trail from the corner of my mouth, over my jaw and down my neck. I stare up at his blank ceiling and lose myself to his touch, bucking my hips in response to his hands cupping over my breasts.

Lifting up my shirt to expose my bra, Will growls at the sight. Without a moment of hesitation, he pulls down my bra to reveal my pointed nipples. He wastes no time in trailing slow, painstaking circles around my nipples, every so often popping one into his mouth.

I'm breathless, on cloud nine, and Will has barely touched me. I could explode right now, the way he knows how to perfectly flick my breasts with his tongue is enough to make me become undone.

Will lifts his head, leaving a cold chill to fall over my skin. He unbuttons my jeans and tugs them down, then tossing them to his floor without a second thought. I am now lying beneath him in only my matching black lingerie, made up by a black lacy bra and panties. My shirt is also bunched up over my chest. He takes notice of my lingerie and hovers over me with a quirked brow, hooking the elastic of my underwear in his index finger before snapping it against my skin. "For me?"

"Isn't that what fake girlfriends do?" I can barely breathe, let alone speak. "Wear lingerie for their fake boyfriends?"

His response comes in the form of trailing kisses down my flat torso, until he reaches the top of my panties. "I want to ask you something."

The last thing I want to do right now is talk. When Will adjusts so his face is in my direct view, I grab the hem of his shirt and rip it off over his head. God, he's even more gorgeous than I remember. The scar still seems freshly healed, I wonder if he will ever tell me where he got it.

All thoughts vanish when Will slips his hand under my panties and hovers his hand over my warmth, teasing me with how close his fingers are to my bundle of nerves.

"Have you touched yourself at the thought of me?"

I bite down hard on my bottom lip to prevent from moaning, confirming my answer. I want to lie, tell him that I've not replayed those moments in my head, touched myself and imagined it was him in the backroom. What was the point in lying now?

"Yes," I whisper.

Will seems pleased with my answer, rewarding my honesty by dipping two fingers deep inside of me. Circling me exactly how I like, rising my hips to meet his hand I grind against him. I knock my head back against his pillow, his scent wrapped around me as I fuck his hand.

He quickens his movements, the wetness between my legs slapping against his fingers. I am chasing the orgasm, so close to release I can almost taste it, when Will pulls his hand out from me and unbuttons his own jeans and pulls them down, along with his boxers.

Fumbling at his side table, he pulls out a condom and rips the foiling with his teeth, quickly wrapping it over his hard length. "You have no idea what you do to me, Lucy."

I never knew words could cause such a tidal wave between my legs. Will removes my shirt and underwear, and tosses them next to my clothes. There is no barrier between our bodies, how it should always be.

When Will slips his cock inside of me, I open my mouth wide as a silent gasp exhales from me. His cock fills me, pushing against my core and sending me spiralling into a pool of pleasure. Will lingers for a while, his face hovering over mine with an oddly thoughtful expression. He brings his hand up to my face, and I guide his thumb into my mouth and suck hard. This causes Will to thrust once, hard. My breasts bounce like jelly from the action, still sucking on his thumb.

"You're so fucking beautiful," and before I even get a chance to respond, or read into his words, Will begins fucking me, hard. Completely and utterly satisfying me with his cock, sliding in and out in a fast rhythm.

Will slips his hands around my back, and rolls me so I am on top of him. He keeps his hands firmly on my back as I writhe against him, our skin colliding like I have be thrust against a cloud.

Pushing myself up from his chest, I watch the equal desire and hunger in his eyes as I grind my hips against him. Continuing to climb until I am high in the clouds, anticipating the epic fall back to earth. There is something about the way this feels, it doesn't feel like it's just sex between friends with benefits. I can't help but feel like this means something, like we enjoy one another's company. That hope that has become all to familiar claws it's way back into my chest. I want this to be more, I want to keep seeing him even after his father has met me.

I hope I'm not wrong but, I'm starting to think that Will may want that too.

Chapter Twenty

I wake up for the first time feeling completely at peace. Lying on my side in Will's bed, his arm wrapped around my stomach and my back against his chest. He sounds so peaceful when he sleeps, and doesn't snore like someone is strangling him through the night.

For just a moment I can pretend that I am waking up in the arms of my boyfriend, that this isn't a fake relationship type of deal. I shouldn't indulge in the fantasy for more than a second, but what's the harm in one minute?

I stroke his fingers as he remains still behind me. His hands are so much bigger than mine, so much stronger too. I could wake up like this every morning and feel content with my day, and return at night to forget all of my worries.

I feel movement behind me, and I can't help but grin, as Will places a hand on my waist and pulls me to look at him. I keep his sheets over my breast, not that there is much point since he has seen every inch of me at this point.

How does he look even more handsome in the morning? His black hair is ruffled in multiple different directions thanks to my hands needing something to hold onto.

My eyes trail down to his chest and over his scar, I feel him tense beneath my hand when I press my fingers against it, tracing the deep slash. "How did you get this?"

"It's rude to stare," he slips his hands around my waist and pulls me on top of him. I ensure to keep my gaze locked to his eyes as I straddle him.

"You know," he says, as his green eyes trail down to my exposed breasts. I feel him harden at the sight. "I've never slept with a 'one night stand' more than once."

"Aren't I lucky?" I roll my eyes and lower myself down to kiss him.

"I'd say unfortunate," he mutters against my mouth. He exudes so much confidence in himself, he knows he can get any girl he wanted, I don't understand why he hates himself. There must be something in his past, something to do with Greg, that has made him this way. I can't imagine whatever he did was so bad, since his family still talks to him. Rosie loves him like any other mother would her son, she clearly adores him.

"I'm grateful you're in my life, Will."

He pauses beneath me, his body tensing again at my words. I pull away this time and he can't look at me. It's clear he is trying to hide his emotions, what he is truly feeling right now, but he can't. There is no mask thick enough to cover it.

"Will," he allows me to cup his cheek but he still doesn't look at me. "I mean it. You're so — "

"Stop."

I remove my hand, my heart is being pulled apart right now. I thought I was saying words of encouragement, that it might show him he is cared for. It's clear now that Will wants someone who can lie to him, pretend that feelings aren't real…I'm not so sure I can be that person, even if it is just pretend.

Removing myself from his lap, I pick up my clothes from his floor and start redressing as fast as I can. Tears threaten my eyes, I ensure to keep my back to him so he can't witness how upset he has made me.

"Lucy, you don't need to go — "

"No," I say with a fake joy that you wouldn't need a lie detector to pick up on. "This was just sex, there's no need for me to overstay my welcome."

I hear him sigh and the sheets rustle behind me. "You could never overstay your welcome," he's behind me now, and his hand makes contact with my arm that I instantly brush off.

"Don't, Will." The tears burn in my throat, it hurts to swallow. "There are no feelings involved with us. It's just pretend until your dad is happy, right?"

My heart is screaming, begging, for him to say no. I want him to say that this is more to him than sex. That he has acquired feelings for me, just like I have for him.

Instead he says, "Right."

"Great," once I'm dressed I walk so fast that it could be mistaken for a sprint. "Well, I will see you — " I open up his door and find Rosie happens to be walking past her son's door, dressed in a pants suit, much different from her usual casual attire in the store.

"Lucy!" She pulls me in for a hug, giving me a chance to force the tears back from my eyes. The last thing I want is for her to think anything wrong between Will and I. We've been pretending for so long if it's ruined now it will be a waste of time.

"What perfect timing, Raven and I were just about to head out for breakfast. You should join us." She looks over my shoulder, presumably to Will standing behind me. Luckily he put on some pants before I opened the door, I imagine that would have been an unfortunate sight. "Unless, I am interrupting something?"

I cringe at the thought of a shirtless Will behind me. It doesn't take a genius to figure out what happened last night. "No!" I step out into the hall, tucking a strand of my hair behind my ear. "I'd be happy to join you."

"Amazing," Rosie looks back to me. "Raven is downstairs, I'm so happy to finally be introducing you." She goes to leave, and I start to follow her until Will's hand grabs my wrist and pulls me back. There is that guilt on his face that I recognise, it's the same look he gave me when I told him of my grandfather's passing.

"Lucy…"

"I'll meet your father soon," I say with finality. "We'll make it seem like we're together for another month, and then we can break up. At least me leaving your room makes it seem real, it should have eliminated any doubt they might have." I snatch my wrist back, the tears betraying how much I actually hate the truth of our situation. "No one gets hurt this way."

No one but me.

I've come to realise that the entirety of Will's family could be an empire of models. His sister is possibly the most stunning woman I have ever seen in my life. Her black hair has a tint of blue under the restaurant lights, she has it pulled back into a tight ponytail which really highlights the sharp curves of her face. She could have been sculpted from marble with only the best features in mind, a sharp cheekbone that could pierce the thickest of concrete, a square jaw that could threaten any man into obedience and upturned eyes that could make anyone do her bidding.

We've not said more than a 'hello' to one another and I'm already terrified of her.

The waiter takes our order and shortly returns with our coffees. At least I can keep my hands busy until I wait for my omelette to arrive.

"My mom tells me you're a designer?" Raven said, taking a sip of her black coffee. Even what she drinks exudes elegance,

I find myself straightening my spine to be like her.

"I will be once I find someone to hire me," I cringe at myself. A simple 'yes' would have sufficed, or 'I'm currently building my portfolio,' anything else would have been better than that response.

Raven didn't appear to be too impressed with my answer either, as she flicked her eyebrows high and took a glance around the room. She shares the same piercing green eyes with her brother, but hers don't fill me with the same fire that Will's does.

I've said no more than a few words to her and I have a feeling Raven does not like me. I can't tell if it's because of me as a person and my appearance, or if she doesn't like what she's heard about me. Whether she thinks that I'm not good enough for her brother.

Not that it matters, I guess.

"So...what do you do, Raven?" I ask, trying desperately to fill this awkward air.

"I'm a legal administrative assistant at the local law firm."

I can't say I'm surprised. I guess she's not one who would understand that working in a creative environment is equal to the hours she must put in. I can't say I know much, or anything, about working at a law firm; from the movies they seem to be run off their feet.

"Well...if your company ever needs a logo, now you can say you know a designer." Raven locks her glare to me, she tries to pass it off with a smile but the ice just froze my heart.

"She is very good," Rosie chimed in, finally. "She's designing one for the store."

"Why?" Raven huffed. "You will only get bored of it after a while. You pick up and drop things all the time."

Rosie clenches her jaw. I knew if I wasn't here she would tear into her daughter for speaking to her like that. I would never dream of squandering my mother's dreams, no matter what it was. I feel like this would be the equivalent of telling my mother she's a terrible singer, when her passion is rooted in music.

"I told you, it's a passion project of mine."

"A waste of money, more like."

I have never been more thankful for a waiter in my entire life. He delivers our meals and swiftly exits. I was hoping to have him stick around, save me from this dreadful conversation, but alas it seems my luck is still yet to turn around.

The rest of the conversation is limited, and somewhat better than how it started. I feel like I am being punished right now, that the lie for Will is putting me in the most awkward and uncomfortable situations, and I'll only be free once I break the curse.

"I have to use the ladies room," Rosie says, and just to top this morning off I am now left alone with Raven.

"So…"

Raven drops any shred of decency she was trying to show for me by slamming her wrists down onto the table. "Look, I'm going to be frank with you," she says, giving me no room to object. "You're not good for my brother. I know I've only just met you — " she raises her hands in surrender before dropping them back down. " — but my brother has been through a lot, he's *dealing* with a lot. He needs someone to take care of him, someone with more stability and drive."

"Excuse me?"

"You seem nice, you do." She said, just casually applying salt to my exposed wound. "Nice isn't what's good for him. My brother needs someone who can steer him in the right direction, get him onto a real career path and focus on a realistic future. Instead of this fantasy he will become a successful author. And with someone like you with the same delusion of a creative field, it won't help him. It will hold him back from ever achieving anything."

Her words should not matter to me, I shouldn't be hurt by this conversation but I am. Even if I am pretending to date Will, even if this isn't real, she has no right to speak to me like I am a bug on the end of her high heeled shoe.

I rise out of my chair, fists clenched at my sides. "I'm not going to sit here and allow you to talk to me like I am a worthless, *dumb* girl. Just because I work part time in a flower shop, and I'm still working towards getting my foot in the door of the career I want, it doesn't mean I am some incompetent girl you can look down your nose at!" I feel eyes of other customers on me but I don't care. Raven is clearly embarrassed, she obviously didn't expect me to stand up for myself, and I'm glad. It will only be more satisfying to tell her off, it seems she's the type that needs it. "Will may be a little lost right now, everyone is at some point, but that doesn't mean you can decide what is best for him. You can't decide what will make him happy, and neither can I. It's his choice what he wants to do with his life, it's his time, energy and *heart*. Not yours. Just like it is mine to not stand around and take your crap."

Rosie joins our table and looks between her daughter and I.

I don't doubt she heard my little speech but I'm too flustered to care right now. I keep my hard stare at Raven and say, "It was a pleasure to meet you." Before storming out and walking down the street with a big smile on my face.

I feel good about standing up for myself. I didn't feel weak or powerless, I feel strong.

Maybe I am ready to face Simon the next time I see him, show him that he can't walk all over me.

Chapter Twenty-One

I hope Raven isn't amongst the people I need to impress for Will's father to be satisfied he is in a stable relationship. I don't think that meeting could have gone any worse, at least no coffee was thrown in the other's face? Small victories, I suppose.

I cringe every time I play back what happened. The shocked look on Raven's face, how strangers stared at me like I was a madwoman. I never want to get out of this bed, and I certainly don't want to know what Rosie thinks of that little dispute.

I still feel a sense of pride in myself for standing up for myself. I would have just sat there silently a few weeks ago, just taken the insults and thanked her for her honesty. I'm tired of trying to please everyone.

I receive a text and my heart thrashes when I see Will's name.

Will: I heard a little someone got into an argument with my sister ;)

I want to die. Of course she would tell Will. Raven probably demanded that he break up with me right there and then. I bet she will be so smug when we eventually do call this thing between us quits.

Before I can respond, Will sends another text.

Will: I'm flattered to have a fake girlfriend that is willing to fight my family haha

Me: It's kind of hard to just sit there whilst your sister tells me how I am not good enough for Prince Will

The three dots to signal Will is typing appear and disappear a number of times. With my phone clutched in my hand I wonder what he is writing. What was the message he decided to delete before trying again?

Then finally a notification pings.

Will: I had hoped you would never meet my sister tbh. I love her but she can be a pain in the ass about speaking her mind. I'm sorry if she made you feel bad, please don't think you're not good enough...especially for me.

Especially for me.

What does he mean by that?

My throat closes as I stare at those three words at the end of his text. My palms are suddenly sweating, I have to hold my phone tighter or it might slip from my grasp and hit me in the face.

It's my turn now to start and stop messages. How do I respond to that?

Me: She must be bad if YOU think someone is a pain in the ass ;)

Will: She's the worst, but don't tell her I said that lol

* * *

Me: I don't think your sister will be very interested in speaking to me again O_O

Will: I'm jealous lol

I am beaming with pride ever since Rosie approved my logo design for the front of the store. She has requested that I work on flyers and other media to help promote the store. Finally, it feels like life is turning in the right direction. After the headache that has been this past year, I feel like I can finally see the sun behind the dark clouds.

It's been a week since I met her...charming daughter. She's apologised on her behalf, and it's surprising that Raven could come from someone as sweet as Rosie. Which makes me wonder whether her bite is from their father, only adding fuel to my already inflamed anxiety about meeting him.

The bell at the store rings, out of habit I look up and expect to find either Rosie or Will, surprise flares when it is a brand new customer.

A handsome customer at that.

The first thing I notice is that he is very tall, taller than most men I have met. I would be lucky if I could reach his shoulders on my tiptoes. Clean shaven, with caramel brown hair trimmed short, with a jawline that could cut through glass. He's looking around at the displays, mostly at the red roses and my heart falls a little. Of course someone like him is shopping for a girlfriend, he's too handsome not to be single.

He's looking around at the displays, mostly at the red roses and my heart falls a little. Of course someone like him is shopping for a girlfriend, he's too handsome not to be single.

Looking around, I can't help but internally pine at his confusion when taking in the other displays.

He looks so lost and as a thorough employee, the least I

can do is assist him.

I step behind the counter, clasping my sweaty palms in front of my apron, and walk over to him.

"Good morning," I offer my sweetest, employee smile. "Shopping for someone?"

His chocolate brown eyes meet mine, and a lopsided grin that has broken so many hearts tilts on his mouth. "Yes, I have no idea what I am looking for."

"Maybe I can help? Who is it for? A girlfriend, wife..."

"No, no." he chuckles and shoves one hand into his front jeans pocket. "My mother's birthday, actually. She's a bit of a snob when it comes to flowers, so I have no idea what she would like."

"We have some ready-made bouquets, or I can create something unique for her?"

The gentleman looks around at our displays, I can tell nothing is really catching his eye. "If it wouldn't be too much trouble," he's so polite my knees might give way. "You will probably have a better eye for this stuff, working in a flower shop and all."

I nod, I've gotten better at my flower arrangements. All of the ones on display are of my own hands, but it's a lot more fun to create something unique for one person. Most people shopping for mother's tend to love the hat-boxes. I grab the pastel pink one and start arranging the flowers to match. Sometimes simplicity is best, you don't want too many flowers to distract from the individual beauty. I get to work in positioning white, pastel orange and pink roses in purposely placed positions.

Topping it off with white allium flowers and rich green ivy to break up the pastels.

I wrap the spines in a pink bow to hold them in place and position them into the hatbox. I do a few last minute adjustments and present them to the customer. I was always anxious about what customers thought of my designs/arrangements but most people now adore what I create, and this customer is no exception.

His eyes ignite from the arrangement and he pulls out his wallet, "She will love this, thank you. How much?"

"Thirty dollars," I punch in the amount into the register and take his money.

The way he holds the hat box is like something from a romance novel, it's enough to leave me swooning anyway.

"Thank you so much for this," he said. "You've got a real talent."

I blush, and dip my head. "Thank you, that means a lot."

I can feel his eyes on me, and when I look up again he is smiling, as though I have done something to amuse him. "I hope you don't mind me saying," he said. "But you're gorgeous."

"Oh!" No amount of make-up would cover the redness of my cheeks right now. "Well...I..."

"What's your name?"

I feel like I am back in high school again, and the most popular guy in school said a simple 'hello' to me. "Lucy."

"I'm Erik," a name that fits his face. "Listen, I'm sorry if this is too forward but would you like to have dinner with me tomorrow night?"

My eyes now wide, my mouth suddenly dry. Someone as handsome as him is asking me out? And there is no hidden agenda like he needs a fake girlfriend to impress his parents? He just wants to go out with me because he *wants* to.

If I say yes, is that technically cheating? Will and I aren't even together, am I supposed to wait around until he realises he has feelings for me? I won't put my life on hold whilst we fake dated, so I can't see why I can't give this Erik a chance.

"Yeah, I'd love to."

"Great!" Erik grabs my pen and writes his number on the

back of his receipt. "Shall I pick you up here at around seven?"

I nod, taking his receipt and clutching it to my chest like it is a lovers note. "Sounds perfect."

"Awesome," he says and goes to leave. "See you tomorrow, Lucy."

I stare at the door he just walked out of, still with the receipt clutched to my chest. That was all so sudden, yet I feel an overwhelming glee fill my veins. It's like I'm going out on my very first date. Come to think of it, I think this *is* my first date. Simon and I would sneak around when we were first together, and he never took me out when we became official. Next is Will, but he and I aren't a real item and he's certainly not taken me anywhere that would be deemed date worthy.

It makes me wish that I hadn't spent most of my teenage years with Simon. That I had the chance to go on dates with different people, everyone is awkward in their teens so it would just be another experience for adulthood that I would feel more ready for.

When the bell to the shop rings again, I am secretly hoping it is Erik to say he had forgotten something. Instead I am greeted with Will, who looks more pissed off than he does on most days. When he takes in how I look, beaming like a lighthouse through a storm, he cocks a suspicious brow. "Why are you so happy?"

I'm not letting him ruin this for me, when he walks to my side behind the counter and begins rummaging through the shelves. "I have got myself a date tomorrow night."

Will freezes for an entire second, like what I had said shocked him enough to warrant such a reaction. "I'm not completely undesirable!"

Will straightens but doesn't look at me, which is odd. "I never said you were."

I find it odd that he has no emotion in his tone. Could he

actually be bothered by it? He shouldn't be, and even if he is it's not my problem because we aren't dating.

"You not going to ask who with?"

This actually makes his upper lip curl, and I regret trying to be playful with him, he's clearly not in the mood. "I don't care, Lucy. Date, fuck, be with whoever you want."

With that, he storms into the backroom and slams the door behind him.

Asshole.

Chapter Twenty-Two

Erik picked me up on time in his car.

When we arrive at a quaint restaurant, he gets out and opens up the door for me like a true gentleman. He offers his arm and I take it as we walk into the restaurant and to our table. Erik pulls out my chair and helps me in, I feel like a princess tonight.

Erik sits opposite me and presses down his red tie against his grey shirt. The glow of the candle light really shows off the handsomeness of his features.

We order our food and Erik starts the conversation. "Do you work at that cute flower shop full time?"

"Part time," I pull at the skirt of my dress, trying to calm my nerves. "I'm actually hoping to get into the world of graphic design soon." I don't mention that I had technically started my journey at a company before I was fired for not being good enough, or meeting their expectations. The last thing I want is to bring down this mood.

"Funnily enough I actually work as head of design for a publishing company," he grins. "If any jobs come up I'll let you know."

I want to cry from appreciation, but that would be weird. Instead I offer my biggest smile and repress a squeal. "Really? Thank you so much."

"Of course."

The rest of the night feels like a dream. We laugh, make jokes, and talk about our lives. Erik is a sweet guy. From the sound of his upbringing, he really clawed his way up the ladder and earned his way to the top spot.

We had a great time tonight. He told me about his past, that his father passed away when he was young and he has two sisters that tease him about how tall he is. He's apparently been gifted with the nickname 'tree-man' which is weirdly adorable.

At the end of our date I asked him to drop me back off at the flower shop. I left the key to my apartment in the backroom before I left. Erik was a perfect gentleman and walked me to the door. Now, I am looking up at him with the glow of the moonlight outlining his silhouette.

"I had fun tonight," I said, my cheeks flushed.

"Me too," Erik said, a thick layer to his voice.

Minutes tick by with us just standing in front of one another. Erik is drinking in every feature of my face, a small smile on his lips.

"Can I kiss you?"

I roll my lips inward before releasing them, I answer with a light nod of my head.

Before I know what is happening, Erik steps forward and kisses me and the kiss...is interesting. I can't pick up on the movements he is making, I swear I feel his tongue lick my teeth. I first thought it was an accident but he does it a number of times, and my instinct is to clamp down but I don't want to hurt the guy.

He opens up his mouth far too much, I am convinced he is trying to eat me.

There is not a single thing I like about his kiss, my lipgloss has been licked clean off like I am the leftover sauce on a dessert.

Finally, he pulls away and I am actually speechless, not in a good way.

"Good night, Lucy." He says, looking like he achieved something as he gets into his car.

I can't even speak, my mouth feels wet and I don't want him to see me wipe my lips as he drives away.

When I open the door to the shop, I'm surprised that it's open. Rosie must be here, she did mention she likes to sneak away after hours and place orders for deliveries.

I get inside and head straight for the backroom, inside I don't find Rosie but my fake boyfriend sitting at the desk and his nose deep into his laptop screen.

"Hey," I say.

Will jolts, dragged him out of whatever he was doing. He turns to face me and offers a small smile. "Fun date?"

The kiss from merely minutes ago comes to my mind, it's like I can see it from an outside perspective. How awkward it must have looked to anyone passing by. I can't help but smile, eventually that bubbles into a chuckle and then full blown hysteria.

"What?"

"He is the *worst* kisser!"

Will cocks a brow, "I thought you dipped your face in vaseline, I'm assuming he's to thank for that?"

I shudder and drop my purse down on the desk, finally wiping away the lingering saliva from my face. "How can someone be that bad?"

He doesn't say anything, the mood he was in yesterday still seems to be lingering. I wish he felt comfortable enough to confide in me, sometimes talking about it takes off some of the weight.

"I'm sorry about yesterday," Will says. "I just…"

I slip my hand over his shoulder, making him meet my gaze. "It's okay. We all have our moments...you more than most."

This gets a chuckle out of him, enough to make his dimples form. When he smiles like this, it's hard to believe I found Erik more attractive at that moment. I don't think it's fair to compare anyone to Will. He's possibly the best looking guy I have ever seen.

"This guy was a bad kisser, huh?"

"It was like he was trying to eat me." I sit on the edge of his desk and roll my eyes. "Actually the worst. I may never kiss anyone again."

Will suddenly stands, and I thought I had shared too much information with him. I half expected him to storm out, instead he stands and positions himself between my legs. My breath hitches as he touches my cheek, his nose almost touching mine. "I could restore your faith?"

I clamp my mouth shut, repressing my smile. I reach out and play with the collar of his t-shirt, "I think that is the *least* you should do." I meet his hungry stare with my seductive gaze. "I might have been put off other things that may need restoring."

"Oh?" He sinks his teeth into his bottom lip. "I'm not sure you deserve it." Will lowers his head and runs his tongue over my throat.

"Why not?" I whimper.

"You did technically just cheat on me," he softly bites my jaw, and my legs naturally open for him.

"Fake cheating," I retort.

I suddenly think back to my conversation with Raven, and how she practically screamed I am not good enough for him. All of my insecurities rise to the surface, that I'm not beautiful, or smart enough for him. Of course I'm not, that's probably another reason he won't ever want a real relationship with me.

"What's wrong?"

I must be wearing my heart on my sleeve again. How can I tell him? What would it matter? This isn't real, I'm just someone he can have sex with to pretend he can have a committed relationship.

I swallow back my hurt and kiss him deeply on the mouth, making us both forget that there was ever a hitch in this meeting.

Will trails his fingers down the lace of my dress until he reaches the end, his hand grabs my thigh and he positions it firmly against his waist. "What a waste of a pretty dress," he said. "You deserve nothing but the best. To be cherished."

My lips actually part, I hadn't expected him to say something like that. Will kisses me, and it's as perfect as a kiss could be. Soft, yet full of so much desire it's enough to make me weak. I position my other leg around his waist so I am keeping him pinned in place.

His kisses are so intoxicating, so deliciously addicting that I can't help but crave more from even the simplest of touch. Will trails kisses down my throat and all the way down to my breasts. He grabs my breast, and I have never been more thankful to not be wearing a bra. With his thumb, he circles my nipple causing me to buck my hips in response. Knocking my head back I open my legs, inviting him to touch me.

Will is not one to disappoint, with one hand on my breast he dips his finger beneath my underwear and slips it inside of me. I start fucking his hand, my release on the horizon. I lean back until my head rests against the wall, I'm thrusting my hips so hard that I might break this table. Will doesn't slow his movements beneath me, he continues to work his fingers as I selfishly enjoy all of the attention. The one thing I can rely on Will for is that I won't last long until he makes me reach my climax. He knows exactly where to touch me, exactly what I like and how I like to be touched. Even with the simplest of kisses, it's perfect for me.

When I become undone, Will removes his hand from me. Instead of walking away, he surprises me by kissing me again. It's a gentle kiss, not what I am used to from him after a time like this. He kisses me like his life might depend on it, and I kiss him back with the same intention.

He pulls away; not fully. He leans his forehead against mine, his eyes closed and with a fast panting breath.

For a while we are like that, just together in a cloud of my pleasure. I'm not sure what this is, or why Will seems so strange. Could he have been jealous that I went out with Erik? If that were the case, wouldn't he have said something? Will isn't exactly shy about confessing something he doesn't like. Or have I gotten him completely wrong this entire time?

I surprise Will by standing to unbutton his jeans and dropping them to the floor. I sink to my knees and start tugging at his boxers, until his hand covers mine to halt me. "Lucy, you don't have to do that."

I smile up at him, "What if I want to?"

He bites his bottom lip, accompanied by a pained expression. "I can't even tell you how sexy you are just looking up at me like that."

I proceed to pull down his boxers, and this time he doesn't stop me yet he still has his hand over mine. When I dropped his boxers to gather around his ankles, I am greeted by his full erect length in my face.

"Besides," my voice is thick. "I want to make it up to you since I just fake cheated on you."

I open my mouth for him and wrap my lips around his length. I take him as far as I can, and Will squeezes my hand as I slow my movements. When I use my tongue to taste him, I can hear his breath hitch, that is shortly followed by a deep throaty groan.

"Fuck," he hisses as I start to pick up the pace with my movements.

I used to hate giving blow jobs for Simon. I hated it mostly because I was always me putting in the effort to please him, he would never do anything for me in return. However, Will is the one to ensure that I am taken care of. It never even crosses his mind to *not* make me feel good. Every time we have slept together, or done anything together, he always ensures I am satisfied first. Even now, he didn't want me to do anything I wasn't on board with.

I can't be wrong to think that Will cares for me more than a friend, can I?

"God, Lucy..." he grunts. "I'm not going to last much longer. I don't want you to..."

I remove my mouth from his cock, and I give him a seductive glare. "Come in my mouth."

"Fuck," he can't say anything else before I am back on his dick and sucking, licking, faster than before. I can feel he is close to release, his hand squeezing mine so hard that my fingertips are tingling.

Will climaxes, and I taste every drop of it as it coats my tongue. I swallow every last bit until I am satisfied he is done.

Getting back up to feet, Will looks defeated — like he could pass out from pure bliss. He opens up his arms and pulls me in for a tight embrace. I rest my head against his chest, and he cradles the back of my head. As we stand like this, a wash of sadness comes over me because I don't want this to end.

I want Will to be mine. I don't want him to find this kind of bond with anyone else, to fall in love with someone else, I want to be with him.

I'm just so in the dark as to whether he feels the same way.

Chapter Twenty-Three

The year seems to have flown by in a blink of an eye. One moment the sun was scorching my skin and now the snow has settled on the ground outside. Will and I have had to extend our fake dating relationship as his father keeps cancelling our plans to meet one another. I don't mind, it's been three months of sex and trying to figure out exactly what he feels for me.

"I really wish you would have a tidier tradition, Mom." I grumble as I help untangle Christmas lights for the tree.

"Or at least put them away properly the year before," Dad comments, being very unhelpful as he sits and eats a cookie on the couch, just watching as Mom and I struggle to untangle the lights. Every year my mom waits until Christmas Eve for us to put the lights around the tree, it's a tradition she started when we were kids, as a way to make Christmas Day even more magical for us. When Harry and I grew out of it she still insists on doing it.

"Caleb, call up to Harry and ask him to bring down the gifts I have in the wardrobe."

I catch Dad rolling his eyes, he's clearly just got comfortable on the couch. As he leaves there is a knock at the front door.

"Could you get that!" Mom calls, and looks to me with a

curious brow. "We don't usually get visitors on Christmas Eve."

I shrug, "It might be carollers."

Mom glances at the clock on the fireplace. "This early?"

I don't know why she thinks I can see through walls. It used to frustrate me when I was younger that she had to know everything, or she would be on edge for the rest of the day. Now that I'm older I can see that she just has a high case of anxiety, and it's best to just reassure her most of the time.

"That was never a thing in England," Mom continues. "When I first moved here I..."

"Lucy," Dad interrupts Mom's story, and I turn to see Will standing beside my dad with a large bag at his side.

My heart is racing a million miles an hour, his nose and cheeks are red from the cold. Not even his striped wooly scarf could save him.

I drop the lights I just spent the last half an hour trying to untangle, and stare at Will. "What are you doing here?"

He shrugged like it's nothing, "I was in the neighbourhood, and figured I would drop off some gifts for you and your family."

"Aw, Will you didn't have to get us anything." Mom gushes.

"It's nothing," that charming smile could melt the snow surrounding our house. Did he drive in this weather just to see me? Or was he actually in the neighbourhood?

"Isn't that sweet, Caleb?"

Dad pats Will on the shoulder, and I can't help but blush when his eyes find mine in this chaotic room.

"I'll pop them under the tree, ready for tomorrow." Mom takes the bag from Will and starts unloading the gifts and placing them under the tree. This wasn't a last minute shop, there is a ridiculous amount of wrapped boxes that would make any kid envious.

"Are you spending Christmas with your family?" Dad asks, unabashed about the directness and invasion of his question.

"No, actually." Will dipped his head slightly, the tips of his black hair brushing against his forehead, revealing a few flecks of snow melting into his hair. "My parents decided to go to Washington this Christmas, and my sister is with her boyfriend."

I see Mom's mouth drop open, "You are not spending Christmas alone."

"Really, Ma'am it's fine — "

"Nope, you are Lucy's boyfriend and we would be more than happy to have you spend Christmas with us."

Please say yes.

My heart is in my mouth now, I've barely said anything because I have been too transfixed on Will, and how adorable he looks right now. If he was blushing I wouldn't be able to tell, because the cold had gotten to his cheeks first.

When he meets my gaze again I feel weak in the knees. "Only if you want me to."

I try to act cool, like it isn't eating me up inside that I want to pounce on him this very second. "Of course."

His smile widens, revealing each of his dimples that I have kissed so many times.

"Perfect!" Mom chimes. "Which means…" she bends down and scoops up the portion of tangled lights she was working on, and hands them to Will. "You can help Lucy untangle these lights. Since *somebody* — " she sticks out her chin to Dad " — can't call for his son like I asked five minutes ago."

"I was just about to," they playfully bicker as they escape upstairs.

Will sits with his legs crossed in front of me as we get to work untangling our portion of lights. I'm nervous suddenly, like I don't want to say the wrong thing and ruin this glee that's forming in my chest.

"I can see why this is a two man job," he chuckles.

"Yeah, it's like this every year."

Will is doing a better job than my mother at untangling the lights, his fingers are like magic as he straightens the green wires. "My dad has invited you to his birthday party next month. To meet you." He avoids looking at me the entire time.

"Oh, okay." My heart sinks a little. I've gotten so used to Will being here, being my 'boyfriend' that it's suddenly hit me that it's coming to an end soon. "Of course, that's what all of this was for right? The big meeting." I try to add a playfulness to my voice but I'm not an actress, my emotions are always front and centre.

"Yeah," is all he says.

"Do you mind me being here?" Will asks. "I know that you don't want your family involved with the lie."

I know if I said no right now he would leave. He's right, I don't want them involved, but I also don't want him to be a *lie*. Plus, how much of a bitch would I be if I made him spend Christmas alone? I don't doubt he'd be celebrating with a bottle.

"I want you here, Will." I finish untangling my portion of lights. "You may be my fake boyfriend, but that doesn't mean I don't enjoy your company."

He smiles at that, both of his dimple making their arrival. That genuine smile is enough to make me ache. How I wish I hadn't gotten myself into this mess. I can feel myself falling and Will won't be there to catch me.

It's strange for Will to be in the room that I spent a lot of my childhood. It feels so personal to have him at my parent's house. For him to bring gifts too, a lot of gifts by the look of

Mom emptying the bag under the tree.

"Want to watch something?" I say as I grab the remote and flick through the apps, mostly to distract myself from his presence.

Warmth fills my body when Will sits behind me on the bed, brushing my hair out the way of my neck. His feather-like lips plant kisses along my skin, and I curse myself for closing my eyes and embracing every moment.

"I'm curious," his voice is thick as he trails kisses up the side of my neck and along my jaw. "If you could have one thing this Christmas, what would it be?"

My immediate thought is: *you.*

Instead of confessing that, I ask. "What do you mean?"

Will's warm hands slip around my stomach, under my jumper, and slowly make their way up to my breasts. I sharp gasp of pleasure bursts from this simple action, his large fingers now pinching my perky nipples, causing my hips to roll in response.

"Is there anything *we* haven't done that you'd want? Anything you like?"

"I don't know," I whisper.

His hands freeze over my breasts. Have I said something wrong? Did I confess something whilst he tortured me with pleasure?

"You don't know?"

"I've not done a lot of stuff," I chew on my bottom lip. "Just sex, and the stuff we have done."

Suddenly, Will removes his hands from me entirely. Coming around the bed and kneeling in front of me, he looks at me with such a fiery intensity I might combust. "Didn't you try stuff with your ex?"

I shake my head, "No. He didn't want to do things like that for me."

A single eyebrow raises on his gorgeous face, he seems to

be genuinely annoyed at that. "Why?"

I shrug, suddenly feeling self conscious with my own body. "He said it was gross."

"Did you do anything for him?"

I shrug again, trying to play it off like it's nothing, that it doesn't upset me as much as it does. "Yeah."

After a beat I thought Will was going to leave it there. That now I have said it out loud he can see what Simon meant, that I am gross. Instead, Will lifts my jumper to reveal my naked chest, and pulls down my pants, including my underwear. Tossing them aside like they are in inconvenience.

"Let me assure you, touching you — pleasuring you — is the furthest thing from 'gross.'" Will's nostrils flare from an anger. "Your ex was a fucking stupid moron. A fucking prick and you are so much better off without him."

He's not wrong.

Will gestures for me to lie back on the bed, and I obey. I place my head on my pillows and lay flat as a plank of wood. He's seen me naked before, he's done things to my body that no one else ever dared to, but this feels different. I feel like he is really looking at me.

Will climbs on top of me, still clothed. He kisses me firmly on the mouth, his hands exploring my chest and torso, until one hand settles over my breast.

I feel his hard erection pushing into me through his jeans, and I want nothing more than to rip his clothes off. I go to do so, until he halts me in place. "This is for you," he whispers, and pins my hands above my head, as he kisses along my jaw and neck.

"What if I want to touch you?"

He rumbles a dark chuckle. "Too bad."

I bite down on any sounds that attempts to leave my throat. We can't be loud here, there are others in this house who will not want to know what we are doing.

Making his way back up to my ear, Will whispers. "Did he ever make you come?"

I shake my head, I don't have to think about the answer because sex with Simon was more of a chore than fun.

"Have I?"

I can feel him smiling because he knows damn well that every time we have been intimate he has. I blush as I nod my head, all words failing on my tongue.

Satisfied with my answer, Will kisses me again. Only this time he is making a long, painful trail with his lips. Every so often he will bite my skin and lick me with his tongue. Then he settles between my legs and opens them wider.

A flurry of paranoia fills my mind, the fear of him finding me disgusting down there has taken over any pleasurable thoughts I just had. I sit up, to find his mouth dangerously close to my heat.

"You don't have to...if you don't like it, I won't be — "

Will looks at me seriously through his desire, "I want to, I *like* this." A smirk tickles his lips. "Especially if it's for you."

I'm about to protest, I don't want him saying this to make me feel better. Only, I don't get the chance for he kisses my flesh in between my legs, and flicks my clit with his tongue in deliciously long strokes. I fall back onto my pillows and bite my hand to prevent from moaning too loud. It's a strange sensation at first, something new that I want to kick myself for not demanding be done before. Yet, I can only imagine it feels this good because it's Will down there. The only man that can make me feel beautiful with a single flick of his tongue.

He feasts on me, and I can hear his own moans with each kiss. My breaths are shallow as the intensity builds at my core, desperate for release.

I fall apart at a certain flick of his tongue, biting my finger to prevent from screaming the house down. Convulsing, and eventually dropping my arms and legs like flubber, I look over at Will who is now hovering over me. He's wearing that shit-eating-grin that I wanted so desperately to smack off when we first began this 'relationship.'

"Goodnight, Lucy."

I didn't realise I'd closed my eyes. I roll onto my side and nuzzle my face against his firm chest, pretending for one more night that this is real.

"Goodnight, Will."

Chapter Twenty-Four

I wake up with Will's arms wrapped around me, fully cocooning me with his warmth and strength. His breath tickles the hairs on the back of my neck and I shuffle back to be pressed further against him.

This causes him to stir, only tightening his hold around my body and nuzzling his nose into my hair.

I could have spent the entirety of Christmas Day in bed with Will, but that is rendered impossible when the Christmas music starts blaring from the living room. It's actually making my pillow vibrate.

It's always like stepping into a cheesy Christmas movie, and it still never fails to put a smile on my face. I know exactly what I will find when I walk downstairs, Dad still half asleep, Mom dancing around in her ugliest Christmas jumper, and Harry glued to his phone pretending he's too cool to get involved with the Christmas joy.

I feel strangely excited that Will is here to share this with me. I used to dread bringing Simon over for the holidays. It's not that Christmas is about the presents, it's about spending time with family. Yet, he never brought anything for my family when I would be sure to splurge on his. Even when my parents gave him a thoughtful gift, there was zero gratitude.

Why did I waste so much time with him? Was it because of habit? There must have been something worth sticking around for.

"I'm guessing your mom loves Christmas?"

I giggle, and roll over to fully face him. He's still got his eyes closed, but a drowsy smile curving his mouth.

"What makes you think it's my mom? It could very well be my dad."

Will opens one eye and gives me a look that says, *do you think I'm stupid?* He only adds to this look by saying, "You dad doesn't seem the type to play festive music."

I somehow drag Will out of bed. He changes into what he wore the night before and I pull out my ugly Christmas jumper that mom has nagged me to wear for the past two weeks. It's a knitted snowman in a snow storm, with a blob that I guess is supposed to be an igloo in the back.

"Ta-da," I show it off, striking a pose to Will and he fails to hide his amusement, he doesn't even try. A smile stretches over his face, causing the corners of his eyes to crease.

"I'm jealous," he says, shaking into his jacket.

Even as I stand in this ridiculous jumper, I can't help but blush at the look he is giving me. I could be standing in a chicken costume and he would make me feel like the most beautiful girl to ever exist.

The rest of the day goes by in a flash, we watch movies, eat a lot of food and collapse with our guts out in the living room. "Time to exchange gifts," Mom sits under the tree and pulls out each and every gift. "Do you have any traditions at your house, Will?"

"Not really," he leans back on the couch. "Aside from arguing who gets to open the first bottle of brandy."

Mom laughs, and hands Will a gift that he clearly wasn't expecting. "I tried to ask Lucy for ideas on what to get you," she said. "But I'm sure you've figured out how helpful she is." She nudges my arm when I settle in on the floor next to her.

I can't take my eyes off Will, he seems to be in awe that my parents brought him something. Like he is apart of the family, and the sight warms my heart. Will tears the wrapping and is presented with a personalised notebook, with his name embossed in leather. "Thank you so much," he says and nods to my mom and dad.

"Lucy mentioned you're a writer, I figured it could come in handy if you need to jot down any notes."

Mom worries so much about getting people the perfect gift. It's sweet, in a way, watching her explain the gift she buys for anyone she struggled with. But based on the genuine smile, revealing each of Will's dimples, I'd say she was successful. "It's great," he said. "I really appreciate it."

"Better than the socks I'll probably get," Harry laughs and Will joins in.

I'm surprised at how much Will remembers what I told him of my family. He must have stored each person's hobby and interest in the back of his mind whenever I mentioned it in passing, only to shine at Christmas. My mother receives a speaker with lights that, according to the box, will change colour based on what music she is playing.

My dad gets a brand new tool set, from what I can tell it is an expensive brand that my dad seems to be over the moon about. I can hear him muttering about plans for the barn and new projects he can finally work on.

Even Harry gets a bottle of his favourite whisky that he only ever treats himself to once a year.

"You have spent far too much on us, Will." My mom gushes, but can't stop smiling. She's always in her element at Christmas, and she deserves it more than anyone. It's been a difficult year for her, and Will gifting my family with such thoughtful presents makes me appreciate him a lot more.

We exchange more gifts, my parents treated me to a brand new bathrobe that I have desperately needed for a long time.

Mom's eyes ignites when she pulls out a large rectangular box, she has to hold it with two hands and she makes a face like it's heavy. She reads the tag, and I swear she was moments away from squealing like a school girl.

"This is for Lucy, from Will."

"Oh," I take it from her, and I can see why she pulled that face. I settle it on my lap and I feel like my knees might shatter. Did he buy me a dining room table? What even is this?

I'm always so awkward opening gifts, but now it feels ten times worse because Will is watching me. I can feel his warm gaze burning into my skull as I tear at the paper.

A gasp lodges in my throat when I see what he has brought me. It's a drawing tablet…not just any drawing tablet but the most *expensive* tablet that I have been pining over ever since they released it. It seemed like something I could only ever have in my dreams, because there was no way my previous or current salary could pay for it.

I snap up my gaze to his, mouth open to say thank you but those words don't seem like enough. "How did you…"

"I thought it would be handy for your designs," he says, a sweet smile that I want to kiss right now. "Saves you drawing on paper."

I look down at it, and I hold it in a firm grip. I could cry right now, I feel tears burning in the back of my throat because this is the most thoughtful gift anyone has ever gotten for me. Regardless of the price, he could have brought anything meaningless and handed to me and beam with pride because he spent a lot, but *this* means everything to me.

"Thank you," I finally say after forcing my tears down. "I feel bad that my gifts are lame in comparison."

Will chuckles and shakes his head, "Nah, I love them."

For a moment I imagine he just said that he loves me, and how perfect it would fit to my ears. What saddens me the most is that was probably the closest I will get to hearing Will say that to me.

Later that night Mom and Dad visit my Aunt Sam and Uncle Lucas to drop off gifts to their family.

I unbox my drawing tablet in my room. Will sits on the edge of my bed and picks up the remote to the TV and begins flicking through the apps until he finds *Netflix*.

"Do you like your present?" He said, with a coy smile on his lips knowing full well that I do. I haven't been able to keep my hands off it ever since I opened it. It's as though I am afraid it will vanish if I spend more than two-seconds away from it.

I get up and pull my laptop out from under my bed, "I wasn't going to class this as a gift," I say and click through my design folder. I browse until I find the mock-up cover I created for Will's book cover. I open it up so it fits my entire screen, before showing it to Will I say, "This is *nothing* compared to what you got for me, but I figured you might like it?"

I hand him my laptop and he takes it from me, settling it onto his lap. A smile beams on his mouth, his full set of teeth showing and those goddamn dimples making their appearance. "This is everything I wanted it to be," he said, turning to me with a warm expression filling my own body with heat. "Thank you."

I look at him, and an urge rises in my throat to admit him what I feel for him. The way his eyes scan over my face I get the sense that he is coaxing me to admit it, almost silently begging me to.

"Will, I..."

I am suddenly interrupted by my brother yelling at the

bottom of the stairs. I snap my head to my bedroom door, trying to listen to what is going on. I hear another voice that doesn't belong to a member of my family.

Without thinking, I scramble out of bed and run down the stairs to find out what's going on. I freeze when I see Simon at the front door, arguing with Harry. I can already guess who this is about.

"Get the fuck out, Simon."

"Not until I talk to her."

Simon's cold eyes snap to me standing on the stairs and I feel my soul shrivel in my chest. There is that fake softness to his face when he is trying to worm his way back into my life. My hand tightens around the banister, holding me up so I don't collapse.

"Lulu," Simon pleads. "I just want to talk to you — " his eyes then look over me, to something over my shoulder and that mask slips into rage.

It's only when Will places a hand over my shoulder do I realise that I'm shaking.

Simon points at him with a spite in his next words, "What the fuck is he doing here?"

Harry shoves Simon back, not enough to get him out the door but enough to make him stumble. "It's none of your fucking business, Simon."

"I just want to talk to her!"

The rage boils in my blood that he talks about me as if he's entitled to me. As if I am his property that he is here to claim because *he saw me first.* I've had enough of living in fear, I don't want to run away and be looking over my shoulder when simply shopping for groceries.

"I'll talk to you," I say, Will's grip tightens over my shoulder.

Harry glares at me, "No, Lucy - "

"I'm talking to him," I storm past my brother and out onto

the porch. "If I need you I will call."

Harry starts protesting, and Will has an unreadable expression from his spot on the stairs. I wait for Simon to step outside with me before closing the door.

Simon starts pacing around on my porch, "I'll call if I need you," he grumbles before turning to fully face me. "What? Like I'm going to hurt you? What the fuck, Lulu?"

"Why are you here Simon?" I fold my arms over my chest, regretting not putting a coat on before stepping into the snow. "It's Christmas Day, why are you showing up here and fighting with my brother?"

"Because I just want to fucking *talk* to you." He snaps. "You've blocked my number, that asshole throws me out of the store whenever I try to come in."

"And all of that isn't a sign that I don't *want* to see you? Besides, aren't you with Melissa now, why can't you focus on her?"

"I don't want her!"

"You wanted her when you fucked her whilst we were together."

Simon is speechless, the colour draining from his face. Clearly Melissa hasn't told him about our little meet up a couple of months ago. He is really trying to stand here and act like the love sick puppy, desperate to have his heart healed by the 'love of his life.'

What bullshit.

"Lulu, I - "

"Stop calling me Lulu!" I yell, that confidence I felt from yelling at Raven returning. "I've always hated it. I am going to make this very clear for you. I do not want to be with you. I don't love you, and you know what, I don't think I ever did!" I am smiling like a madwoman to get this off my chest. Maybe the last part isn't entirely true. I did love him in a way that I cared for him. It was more like puppy love, a teenage infatuation. "I can't believe I wasted five years of my life with you. I almost jeopardise my relationship with my brother over a scumbag like you."

I was so lost in my rant that I didn't notice Simon take a step closer to me. I stick out my chin, not showing any weakness. If he sees that I am not scared of him, that his presence means nothing to me maybe he will finally take the hint.

"How long have you been fucking that guy?" He tilts his head to the house, signifying Will inside.

"That's not your business," I snarl. "But if you must know, I was single when we got together."

Simon hates that he is fully to blame. I can see the fire in his eyes, he could melt the snow beneath his feet. "I *love* you, Lucy." The words that are supposed to be filled with love are spewed with hatred.

I can't allow him to think that there is a chance for us to get back together. That if I tell him there was a time that I did love him, he might think there is a way for him to crawl his way back. If lying to him is what it takes for him to leave me alone and never look back, I will lie to my hearts content.

"I *never* loved you."

Simon raises his hand high and before I can register what he is about to do, he slaps me across the cheek. Hard enough that my head faces the side.

I'm in shock for a moment, and don't even acknowledge that the front door has swung open and out runs Will and Harry.

My brother pulls me back as I cradle my stinging cheek.

Will grabs Simon by the scuff of his shirt and lands a solid punch across his cheek. Blood pools out from Simon's nose and leaves red dots in the snow. "Do not come fucking near her again. You understand me?"

Simon tries to meet my eyes, and I don't hide away. I show

him exactly what he has done, the tears he has caused the pain he has inflicted and I think I see something change in his eyes. A daunting realisation that everything I said is the truth. It's like the past five years, these past few months, are flashing before his eyes without the delusional goggles blocking him.

"Lulu," he breathes. "I'm...I'm sorry."

"If you're truly sorry," my voice trembles with every word. "You will leave me alone. Forever."

Simon doesn't say another word, he doesn't give me the courtesy of confirming whether he will abide by my request. Instead he walks away into the night, and I feel like my heaviest weight has been lifted from my shoulders.

Chapter Twenty-Five

Harry hands me a mug of hot chocolate and places a hand over my shoulder. "This isn't the first time he has done something like this, is it?"

I sigh and take a sip from my drink. "No, but it's over now."

Harry huffs, anger slipping over his face. He runs a hand over the length of his face, seemingly wiping away whatever it was he was going to say. "If he comes back," he says. "Let me know. We'll go to the police, file a restraining order, anything." Harry shakes my shoulder. "Don't go through stuff like this alone."

I offer a smile, biting back tears. "Thanks, Harry."

Harry nods then leaves me and Will alone in the living room with a fire burning. I warm my hands with my mug and stare out at the dancing golden and orange flame.

"I'm sorry," it's all I can think of to say to fill in this silence. Tears slip down my cheeks, "I shouldn't have agreed to talk to him outside, I - "

"Hey," he whispers, taking my hot chocolate and placing it down on the coffee table. Will cups both of my cheeks with his hands and I flinch at the contact to the sore spot from Simon's hand. When he realise it hurts he releases his grip over my sore cheek, but brushes his thumb over my skin. I look him in the eyes, and the sadness that I am all too familiar with is present. Only this time, it's in relation to me. "It was brave what you did. You stood up for yourself."

I try to deny it, shake my head but Will keeps my face to his. "It's true, Lucy."

I swallow and stare at his lips, "Thank you for stepping in. I think you scared the shit out of him."

Will doesn't laugh, "I couldn't let him get off easy, especially after hitting you."

I don't know what else to say, instead I lean over and kiss him firmly on the mouth. Will continues to cradle my face as his lips explore mine. It's not fast and passionate like it usually is, but right now he is slow and tender. His lips graze over mine in a painstaking motion.

God, my heart is heavy in my chest right now.

How could anyone possibly compare to Will after we 'break up?' His kiss is so addictive, like my own personal brand of chocolate for my lips only. The idea of him walking away, no longer having him in my bed, sitting in his arms, is the most painful thing my heart will ever have to endure.

Oh my God.

I'm in love with Will Dawson.

I have avoided Will since Christmas Day. I can't quite look at him ever since I realised that I am ridiculously in love with him. He texted me asking if I will be his date for a New Year's Eve party at his friends place. I haven't responded to his text, I'm not sure if I can do this anymore. How can I keep this up when my heart has stupidly fallen deep into the pool of love, forever searching for the bottom in a bottomless ocean of Will?

Instead, I invite Jeremy over for our catch up rom-com night.

When knocks on my apartment door, he greets me with a

wide smile but I'm confused when I see him fall into sorrow.

"Lucy?" He places his hands over my shoulders and looks me in the eye. It's only when I feel the cold tear stream down my cheeks do I realise why he is so concerned. "What happened, Lucy?"

"I...I..." I hitch a breath before I whisper. "I love him."

Jeremy arches his brows and the look of pity will never be washed from my brain. He knows why this devastates me, because our relationship is fake. As much as I can pretend that Will might one day return my feelings, that I can crawl my way into his heart, it will never happen. He will never love me.

Jeremy opens up his arms and pulls me into a tight hug. I cry into his chest as he squeezes me tight as I sob.

If there is one thing that will never fail me, it's Jeremy's ability to cheer me up. He stuck on the lowest rated rom-com, ordered take out and sat on my couch making my living room a pigsty.

When the movie credits roll, I expect Jeremy to stick on another film, instead he turns off the TV and turns his body to face me. Resting his head against his fist, he stares at me with a small smile. "Why don't you tell him?"

I deflate and snuggle back against the arm of the couch. "I can't."

"What have you got to lose?" He asked, taking a mouthful of his Chinese. "He might feel the same way."

I shake my head, the very idea of Will loving me is ridiculous. "He made it clear from the start. He doesn't want to love anyone, he doesn't want a relationship."

"Listen, you cannot spend almost half a year with someone and feel nothing." Jeremy says. "Not with someone you have kissed — had sex with — and feel nothing."

"People who have friends with benefits seem to manage

just fine."

Jeremy glares at me. "That's not what this was though, right?"

I sigh, inhaling a fork full of noodles. The tears are threatening my eyes again, and I swallow them down with a burning sensation heating up my food on the way down my throat.

When he sees the tears, Jeremy shuffles over to me and pulls me into another tight hug. "Tell him, Lucy." He mutters against my hair. "Even if it's just to save your future from a bunch of *what ifs?*" He plants a kiss against my hair as more tears fall from my eyes. "Even if it's just to give you closure."

That night I lie in bed and open up my texts from Will. There are three that I have ignored, including the invite to his friends party on New Year's Eve.

Will: My friend is throwing a New Year's Eve party, would you accompany me as my beautiful date? Xxx

Will: We don't have to go, just thought it might be fun for us to have a night out xxx

Us? Damn my heart for skipping a beat, yet another moment of my heart mistaking this as something real.

Will: I hope you're okay xxx

No, Will. I'm not okay, I want to type. *I'm so madly in love with you that I can't stand to see your stupid, beautiful face.* I don't respond with any of that, instead I text him:

Me: I'd love to xxx

Chapter Twenty-Six

Maybe replying with 'I'd love to' was too strong a phrase. Of course I want to spend more time with Will, being on his arm and finding out more about his life. Going to a party hosted by his friend is a good start, they could provide me with some interesting information to get a better understanding of Will. I'd like to know whether he was always this distant, if he had girlfriends in the past and how serious is he about not wanting a relationship?

Sand dries my throat at a sudden thought. What if this entire time Will has been open to having a relationship, he just can't see it working with me?

I jolt out of my depressing thoughts at my phone vibrating in my clutch bag. I check and see it is Will calling me. Even seeing his name light up my phone makes my heart thrash around in my chest. He's here to pick me up. Before I head downstairs, I check my outfit to ensure there is no boob out of place, no streaks in my make-up, and certainly no part of my dress tucked into my panties. That is one mistake I do *not* want happening again.

Once I'm happy that my silk red dress won't embarrass me with accidental nudity, I head downstairs and meet Will in his car.

I check my make-up in his rearview mirror, and the car is

weirdly silent, even for him.

When I turn to look at him, he is practically drooling over my appearance. With his lips parted and his eyes taking in my cleavage, that I will admit is on display more than I usually would. How the silk hugs my slim frame also is probably as sweet as candy to him right now.

I shove him back, my cheeks flaring up with heat. "Like what you see?" I tease.

Will shakes his head, seemingly coming back to reality and keeping his eyes locked on the road ahead. "Very much so."

I wish it wasn't so dark, and his trousers weren't black, so I might be able to catch a glimpse at exactly how much he likes how I look.

Feeling a boost of confidence in myself, that Will certainly has some level of attraction to me, I straighten my back and sit a little higher. All the while Will has both his hands firmly around the wheel and races us off to his friend's party.

If he's lucky, maybe we can sneak off and find a closet somewhere.

Stepping into a party that is clearly an entirely different class level is more overwhelming than I was expecting. Suddenly, the dress I felt confident in only moments before felt too short, it was too tight against my skin, and not appropriate for this party.

I look around the room and try to find another girl with a skirt the length of mine, a dress shorter than mine, but I find none. These women are elegant, beautiful, and here I am in a scandalous red dress.

"Give me your coat," I hiss to Will, my hands clamming from anxiety.

"What?"

"I - I…my dress it's way too…"

"Hey," he steps in front of me and cups his hands over my

cheeks. "Calm down, you look perfect."

Tears prick my eyes, "But it's so short...so revealing."

Will silences my new words of insecurity with a kiss. "You're perfect."

When I look into his eyes there is no doubt that I am truly, madly, ridiculously in love with him. How bad would it be if I told him? The sincerity, the sweetness, of his words can't mean nothing. They can't.

"Will, I..."

"William!" a short gentleman emerges from the crowd with a champagne flute to add to his snobby exterior. Wearing a suit that probably costs more than my apartment and furniture combined. He takes another champagne glass from a waiter's tray and offers it to Will. The sight of the glass makes Will tense, like the very sight of it frightens him. I'm not sure why he had that reaction, he's not against alcohol, I picked him up drunk out of his mind a few months ago. However, I haven't seen him touch a drink since then.

That moment of awkwardness vanishes as he composes himself. "No thanks, I'm driving."

I try not to look this guy in the eyes, there is something about his lingering stare that makes me uncomfortable. When he does finally acknowledge my presence, his eyes immediately darken to my cleavage.

When this sleaze does decide to look at my face, his mouth quirks to a grin. "I'm Billy, nice to meet you."

"Lucy," I don't want to talk to him more than I have to. I keep my answers short, hoping this guy will not be interested in engaging with me. It seems to work, since he turns to face Will and barely acknowledges that I am standing right in front of him.

"It's good to see you out and about," Billy says. "We were surprised to hear that you were coming tonight."

Will shrugs, "Who doesn't love a good New Year's Eve

party?"

"Have you spoken to Jade?" Billy's voice dips into a whisper, it's loud enough for me to hear but quiet enough for him to pass it off as trying to be discreet.

Will works his jaw at the question, "No, I'm sure I'll run into her at some point."

"Make sure you do," he says. "She's missed you."

Billy gargles a laugh when takes a glance at my reaction, which is clearly what he was looking for, and leaves us in a cloud of unease. I can't help but notice the shift in mood, he is someone who I will be happy to never cross paths with again.

"Who's Jade?" The question slips past my mouth before I can catch it. I can't take it back now, it's clearly a topic sore for Will. I'm not sure if I could handle it if she was his ex girlfriend. I already know I will be comparing myself to her more than anyone else in this room.

Will sighs and runs a hand through his black hair. By the look on his face I can tell he is considering not telling me, he knows I won't like the answer.

"Jade is…" he rolls his eyes. He really likes to make me suffer with dragging out the truth. "She's the one my parents were going to set me up with." He looks at me. "To marry."

My heart freezes over, like it has been dropped in a pool of water in the Antarctic.

It was always easy to pretend that the threat looming over Will's head the entire time was just a ghost. Just an empty threat parents give their children, the equivalent of saying 'I will turn this car around if you don't behave' knowing full well that the car will continue down the same track, regardless.

It was easy to pretend that Will just wanted a fake relationship because he didn't want to attach labels to it. Now knowing the woman is real, that she exists and has a name, I feel a wave of sadness overcome me. Just the idea of Will marrying someone else, kissing her, holding her, *being* with her, is enough to break the last shard of glass holding together my heart.

"That's why I'm here," my voice is low. "So she will report back to your father that you are in a committed relationship."

I have no right to feel this way. This was fake, it's always been fake. It's my fault for stupidly falling in love with him, when from the beginning he told me he didn't want a relationship. Just because I shouldn't feel this way, it doesn't mean I can't.

Will steps in front of me, "Lucy..."

I don't want to hear his explanation. The knife is in at the handle, he can't twist it anymore. Instead of hearing him out, I walk away and lose myself in this crowd of upper class strangers. When I look behind me, Will is no where in sight.

Chapter Twenty-Seven

Why is it that being left along for a few minutes at a party feels like an entire lifetime? As I stand in the darkest corner I still feel like eyes are on me, questioning whether or not I've stumbled in uninvited. It's fine when I have Will, he easily distracts me from my anxiety. All he'd have to do is slip his hand around my waist and all my troubles would vanish.

Maybe if I recognised one other face in this room, or actually had any people skills, this time alone would be less humiliating.

Suddenly, a goddess in gold approaches me. I look around to see if she could be walking towards someone near me, but I am the only one in this section. She looks as though she has just stepped out of the cover of a magazine. Her rich black hair is twisted into a high bun, really elevating her cheekbones that I would die to have. Her face is elegantly painted in make-up, with a smoky look to highlight her dark brown eyes. She is so gorgeous, and I might pass out just being in her presence.

"Hi, you're Lucy, right?"

"Yeah," I offer my sweetest smile, to somehow mask the intimidation that I feel.

"I'm Jade, it's nice to meet you."

My heart stops at her name. This is *the* Jade. The one that

Will's parents were going to set him up with, the one I was supposed to be impressing. In all honesty, she could easily steal Will from me and I wouldn't be mad at her. I got the implication that Will and Jade knew each other prior to this arrangement, why on earth would he say no to marrying her? There must be a flaw hidden beneath her golden exterior.

We make small talk, and so far I find absolutely nothing wrong with her. She is easy to talk to, like she isn't here to pity me and actually takes an interest in what I have to say. It's refreshing, considering   most people here won't even acknowledge my existence without Will by my side.

I find out that she is head of finances at her father's company. Her father and Will's father have known each other since high school, which explains why he would be eager to set them up for a marriage.

"How did you manage to snag Will?" She asked, her glossed lips still turned up to a smile. "I'm sure you've heard that there was plans for us to get hitched."

I don't know if she was expecting to surprise me with this news, and I will admit the idea still stings, but I nod and pick up a champagne flute. "I did hear. I guess it was just…perfect timing on my part."

I hate how effortless it has become to lie about this. I know that it has become something more for me, and in moments like these it's easy to pretend that I mean something to Will. That him and I are a real couple, and I could walk in here with pride in my step knowing that Will is mine.

There is something painful twisting in my heart knowing that that isn't true. Knowing that this is all fake, and I'm not sure what it say about me that I so desperately want this to be real. The moment we slept together again, becoming whatever we are now, was when it should have ended. I became too intimate with him, giving him so much and pretending I could handle it was a mistake on my part. I should have thought this through…all of it.

I'm not someone who can sleep with someone and not get attached. I truly envy those who can, I wish I had a stronger barrier over my heart, but I don't. My heart has been shattered so many times, and even when I manage to put the pieces back together, it will never be what it once was.

"Listen Lucy," Jade drops her head and takes a small step forward, creating an intimate bubble around us. "I know how this is going to sound, and I can't think of a better way of putting this, but are you sure you belong with Will?"

I clutch the flute so tightly I'm afraid it will crack in my grip. How am I supposed to answer that? Luckily I don't have to, because Jade elaborates. "You seem like a lovely girl but Will needs someone who is on his level, do you understand what I'm saying?"

My cheeks are flushing from embarrassment. I know she isn't intending to cause me hurt, I can see she is thinking of Will's best interest because she cares about him, maybe even loves him. Maybe she's right, I'm not what's best for Will, maybe everyone can see that and I've purposely blinded myself to it.

I wonder if Jade and Raven are friends, or if both of them know what is best for Will? If everyone has this same impression, am I the one that is in the wrong?

"He seems so happy here at this party," she continues. "Back in this crowed with his old friends. I just think he needs to be in a circle where he belongs, with someone who can suit his needs."

I feel a lump burning in my throat, it hurts to swallow. I simply nod, and somehow I manage to compose myself. "I understand."

Jade offers a sad smile, and lightly taps my arm to offer a silent apology.

I am suffocating in this bubble, I need to break out. "Please excuse me, I need some air."

"Of course."

I rush to the back door and burst into the cold winter night. The chill from the air helps extinguish some of the flames burning my heart.

I lean over the balcony and take a long inhale through the nose. Staring out at the stars, I will my heart to calm itself but with no avail. It's screaming Will's name, demanding that he be here, like a toddler throwing a tantrum.

The tears from earlier are back, and I feel like I am breaking. Jade is right, Will belongs with these people. I'm not even his *real* girlfriend, there was never supposed to be any emotion involved. I knew from the beginning that he didn't want a relationship, he flat out told me so I have no right to cry. It doesn't help ease my pain, if anything it makes me hate myself more for allowing myself to fall for him as hard as I have.

Everyone can see that I am not right for him, his own sister can see that.

I'm not going to be the one that he drops everything for. I'm not the one he will love. I'm not the one he will risk it all and have a relationship with despite the world that is against us.

I'm not the one.

"Hey, I've been looking for you." I would recognise that voice anywhere, and so does my heart.

I don't turn around to face him. I try to bite back the tears that are freely spilling down my cheeks. I am just thankful I put a minimal amount of make-up on tonight, otherwise I would be walking home with eyes that rival a raccoon.

What is wrong with me? Why am I so weepy recently?

Will steps to my side, and I feel his emerald eyes try to meet my own gaze. As much as I try to hide it, he can see right through me. He knows when I am upset, when I'm happy, but he can't see how much *he* means to *me*.

"I saw you talking to Jade," his voice is soft, careful, which somehow makes me feel worse. I want him to be horrible, to yell and scream at me. I want him to force these feelings out of me, I want to hate him because it will be a lot easier to deal with than loving him.

"Did she say something to you?"

I shrug. I don't want to cause a rift between them, especially when she was only doing what she thought was best for Will. It's obvious she has feelings for him, she's known him longer and she probably does know what's best for him.

I have no idea, I barely know what is best for myself. Every time I try to make a change it always leads me down the same path of pain. Maybe I'm the problem, I'm the common denominator. Perhaps I'm just not meant to be happy.

I grip my hands firmly around the wooden plank that makes up the balcony. My knuckles start to turn white from squeezing so hard. Finally, I look over at Will and push out a smile, stretching over my row of teeth. "You should be with her."

He is physically taken aback by what I said, clearly he was not expecting that. If I wasn't mistaken, I could have sworn I saw a hint of hurt.

"She's just so perfect in every way, Will." I flick away the few tears that are falling and look out to the bright lights this balcony overlooks. "She's smart, career focused, *nice* and my god she is probably the most gorgeous girl I've ever seen." I release a baffled laugh that someone as perfect as her exists and I'm the one on Will's arm tonight. "She would be perfect for you."

Will is silent for a while, I wonder if he believes me. That only now that it's been pointed out to him does he realise how much time he has wasted on me when he could easily get an angel like her.

"A lot of people have been saying that to me," he says. "Everyone but me."

My heart leaps when he covers my hand with his, immediately filling my cold body with warmth, like I have just been seated in front of a fire in a winter storm. When I look over at him again, his eyes are intently focused on mine and he draws his other hand to my cheek. Slowly, he traces a small stroke over my skin and I settle into his palm. "I don't think you realise, Lucy Wilson, that you are also all of those things you just said…and so much more."

I want to believe him, to leap into his arms, allow him to kiss me like most couples would in a moment like this. Instead, I roll my eyes and scoff, because this isn't what I want it to be. We aren't a couple, he just wants me to stop crying before walking back into his party of friends.

"You are, Lucy." He smiles just enough to reveal a hint of his dimples. "You are too hard on yourself. You are career focused, it may not seem like it working in the store, but you're building the foundation of your career. You're smarter than most people I know. And *nice?* Lucy," he scoffs a laugh of his own. "Right now, and everything else you have been doing for me, is on a whole other level of nice. Saints would probably do less, especially for a pain in the ass like me."

I can't help but laugh at that. He is an ass, and he's the one that my heart wants.

"You are…" his breath actually hitches, his face pained. "You are the most beautiful, stunning,…*God* there isn't enough words to describe how gorgeous you are. I feel lucky that I can kiss, touch, and do things to you."

The smile fades when his thumb stops abruptly, his fingers gripping tighter against my skin. "In all honesty, I envy the man that will one day claim your heart."

That man is you, I want to scream. Why can't he see that

194

he's the one I want? Why can't he just *see?*

I reach up and kiss him softly on the mouth. Will returns my embrace without a moment of hesitation, his hand still over my cheek and the other now circling my waist. Clutching my hands against his chest, gripping the fabric of his shirt in my fists I push my face into his. I breathe him in as I press my body flat against his.

"Will?" I lick my bottom lip as I pull away, leaning my forehead against his and drinking in the silence.

"Yeah?" His voice is rough, laced in thickness.

"Let's just keep pretending, okay?" My voice trembles with each word. "Until we can't anymore, let's just pretend."

Will raises his head to look at me again, a soft smile on his lips. He leans down and kisses me again, barely touching my mouth. "That sounds good."

This is my first time in Will's condo, and it screams money. If felt scantily dressed before at that party, I feel like I am in nothing but a potato sack right now. If I lived here I'd feel like I'd have to change into a ballgown to simply lounge around.

"Tell me again why we spend more time at my place than yours?" I run my fingers over the leather sofa, my eyes focusing on the built in fireplace sitting beneath the flat screen TV.

Will's hands creep up over my shoulders and slip down my bare arms. "Your place is more comfortable."

I bark out a laugh and turn around to fully face him. "Than a literal condo?"

A chuckle rumbles up his chest, then dips his head to trail kisses over the curve of my neck. I knock my head back to give him better access, his hands slipping over my sides, completely vanishing any further thoughts I may have had.

"I want to show you something that might melt your troubles away."

If that is an innuendo I swear I will slap him. The patch on my neck feels cold when he removes his lips, he intertwines our fingers. There is a mischievous look on his face, with his front two teeth biting his bottom lip.

Will guides me through the wide space that is his home, and out onto the balcony. Outside there is a hot tub built into the wooden floor. It lights up the water with a cold blue glow, the wind causing small ripples over the top layer.

"I'm not sure whether to be impressed or mad that you didn't bring me here sooner."

Will laughs and kisses my temple. "We can drive to yours and pick up a bathing suit, preferably a revealing one."

"I don't know where you think I spend my free time to own a bathing suit." I flick an eyebrow at him. "My family vacations are in England, not exactly a place for a summer holiday."

Releasing his hand I look over the town, a slight breeze causing goosebumps to raise on my arms. I can't see anyone around, there are no neighbours in sight and anyone below would have to break their necks to look up this high. I still have to ask before I make a huge mistake, "Can anyone see us from here?"

"Nope."

My cheeks flush, maybe it's the champagne from the party, but I act upon my desire. I hook my arms behind my back and pull down my zip until it stops at my hips. The silk releasing its tight hold over my ribs.

Will watches me with an intense focus. Even when I drop my dress to gather around my ankles, my entire body is exposed, aside from the section covered by my panties, Will's eyes do not waver from my face.

Stepping out of my shoes, I then drop my underwear to gather next to my dress. I step into the hot tub slowly, the entire time I keep my longing stare on Will's. I don't sit, I allow the warm water to soak my body, my breasts above the water. "Care to join me?"

Chapter Twenty-Eight

I can't help but bite my bottom lip as I watch Will undress entirely. If I had any uncertainty as to whether Will enjoyed watching me undress and stand in his hot tub naked, that has been well and truly rectified. He is hard when stepping out of his boxers, and it does not ease up as he joins me in the water.

We sit opposite one another, the desperation to be closer is becoming unbearable.

"I can see why you didn't want to bring me here," I say, sinking further into the water so my shoulders submerge.

"Why is that?"

I offer a smile, with my front row of teeth sinking into my bottom lip. "I might never leave."

Will runs his hands through his hair, the water reflecting the moonlight over the thick locks. Then he gets up and makes his way over to me. He stops in between my legs but keeps his hands to himself. "Wouldn't that be dreadful?"

My breath has quickened at the closeness. I want him to touch me, I want his hands all over me right here, right now. Why is he just standing there? Does he not feel this intense pull in his chest?

"Touch me," I whisper.

Will takes a small step forward, the glow from the hot tub highlighting the strong features of his face. They make his green eyes ignite, like there is a strong power building behind them. His black hair is wet, with droplets of water slipping down his nose.

He abides by my request — demand — and wraps his arms around my body, pulling me to straddle his lap. With the head of his erection pressed against my entrance, I have never been more thankful to be on the pill. I actually considered coming off it, since we mostly use condoms for sex, but the universe is in my favour tonight for not making that decision.

I rub myself against the head of his cock, slowly. I want to slide myself down on him, but I also want this evening to last. I adjust myself so that his cock isn't near my entrance. I slip my hands around his neck, his wet skin against my palms makes me feel powerful. The way he is holding me, looking at me like he might actually think I am beautiful, is driving me over the edge.

"Will," I whisper his name for no real reason.

He kisses my mouth in such a painfully slow way that I exhale a sigh. Will presses my back against the edge of the hot tub as he blankets my naked wet body with his own. Removing his hands from my body, he braces each side of me on the edge of the hot tub, all the while kissing me.

I reach up and hold his face as we become fuelled with desire from this simple action. Between my legs aches for more, for him to satisfy me like he has done every time before. But he doesn't touch me, he only kisses me.

It's so easy to lose myself in his kiss. I've never enjoyed kissing someone as much as I do Will. I always thought I was doing it wrong, or kissing isn't as magical as the movies make it out to be, but Will proved all of those theories wrong. It's enchanting to be the centre of his attention, it's like he is casting a spell of lust on each patch of skin his kisses.

"You're so confusing," he suddenly says, and starts trailing kisses down my throat. I tip my head back to give him easier access, but it doesn't make the words vanish from my head.

"Why?"

Will pauses over my throat, his lips still stuck to my skin. He softly bites my flesh, enough to make me bite my own lip, imagining him doing that down there. "How you make me feel."

This causes my entire body to pause, and Will must have sensed it because he raises his head to meet my shocked stare.

"Do you have feelings for me?" I shouldn't have asked that, I don't want to know the answer. If I could turn back the clock and zip my lips shut I would.

Surprisingly, Will doesn't storm out, bark in my face that that could never happen. He chuckles softly, not to mock me, and then he kisses my lips gently. "If I felt nothing I wouldn't be touching you like this."

Before I can ask what he means, he slips two fingers between my folds and I inhale a startled gasp. I bury my face in his neck as he works his fingers. I raise my hips to meet his hand, and I grind against him. I hold him close to me, sinking my nails into his soft, wet back.

I find my release with a shudder, and I relax in Will's arms. When he removes his fingers from me, he holds me close to his chest. Both hands pressed against my back, as if he is afraid of letting go and losing this moment.

"If I were a better man I would never let you go," he mutters into my hair. "But I'm not a good man, Lucy. And you deserve the best."

I never thought words could make my heart collapse into rubble. I didn't think they would be powerful enough, but Will caused it to crack and entirely fall in just a few words.

"You'll find a man that will be worthy of your time, because you deserve nothing less than the world."

Why does this feel like a break up? Like this will be the last time we are together?

This can't be over. Not yet. I don't want to think about not having Will in my arms like this.

I brace my hands against both of his shoulders and guide him so he is now pinned against the edge of the hot tub. I hook my legs around his waist and straddle him, my eyes intently focused on his. "You are a good man, Will."

His lips part, and then the pain is back in full force from my words. As if to silence me, not wanting to hear my truth, he kisses me and holds my head in place.

I grind against him, needing to be filled by him. Without taking my lips from his, I guide his hard cock to my entrance and slide myself down until he fills me entirely. Will grunts against my mouth, stealing the breath from me.

I roll my hips, water splashing and crashing around us as I pick up my movements. "You are a good man," I whisper, and Will brings up his own hips to meet mine. No matter how hard he fucks me, no matter how many times he kisses me, it won't distract me from the truth in my heart.

"I wish I had met you before," his voice is quiet. I'm not sure if he intended to say that out loud, and the frantic passion caused him to speak without reservation.

"Before what?" My hands grip on tightly to the ends of his black hair, needing to hold on to something.

Will's rhythm slows for just a few seconds, before he is right back fast and erratic strokes, our skin slapping together beneath the water.

"Before my world shattered," he grunts. "Perhaps if you were there…I might have had a chance to put the pieces back together. With you…being here with you…I…"

I hold on tighter, this confession feels so intimate and not just because we are having sex.

"God," he growled. "I wish I could be yours."

My heart swells, my lungs restricted of air.

I love him. I love him with every fibre of my being, my soul is wrapped around him like a thick piece of rope, even the strongest scissors couldn't cut it now without leaving a permanent scar.

"You can," tilting my head back, I give his lips access to my throat. An intense pleasure flickers down my entire body, down, down, down.

"I can't," those two words broke me. "But we can keep pretending, right?"

There was nothing left to say. We would keep pretending until we couldn't anymore, simple as that.

We both become undone, finding release that leaves us breathless in this midnight silence.

"My dad's party is next week," he murmurs. "It's going to be a garden party at their house. You'll be a free woman soon."

I don't know how to respond, or if I should even say anything. So I remain silent and hold him tighter as I pretend my tears are just remnants of the hot tub water.

Chapter Twenty-Nine

Before my birthday a party was a rare event for me. It would always be a party for two, consisting of Jeremy and myself. It used to be three before Melissa ditched us but I'm not bitter, I'm not mad at her for sleeping with my boyfriend whilst we were together.

Ever since I met Will, I have been to places far out of my comfort zone. I've never been invited to a garden party before, so I was stuck for a while on what to wear. I eventually landed on a breezy white sundress, that has an open back to expose my spine. It's shows enough cleavage to catch Will's eye but not enough to be deemed inappropriate.

This will be the first time I am meeting Will's father as his girlfriend, and most likely the last.

I do feel a sting in my heart when I remind myself that this is what everything has been leading up to. This is the final test for Will, to convince his family that he can survive in a stable relationship.

This will all be over soon.

I hate to admit, even at times he drove me crazy, that this weird relationship was somewhat fun, in a bizarre way. I still feel wrong involving my family into this. It was supposed to be harmless a favour to Will, but for my family to also be attending this garden party today I can't help but feel like I am in way too deep with this.

Talk about an understatement of the century. I am so far down this rabbit hole that it is impossible to climb out. I am so consumed in Will, falling in love with him was probably the worst thing that could have happened. No matter how many times I tell myself that this is coming to an end, Will can never love me, that single ray of hope with be enough to break me completely.

It was Will's idea last night to invite my parents, because that's what couples do in committed relationships apparently, their parents meet. Forgetting the fact that not once did my parent interact with Simon's, but Will seemed set on the idea.

I'm lying to a lot of people recently. I don't have anyone to blame but myself.

Will calls to let me know he is outside of my apartment. I add a few touches to my make up and grab my purse. I'm nervous, what I'm wearing feels appropriate for meeting Will's father. They come from money, I bet they wouldn't be impressed if I showed up in a plain T shirt and jeans.

I lock the door to my apartment and hurry down the stairs. The sooner we leave the sooner I can get this over with.

Surprisingly, Will is waiting outside of his car like he is picking me up for a real date. It reminds me of a scene from a movie, but the look on his face is something no actor can recreate. If I didn't know any better I'd say he was admiring how I look. I achieved one thing at least, I wanted him to like what he saw. I wanted to impress him with this few extra touches of make-up, with a bold winged eyeliner and red tinge to my lips.

"You look really…"

"Is that?" I pretend to investigate his bottom lip. "Drool I see?"

He shakes his head, with a warm laugh. "No."

I don't know whether to be insulted that he didn't

comment further on my outfit. Instead, he climbs into the drivers side. I fasten my seatbelt once I am settled into my seat. As soon as Will is on the road and driving he keeps his gaze focused on the road. I narrow it down to him feeling anxious about introducing me to his father.

Before Will announced this garden party I got the feeling Will had been putting off this meeting with his father. Rosie had mentioned a few times about him being back in town for a while from his business trip, and Will would either ignore her or change the subject.

There must be something about today that made him feel like it was the right time. Maybe he's ready to say goodbye to me. Will must be letting go before he gets a chance to hold on.

We arrive at the party, and my family is already here mingling amongst the rich. My mother instantly spots me and hurries over to me with a champagne flute in hand. She looks stunning in her floral dress. It has a square neck and a skirt that dances in the breeze as she walks. My father went for a simple two piece suit, and my brother in just a shirt and trousers.

"This is so fancy," Mom fits right in with her accent, she sounds so posh in a public setting like this. "You look gorgeous — both of you. You make such a lovely couple."

"How much have you had to drink?"

Dad loops his arm around her waist and pulls her against his hip. "Believe it or not that's her first."

"I'm sorry, I just get so flustered." She looks to Will and smiles. "Thank you so much for inviting us. It's been a while since I have been taken out."

Dad responds with a simple eye-roll.

Will dips his head, placing his hand over the small of my back. This simple touch sends my skin into ablaze. "Glad you could make it."

"William!"

We all turn to see Rosie beckoning her son to come and join her. She is standing beside a tower of a gentleman, who I can only assume is Will's father. With his back to us I can already tell he is an intimidating man, and this isn't going to be as easy as I hoped.

As we leave my family to join Will's, he dips his lips to my ear enough to send a chill down my entire spine. "Not that it should be hard, but act like you adore me so much that you'd rip off a limb just to kiss me."

I can't help but chuckle, "Then they would know I am acting."

Will straightens and laughs, it seems to have eased some of the tension from him also. I know I am his fake girlfriend, right now is all pretend. What's wrong with me pretending like this is real? That this will lead to a future with Will? I know I promised not to fall in love with him but it's too late for that. I just wish I had some sort of sign that he felt that way toward me, or if this is just one giant act.

"Hello dear," Rosie kisses Will's cheek and then turns her attention to me. "And Lucy, don't you look beautiful!"

"Malcom, honey." Rosie taps the tall gentleman's shoulder, and he turns around to face us. It's like the wind has just been knocked out of me, like this man has just punched me in the gut without so much of a smirk. There is no doubt in my mind that this is Will's father, they look almost identical. I can imagine Will growing older and looking like a twin of his father. They could be now if it wasn't for his father's strips of grey in his hair and the creases around his eyes and mouth. He even regards me with the same grin that Will has flashed me plenty of times before.

"So, you are the famous Lucy I have heard so much about." When he extends his hand I take it, internally fretting that my palms are sweaty, but Malcom doesn't comment on it. "You must be someone special to get Will to settle down."

Settling down seems like to drastic of a word to describe what we are, or at least what we are pretending to be. I go along with it, because I don't want to disappoint Will's father. "I don't know about special but I try to keep him in line."

Malcom and Rosie laugh, which makes me feel like I have passed some sort of test.

"I hear you have been doing wonders for our little flower shop, I don't think a day goes by when *somebody* isn't singing your praises."

I open my mouth to thank Rosie for the compliments on my work ethic, but I'm cut off by Malcom nudging his son's shoulder. "I don't think he's talked this much about anyone before."

I look up at Will who's cheeks have colour to them. He talks to me so much that it's worth his father's mocking?

"I have to say, Lucy." Malcom says. "We are somewhat relying on you."

I get a sinking feeling in my stomach, Will must sense it as his grip tightens around the small of my back. "Dad…"

"No, no." the kindness in his voice seems to have vanished, as though it never existed to begin with. "I would rather get any and all awkward conversations out of the way. What's the point in saving them when it could be too late?"

"Perhaps not being *rude* is a good point?"

Malcom rolls his eyes, completely dismissing his son's protest. His eyes focus on mine, a small unamused grin curves one side of his mouth. "Raven has told me…a lot about you."

Oh God.

"I am proud to be her father, with her work ethic and drive for success." Malcom picks up a glass of champagne from a tray passing by and takes a sip. "She told me of a little… disagreement between the two of you."

"Oh...well, I - "

"Do understand that Rosie and I hold expectations for our children."

Rosie shrinks beside her husband, I have never felt so small in my entire life. I can't imagine what this was like for Will growing up.

Speaking of Will, he is slowing burning up into a fire of rage beside me. His fingers pressing tightly against my skin and his emerald eyes glaring up at his father.

"My daughter provided feedback on what she thinks of your behaviour."

Feedback? As though I am some sort of employee on probation for a role in their family?

"I would ask that you consider your compatibility with my son," Malcom shrugged. "After all, you're not the most interesting of people — "

"That's enough!" Will barks, causing all three of us to jolt and snatch our attention to him.

I didn't have time to register what his father had just said to me. My eyes are stinging, my throat is burning from holding down the fiery emotions bubbling in my chest.

No wonder Will didn't want me to meet his father, he was trying to spare my feelings. It's easy to see now where Raven gets it from. Neither of them are afraid to speak their minds, no matter how harsh and uncomfortable it makes another person.

"You are lucky I even brought her here to meet you," Will snarls.

"I'm surprised she even turned up after last time." Malcom speaks of me as though I am not right in front of him, a trend amongst Will's circle. There is also a venom in his tone, as though I have personally offended him.

Will shakes his head, "You know what? I am so tired of you deciding my life for me. Deciding who I should and shouldn't be with, and you have the nerve to speak to this woman as though she is nothing but a bug on your shoe, as if *she* isn't good enough for *me*?" His voice raises louder and louder after every sentence, father and son facing off in a glare. "When in fact it is the other way around, and you know that...after what happened."

"William." Malcom warns.

"I'm glad she is nothing like the people you try and set me up with. I'm glad that she is actually fun to be around, and not afraid to be herself and *tells* me when I'm being an asshole. Unlike you, who buries everything, acting as though nothing has happened."

"I am the one who isn't deserving of Lucy." Will snarls. "I should be counting my blessings every single day she decides to spend with me."

"Will..." it comes out as a breath. Before I can say another word to Malcom, or Rosie, Will is dragging me through the garden and into his parents house. I'm too stunned to speak, I just stare at the back of his head as he leads me into the house and into the downstairs bathroom.

Will shuts the door behind us, and before I can come to my senses, Will presses my back against the bathroom door and crashes his lips over mine. He kisses me with such a ferocious intensity that my knees weaken from his touch. I open my mouth, his tongue plunging in to find mine. That same tingling sensation tickles down my spine, matching the feeling between my legs.

"I'm sorry," he whispers between kisses. "Do not listen to any of them. They're all just stuffy pricks."

It's only when a cold line traces my cheek do I release I am crying. I should be used to it by now, what's one more person to tell me I am not good enough?

As if Will heard my internal thoughts he raises his head but keeps his hips firmly pressed against me. Both of his hands cup my cheeks, tilting my head to look deeply into his eyes. "You are a fucking light in this dark world, do you hear me? A fucking beacon of light."

I'm so confused. He speaks of me as though I am a light in his own life. He speaks with such a deep passion that I know there is something between us. There is something more, I can feel it in his touch. I have felt it when we sleep together, that it's not just sex, it's something more.

"They are going to wonder where we went."

Will moves one of his hands to rest on my thigh, his fingers grazing up my skirt causing my breath to lodge in between my lungs and throat. "Let's forget about them for a while."

I can't stop looking at him, completely in awe. I have never had someone stick up for me, especially to someone who they are trying to impress. To defend me to his own father has my heart contorting in my chest, and for him to consider that he is not worthy of me? It's ridiculous.

"Will," I reach up and cup his cheek but he can't look at me. A frown is engraved into his forehead.

I move my hand away from his face and bury my face into his chest. I want him to know how much that meant to me, how full my heart feels because of him. I wrap my arms around him and hold him as tightly as I can. I expect him to stand and wait for me to stop, but Will surprises me by holding me back in an equally tight embrace, keeping one hand dangerously close to my heat.

"Don't listen to them," his lips moving against my hair. "You're a remarkable woman, Lucy."

And you're a wonderful man, Will. Is what I was about to say, until all words vanished when Will moved my panties to the side and slipped two fingers in my folds. I gasp at the impact, burying my face further into his shoulder as he slides his hands up and down until that bundle of nerves swells with need.

I slip my hands down and unbutton his pants. Once I pull them down, along with his boxers, Will grabs my thighs and positions them around his waist. I fill myself with his cock and Will fucks me against the bathroom door in long, fast strokes.

I hold onto him and press soft kisses against his temple, cheek, and mouth.

"You're so fucking perfect," he grunts against my mouth. "Don't let anyone tell you otherwise."

"Will…" I whimper his name.

"You are just too good for someone like me."

Chapter Thirty

It crawls into the afternoon and meeting Will's father went far worse than I expected. I actually don't think it could have gone worse, maybe if Raven showed up and tag teamed me with verbal abuse along with her father.

Will and I are talking with my family, avoiding his at all costs. We are laughing at a joke my dad had made. We're all having a great time, my heart feeling full by being surrounded by the people I love most.

"Hey, it's Willy!" A slurred voice roars across the garden. When I see the drunken man it belongs to I do not recognise him, it's clear that Will does as his entire body stiffens.

This drunken stranger drapes an arm around Will's neck, leaning his body weight on him. Will reluctantly holds him up, I can tell from the look in his eyes he would be more than happy to let him collapse in the mud.

"It's been so long," the drunk grumbles to Will, jabbing a finger into his chest. "How long has it been since I last saw you? Over a year?"

"Probably."

The drunk looks around at my family, with a hazy glaze over his eyes. "Aren't you going to introduce me?"

Will flares his nostrils, struggling to contain his frustration with this gentleman. Not that I can blame him, if I had someone weighing me down and drawing attention to us at a party I would be pissed off too.

"This is my girlfriend Lucy, and her family." He points to the drunk. "And this is my cousin Paul."

"Lulu-Lucy," Paul sings as he drops his arm from Will's shoulder and anchors his hands down. He drunkenly steps into my few and the overwhelming stench of alcohol hits my senses, so much so that I have to take a step back.

"Leave her alone, Paul. You're making everyone uncomfortable." Paul shrugs off the hand that Will places on his shoulder, in an attempt to pull him away from me.

"Why? She seemed to be comfortable enough...at least based on what I heard in the bathroom a few minutes ago."

My heart comes to a complete halt in my chest. Please tell me this man isn't going reveal to my family that Will seemingly snuck off to get frisky in the bathroom, at a party.

"Paul." Will's deep voice is a clear threat, a warning with a single word.

"Don't you want her to meet the family?" Paul focuses his gaze at Will, only with a far less playful expression. "It's a shame they won't meet Greg."

"Don't." Will's tone cuts through the conversation like a knife. We all stand in shock, and it's clear we have gained the attention of the rest of the party.

Paul shoves Will back, causing him to stumble slightly before catching his footing. "I'm so happy for you Will. So very happy that you got to move on with your life, meanwhile your brother is dead because of you!"

My heart plummets in my chest.

Dead *because* of Will? I want to see him deny it, that these are just the ramblings of a drunken lunatic but Will just stands there, with fists clenched at his sides and his jaw locked tight.

"Greg was my best friend, and he's dead because of you!"

Paul stumbles back and looks me up and down with pure disgust, like I have just walked in with manure on my dress and I am stinking up the entire garden. "Well, at least you rewarded yourself with a whore you can fuck your guilt away with. If she's willing to fuck you in a party bathroom I'll give her a go — "

Before I get a chance to slap him myself, speaking of me as though I am nothing more than a sexual object — in front of my parents and brother, Will charges for his cousin until they both fumble to the ground. He grabs Paul by the scuff of his shirt and punches him square in the jaw. The party gasps as they watch is dismay, when Will repeatedly punches Paul in the face and my ears ring with shock. He is putting all of his anger into his fists, pummelling him until his cousin's nose starts bleeding.

I step forward to stop this, he's going too far, until my mother is suddenly beside me, draping her arm around my shoulders and halting me before I can get involved. Surprisingly it's my father who hooks his arms underneath Will and drags him away from Paul.

Will kicks out and swings for his cousin, so consumed by his own rage that he is oblivious to the party around him.

"William!" Malcom's voice booms over the now lingering silence, only filled by Paul cradling his face and whining in agony.

My father releases Will once he settles down, and he looks around at all of the eyes on him. Everyone is shocked, including myself. I have never seen this side of Will before, I knew that there was something his past that he kept from me. Was Paul right about Greg? Did Will have some involvement in his death?

Will sprints out of the garden, leaving the party in a state of disbelief. I go to run after him, until once again my mother holds me back. "Let him calm down. Give him a little while, okay?"

A few people help Paul to his feet and guide him away from the party to get cleaned up.

My father is just as furious. "I don't blame Will for doing that."

"Caleb," Mom hisses.

"After what he said about Lucy? I should have let it go on for longer."

Mom starts quietly bickering with dad, eventually settling it with a quick embrace.

All I can think about is Will and whether he is okay. I already know the answer to that question, but I think it's time I find out the answers to others.

I find Will in his room after giving him half an hour of space. I know I should have given him more time but I am too impatient, I need to know that he is okay. I step inside of his room and find him sitting on the edge of his bed, with his elbows digging into his knees, and his head in his hands. Those large warm fingers are spread through his raven hair.

"Hey," I speak softly and stand over him.

He starts shaking his head, and when I touch his shoulder it breaks my heart that he flinches. He's in so much pain, and not just from his bloody knuckles.

I kneel down in front of him, trying to get a good look at his face but he is doing a wonderful job of hiding it from me.

"Will," I whisper.

I almost break out into tears when I hear a desperate whimper rise up his throat, and his shoulders shake as he starts to cry. "I-I'm so sorry."

"I've done nothing but ruin your life ever since you met me," he whispers.

Will finally lowers his hands to allow my arms to wrap around him, I hold him close to me and he embraces me with a tight, almost frightened, squeeze. One hand surrounds my waist whilst the other cradles the back of my head. He buries his face into my shoulder and I can feel his warm tears spilling over my exposed skin.

"You know that's not true, Will." I kiss the top of his head.

I hold him like this for what could be hours, I allow him to cry and hold onto me as he works through his emotions. It doesn't take a genius to figure out that he has bottled these feelings up for a very long time.

"Will," I say when his sobbing begins to calm down. "If you don't want to talk about it, you don't have to." I pull back from him so I can look him in the eyes. His cheeks are soaked with tears and his eyes rimmed red. "But if you ever need to, please know that you can talk to me. That you aren't alone."

I knew he was broken, but I never realised the extent. I can't be the one to fix him, he has to do that himself. I will happily be at his side and help gather up the pieces so he can put them into place.

Will touches my cheek and stares longingly for a moment. "You've put up with so much crap, from so many people," he whispers. "Don't for one minute think that any of them are right, especially heartless people like my father and sister."

"Will, this isn't about me."

"I need you to know that you are wonderful, Lucy Wilson." His bottom lip trembles. "You are so perfect. And I'm sorry that I suck at protecting you from idiots. I'm sorry that you got introduced to those morons because of me."

I offer a small smile, "I can look after myself, or at least, I *should* start doing that."

Then he slides back, my immediate thought is that he is going to tell me to get out, leave him to deal with his pain alone. To my surprise Will opens up his arms and gestures for me to sit on his lap.

I waste no time in positioning myself. Will gathers me in his arms and settles my head to rest against his chest. I take note of the intense rhythm of his heartbeat punching me in the cheek.

"You know that I had a brother that died," he says. I wish I could look up and see his face, but if this is the most comfortable way for him to open up to somebody about this, I will stay in this position for as long as he needs.

I nod, feeling the soft material of his shirt brush against my cheek.

"It was a car accident."

I don't tell him I already know, I don't want him to feel betrayed by his mother about confessing the way his brother had passed. That's where my knowledge ends though, I couldn't have Rosie continue because it clearly eats her up inside. She and Will are so alike, they can mask their pain when around others.

"It was my birthday and we decided to go out for a drink," his hands clench around my arms. "We got ridiculously drunk, stupidly drunk. I don't remember much of the actual night. All I know is that Greg ended up driving, we got into a bad wreck and he...my brother..."

I slip my arms around his waist and hold him tightly.

"He crashed into the side of a building and...and he died instantly." His voice cracks, I feel his shoulders tense like he is reliving that night. "It's my fault that he's not here. It's my fault that he's dead, all of my family knows it."

I decide to lift myself from his chest, he can't look at me. The moment I make contact with his eyes he drops his head in shame. I'm confused as to what part of that story made him fully responsible. "It was an accident, Will."

"I'm the oldest, I should have taken responsibility that night." He snaps his head up, more tears streaking down his cheeks. "I should have done more. I should have thrown the keys away when he suggested to drive."

"If you can't remember, how do you know that you didn't?"

"Because he still got in the car," Will shakes his head, pinching his eyes shut. "*I* got in the car with him. Raven could have been with us, she cancelled last minute. What if she did decide to come with us, and she got in the car too? She would be…she'd be…Maybe if we didn't drink so much in the first place he would have realised he couldn't drive, what if…"

"You can't keep asking yourself *what if?*" I desperately cup his cheeks and hold his gaze to mine. "You will never find an answer to any of those *what if's* because no one knows. Just like you didn't know the accident would have happened that night. If you *did* know I am confident you would have done everything in your power to prevent."

Will remains silent, staring at me with a glaze in his eye.

"What happened isn't your fault, Will." I need him to hear me when I say it. "It isn't. You weren't the one driving, you didn't cause the accident."

"I know but we went out for *my* birthday."

I shake my head, he is trying to find any reason to hold himself responsible when there will never be a strong enough reason. I understand when people die in an accident they sometimes need someone to blame, and Will would be the perfect person as he was with him the night he died. I'm sure that it has killed him to not be able to grieve properly over his brother, because of all this guilt he is desperately trying to hold onto. As if holding onto the guilt will mean he can't let go of his brother.

I'm assuming that's what those scars are from. It must be why he got so angry about the mention of them, a constant reminder of that dreadful night.

"That's why I despise going to any family event, I can feel

them looking at me — blaming me. Everyone in my family *hates* me for what I have done."

"Your mother and father don't blame you. Your sister doesn't blame you. They should be the only people that matter." The desperate attempts for them to see him settled down start to make sense. It's not to be difficult, it's because they want to make sure he is taken care of. "They want you to be happy, Will."

I'm confident if any of them did blame him, they wouldn't be trying so hard to fix his life. Rosie wouldn't look at him with admiration every time he steps foot into the flower shop, Raven and Malcom wouldn't be so worried about him spiralling into a depressing future.

"The last family event was Greg's funeral," a sad smirk tugs at the corner of his mouth. "That ended in a similar way."

"What do you mean? Did you fight there too?"

Will shakes his head. "No. I ended up spending time with you."

It suddenly makes sense, why he was wearing all black the night we met at the nightclub. He had just showed up to wash away his memory of his brother's funeral.

"If I had just…"

"Will, it wasn't your fault." Tears threaten my own eyes but I fight them back, the last thing he needs is to feel guilty over someone else's sadness.

"But if…"

"Stop." I press a soft kiss to his cheek.

Will holds me tight and kisses me on the mouth. I slip my fingers into his hair and kiss him back with all the love I hold in my heart. Maybe if he knew how I felt, maybe if I told him I love him it might make him realise that he is not a monster. That I love him regardless of his past or the torment he puts upon himself. At the same time, he is in such a vulnerable position right now and I don't want to put him in an even tighter spot if he doesn't feel the same way.

"Can I stay with you tonight?" he whispers against my mouth.

"Of course."

We don't say goodbye to anyone at the party. I text my mom to tell her we have left and she responds with:

Mom: Make sure you take care of him xx

If only Will could see how much of a good person he truly is. There are people that care about him, his family, my family... me.

"Help yourself to anything in the fridge."

"Do you have any ice?" He asks, clutching his cut knuckle.

"Do you want me to take you to the hospital?"

"No."

"But you might need..."

Will kisses me on the mouth, hushing any words that I was about to say. He knows my weakness, make me lose any train of thought, with a simple brush of his lips I am his.

I pull away, licking my bottom lip and pressing my hands against his firm chest. "Ice?"

"Please."

I bend down and pull out an ice pack from my freezer. I turn over Will's hand and place it over his knuckles. He cleaned up most of the blood before we left his parents house, so now it's mostly cuts and a swollen hand. The moment the pack makes contact he hisses and flinches back.

"Don't be such a baby," I say with a playful smile.

"It hurts!"

I look up and the moment our eyes find one another I feel the beating of my heart against my chest. It's so loud in my ears I wonder if Will can hear it too? God, I love him. I love him so much it hurts. I can't be the only one that feels like this, it's too painful for it not to be real.

Just three words. That's all it would take. But why is it so hard?

I remember a quote from Will's book that seems to resinate with me right now. *Words aren't physical, but they can hit us the hardest.*

Wasn't that the truth? It's just three simple words, when separated mean as little as a grain of sand but when combined it's heavier than a bag of bricks.

"Want to watch a movie?" His voice is thick like caramel, his throat bobs as he swallows and I have absolutely zero desire to watch a movie right now.

I remove the icepack from his hand and set it down on my kitchen table. With his injured hand still in my grasp I bring it up slowly to my lips. I make sure to kiss around the cuts, I don't want to hurt him.

I gently brush my lips across the back of his hand, painfully slow with my actions. I start to make a small trail down to his fingers, eventually uncurling his hands so the tips of his fingers are against my lips.

"Lucy…"

"I want you…" I didn't just mean his body. Yes, I want him to take me right here, right now. In the kitchen, the living room, the bedroom, *everywhere*. But I also want *him*. Exactly how he is, I want him to be mine, and mine alone. I want to build a life with him, made of a foundation of trust, support and love.

"I want…" I wish he gave me some inkling on what he feels for me. Any sort of sign. All of his kindness, the actions of him going out of his way to ensure my happiness can't have been fake. He didn't have to go out of his way for me, pay for mine and my families plane ticket to England, support my dreams of becoming a graphic designer, *touch* me in the way that he does if it means nothing.

"I want you to write me as the dedication in your book."

That was the last thing he was expecting me to say, yet it was the only thing I could think of. "If you use my cover design, I think it's the least I deserve."

Will smiles and kisses the corner of my mouth. "Consider it done."

Chapter Thirty-One

It's been two weeks since the garden party, Will and I have remained as fake boyfriend and girlfriend the entire time. Every day I wake up anxious, that this will be the day he decides that we have fake dated for long enough. That he can no longer pretend, and wants to get on with his life.

Today, Will and I spent the day shopping for supplies for the store, which provides a good distraction for my anxious thoughts. I actually had a great time in his company, laughing at the ridiculously stupid jokes he would tell. The way he can naturally make me laugh is something I can't explain. I feel happy to be with him, that he is eager to be with me too, even if it's just to shop around and talk about nonsense.

As the day sets into night, the stars accompanying us on our stroll, we buy a burger to takeaway and sit on a public bench whilst we eat. For a while we just sit and watch strangers walk by us.

"Want to play the question game?"

I swallow the mash of greasy food in my mouth before questioning, "The question game?"

"It's like twenty questions, but with no limits for how many you can ask?" There's a playful smirk on his mouth, like all of his will be designed to embarrass me. "And you *have* to answer honestly."

I snort a laugh, "How would you know if I am lying?"

Will gives me a poignant look. "You get flustered and giggle when you lie."

My mouth drops, probably revealing a few pieces of lettuce stuck in my teeth. "I do not get…"

"*Please,*" he drags out the word with a laugh. "Whenever you introduce me as your 'boyfriend' you look like someone has just been smacked in the face with a pie."

It's my turn to shoot a poignant glare. "I wouldn't find that funny even if it happened."

"Accept if it was to me."

That gets a smile out of me, and I want to kick myself for it. I duck my head down trying to hide it from him, but when he starts chuckling I know hiding is pointless.

"So, what would you like to know?"

"Is that your first question?"

I knock my head back and let out a playfully exaggerated groan. "You are so infuriating."

"What's your favourite colour?"

"Wow, start off with a hard one," I take another bite from my burger as I think. It's hard to choose one, I like different ones depending on my mood. When I'm upset a midnight blue can be a comforting sight, when I'm content a canary yellow is my companion, and when I'm at my happiest it would have to be bright lilac.

"Bright lilac."

"Typical you wouldn't say anything normal like a simple 'red.'"

I shrug, "Being a designer, I can see a difference in a colour pallet."

Will sticks out his bottom lip as he nods. "They all look the same to me. If you showed me different shades of red I would call one red, another dark red and a slightly lighter shade of red."

I roll my eyes, and wrack my brain trying to think of a question for him. All of the ones I have are heavier than asking what his favourite colour is. "What's yours? Red?"

"Blue, actually." Will replies, his cheek full of food that makes him look like a chipmunk storing food for the winter.

"All shades of blue?"

"*Dark* blue."

We laugh as more and more strangers cross out path. Even with this being a public setting, I still feel as though it is just Will and I in this entire town. Both of us with half a burger and laughing at jokes that no one else would find as funny as we do.

"What made you want to become a designer?"

"I loved to draw when I was younger," I smile at the memories of drawing on any piece of paper I could find. I explain to Will that my grandfather would give me a stack of printer paper that he stole from his office whenever I would see him, and I would have an endless amount of paper to work with. All he asked in return was a unique drawing upon every visit.

A guilt burns into my stomach when I didn't arrive last time with a unique drawing, and how I never got to make it up to him. I bite back the tears that desperately want to fall.

"I never really planned on being a designer. It just seemed like a good fit to work on skills outside of drawing, and a lot of my teachers recommended it as a career and so I just went for it and realised I loved it. The more I learned the more I felt confident in my work. Until...well, until I got fired for not being as good as I thought I was."

Although I'm smiling right now, it hurts to admit that my work might not ever be good enough. If I was so good at design, then why do I keep getting rejected after every application? My work is in my portfolio, and no one thinks I am worth taking a chance with. I understand that there will always be someone better for the job, I just need to fight to prove that I am worth investing time into. Yet, companies don't want that. They want someone who is already fully experienced in the field. Where are you supposed to start if *everyone* wants someone with an already established career?

"I really don't think you give yourself enough credit." Will said, all the playfulness gone from his tone. "You designed a cover for my book, and I couldn't have asked for anything better. It's perfect, exactly what I wanted."

I roll my eyes, clearly he's just saying that to make me feel better.

Will takes my free hand in his and squeezes my fingers. His knuckles still look sore, but they have healed a lot these past two weeks. "Just keep fighting, a lot of the time you need to battle before you feel a victory."

I stare at him, a sweet sincerity on his face that makes my heart leap. Is this advice he has given to himself? Is he putting himself through so much pain so when he finally forgives himself it will be a bigger victory? Does he not realise that all of the blame, the torture he puts upon himself, isn't necessary?

"What made you want to become a writer?"

Will's smile widens across his face, revealing each of his frustratingly gorgeous dimples. "Are you going to mirror every one of my questions?"

"I asked mine first."

Will is silent for a while and I wonder if he is going to answer my question. If maybe the reason for his art is too personal to share. I wouldn't blame him, I know just how personal your own work can be and the sometimes crippling fear that comes along with it to share with others. To open up about *why* you need a creative outlet and not having them understand. I hope Will knows that I understand exactly how he feels, it's just a different medium.

"I always liked to create stories," he said, his voice softer. "When I was younger I would imagine what characters in my favourite movies were doing after the credits roll."

"Kind of like fan fiction?"

He brings his shoulder up to his ear, "Sort of. Then I would imagine them in different scenario's, putting them in different settings and wondering how they would react." Will shake his head and seemingly laughs at a memory. "I would sometimes wonder what it was like if a character from one movie met one from another. Like *The Flintstones* and *The Jetsons.*"

"Didn't they already do that?"

Will nods, "Yeah, but when I was a kid I thought I was so smart thinking of the possibility. As I got older, I realised I wanted to create characters that people could relate to. That, if I created a series then my readers would want to visit them, talk with them, and they'd get so invested and *they'd* create their own scenario's based on my characters."

His smile falters. "Then...when Greg died, my characters became my closest companions."

My heart aches at that confession, only now can I see the loneliness in his eyes. The isolation he put upon himself.

"It was easier to escape into my character's head, to come up with a story that was so far away from my own. Writing books only became a true passion born from my own misery."

"Words aren't physical, but they can hit us the hardest."

When Will looks at me, there is surprise in his eyes from hearing his own quote recited back to him. "You actually read what I sent you?"

I beam a smile at him. "Once I started I couldn't stop. And that says a lot from someone who can't read a full menu without getting bored."

I can feel the weight lifted from Will's heart as he exhales a laugh. For a while the questions stop, both of us with greasy hands from our burgers that have vanished into our stomachs. It's like this for a little while, it's not awkward. The air isn't screaming for the silence to be filled, I'm happy to just be with him.

"If were so afraid of your ex, why did you stay with him for so long?"

That was a question I wasn't expecting, and honestly my answer scares me. "I don't know…" I try to pull from my memories that I would revert back to in order keep our sinking relationship afloat. Like the one time he brought me my favourite chocolate bar simply because he wanted to. How at the beginning he would kiss me like I was his favourite person in the world. How he said I was worth risking the relationship between him and his best friend, my brother. Looking back, those reasons don't hold any weight to tolerate the worst in someone. Chocolates are sweet but they eventually melt in the sun if not consumed right away, you can try to maintain it for as long as you want but it will never be what it once was.

I shouldn't have romanticised being a secret, especially since my insecurity as a teenager was far worse than what it is now. Most of all, I should have considered that he may not have cared how it effected his relationship with Harry, but he never stopped to think of mine with my brother.

"When I was younger, I was obsessed with the idea of being with one guy for the rest of my life. That the man I would have my first kiss, first….you know, *everything* with was going to be my true love. I thought that was how it was supposed to be. I made the choice to be with him, give myself to him entirely and I didn't want to admit as time went on that I had made a mistake. That I chose the wrong person to trust with that sort of thing."

"You can be quite stubborn."

I elbow him in the gut and clamp down my smile. "I think

of everything that he did while we were together...how if I was on the outside looking in I would have berated myself for not leaving sooner. However, when you're *in* that situation, and all I had known of relationships was him, I just assumed some of the things were normal — or at least, not as bad as it could have been." I can't stop the warm tears that spill down my cheeks at the memory of the pain he put me through, I rub my cheeks with the sleeve of my jumper. "Isn't it fucked up how we try to rationalise their bad behaviour? That *he* did the wrong thing but I am left with the burden of it."

Will is still holding my hand, and squeezing my fingers in a tight grip. "If you ever need to talk about it, you can."

I rest my head on his shoulder, willing the tears to stop. "I don't want to live in the past, but I might need to one day to create a clear path for my future."

Will presses a kiss to the top of my head, "I might steal that for my book."

I laugh, and wrap my arms around his chest and hold him as close as I can get. I love the smell of him, maybe it's his brand of aftershave, or shampoo but he has made me adore the scent of pine.

"What was your worst kiss?" I ask.

"You," I can hear the shit-eating-grin in that single word.

I punch him lightly against his stomach, that might have been as effective as punching a rock.

"No, it was probably my *first* kiss." He said, accompanied by a small shudder. "It was prom, I know not a cliche at all. She was my date, gorgeous — obviously."

I roll my eyes even though he can't see.

"I kissed her in the middle of the dance floor, right under the disco ball." I feel him cringe beneath me. "But I realised there was something cold and wet pressed against my upper lip. It's only when I pulled away did I realise her nose was running with the greenest snot I had ever seen. When I wiped it off, my hand was coated in literal slime."

I gag at the clear imagery he painted. I still can't help but laugh at a younger version of Will, trying his best to be smooth with his first kiss. At least he can't say it wasn't something to remember, not that he could forget it even if he wanted to.

"What about you? Let me guess, the guy that gave you vaseline face?"

I lift myself up from his chest, immediately wanting to crawl back against him. "How did you know?" A violent shudder skidded down my spine at the memory. He was so perfect in every other way. He was handsome, kind, compassionate and all in all a great guy. He's just a terrible kisser. God, I'm so shallow.

"I am very interested to know what he did to make you look like that." Will laughs. "It looked like he licked off your lipstick."

"I think he did."

Will turns to fully face me, a playful smirk on his lips. "Kiss me like he did."

"What?" My cheeks burn red.

"I am just very interested in how he did it," he shakes his head, not even trying to hide his amusement. "Reenact it on me, I want to share your pain."

"I am not recreating the worst kiss of my life, especially in public."

"Why not? You had to endure it? I'd *love* to share your pain."

He can't be serious. I'm tempted to do it, and worse to make him ever regret even suggesting the idea. At the same time, I don't want him to be put off kissing me all together. As much as he is a pain in the ass, he's probably the best kisser I've ever had.

"C'mon," he insists as he straightens his back and morphs into a regal pose. He flicks an imaginary lock of hair of his shoulder as he closes his eyes, with a strange attempt of a pout on his lips. Taking in his odd stance I only just now realise what he is doing.

"Is that supposed to be me?!" I shriek.

Will immediately deflates into his normal posture, snickering like a child.

"Please? I really want to know how he managed to kiss you that left you looking like that."

I glare at him, and realise he isn't going to let this go until I concede. With a roll of my eyes I shuffle forward and intently lock my eyes to his. "Fine, but I am giving you the *full* experience."

A triumphant grin splits his face.

"So, it was a wonderful night. He was very kind, dropped me back to the flower shop and he even *asked* if he could kiss me."

"What a gentleman," Will comments.

"Yes," I place both of my hands around Will's cheeks, just like Erik and start slowly leaning in. I go as slow as possible, trying to hypnotise Will with the idea of my kiss. He seems to be entranced as his eyelids start to lower, seemingly forgetting why I am doing this in the first place. I almost kissed him like I usually would, forget about former lovers and dates, kiss him like he is mine. It's always a harsh reminder, like a winter storm avalanching over a warm cabin, that Will won't ever be mine.

I open my mouth as wide as it can go and engulf Will's entire mouth and ridges. If my mouth was just a little bit bigger I could probably fit the bottom of his chin inside. Will squirms beneath me, and actually squeals like a school girl as I give him the worst kiss of my life. His hands grip around my waist, I can feel the desperation to push me off but we are both laughing as I continue to eat his face like he is the last slice of cake at a buffet.

I know people are watching this display, probably giving Will with so much sympathy. As much as it is gross to kiss him like this, I'm sure it is just as bad for people passing by.

I pull away after a painful, solid minute of kissing Will like I am trying to fit his entire head in my mouth. I can't help but burst into a fit of laughter when I see the look on Will's face. The instant regret is right there, but I can tell he is trying to repress a laugh. His mouth is clamped down into a razor thin line, and his nostrils are flared.

"That was…disgusting."

"Which was worse, that one or your first kiss?"

"It's close," Will thinks for a moment, like it is a close contender. "It still goes to my first. I don't think you can top snot."

I shudder at the reminder, "The more we talk about it, the more I am being put off kissing entirely."

Will gets to his feet, takes my burger wrapper, and throws both of them into a nearby trash bin. He stops in front of me and extends his hand, I take it without hesitation and stand with him.

"You're not going to ask to reenact your prom kiss, are you?"

"No. I need to wash that kiss out of my mouth," he looks around for a nearby bar but everything seems to be closed.

I suddenly remember Jeremy mentioning a house party he is having, it should be near to where we currently are. "Want to stop off at my friend's house party? Could be fun?"

"You don't seem like a house party type?"

I shrug, "Jeremy always seems to make a night to remember."

Will squeezes my fingers, "Then let's make tonight that. I certainly won't be forgetting it."

Chapter Thirty-Two

Will and I arrive at Jeremy's house and we are greeted by thumping music and drunken strangers taking up most of the hallway. The atmosphere is intoxicating, everyone high on having a good time.

I guide Will through Jeremy's house until we make our way to the kitchen. We manage to find a small space for us to stand and grab ourselves a drink. I pour myself a vodka and coke whilst Will helps himself to a beer in the fridge.

It's like Jeremy and I have a best friend radar. We always manage to find one another in a crowed of people. He shoves his way through drunken guests, wearing a cable knit grey jumper and black jeans.

I hurry over to him and wrap my arms around him, embracing him for a tight squeeze. "And here I thought you wouldn't come and see me," he says as he pulls back.

"How could I pass on you?"

Jeremy's words fall on his tongue when he looks over my shoulder, a devious smirk quirking his mouth. "You're still 'together' then?" He uses air quotes on the word 'together.'

"For now," I take a sip from my drink, pretending that it isn't affecting me as much as it is. It could be tonight that Will decides to break this entire deal off. I haven't seen or heard from Simon since Christmas, I have a confident feeling that he won't be showing up announced anymore.

"I can see how much you love him," Jeremy looks at me with a sad expression, his eyebrows arched and sympathy glossing his eyes. "Why don't you just tell him?"

I shake my head, "I can't. He doesn't want me…"

"Lucy," Jeremy places his hands over my shoulders and forces me to meet his gaze. "If this was just one big scheme to win over his dad, he would have broke it off by now. And he wouldn't care enough to stick up for you."

I told Jeremy everything about what happened at Will's party. Everything other than the things involving Greg, it doesn't feel right to share someone else's story. I trust Jeremy one hundred percent, but it's still something Will shared with me in confidence.

"Why would he spend most of his time with you if he didn't like you?" Jeremy continues. "If he was just in it for the sex that's all he'd ask for. He wouldn't go shopping with you, he wouldn't come to a party with you…*Christmas!*"

I hate that his words are filling me with hope. A small spark has ignited again, lighting up the darkness in my heart. His words from New Year's Eve ring in my ears.

If I felt nothing I wouldn't be touching you like this.

Will outright told me he holds some feelings for me, why didn't I ask him to confirm it there and then? Perhaps it was because of his determination to drill in that he is not a good man. He is confident that I will find another man to spend my time with. I wish he could see that I don't want another man. I wish he could see that he is good enough.

"Go save your man," Jeremy chuckles, looking over at Will. When I follow his gaze I find Will with his arms crossed and drunken strangers trying to talk to him. He's being polite enough, but I didn't stop to think if this kind of setting may effect him due to his past.

I give Jeremy one last hug and head over to Will. When he

spots me coming back to him, he releases a sigh of relief and unfolds his arms. "Jeremy's friends are…interesting."

I smile, "We all are."

I slip my hand into his, lacing our fingers together. "Is this okay for you? We can leave if you're not comfortable."

Will answers by slipping his hand over my hip and planting a light kiss against my forehead. These little actions, so soft, so delicate, somehow mean more to me than the nights of fiery passion. How can I possibly have this with someone else? If Will truly wants this to end, I never thought I would understand the phrase 'the one that got away' until Will. How can he truly be that when he never wanted to stay to begin with?

After a few drinks I have forgotten the troubles that plague my heart. Even though the man in front of me is the cause of said troubles, it's fun to let my hair down and enjoy this house party. I have barged into people with my flailing arms, that I call dancing. I feel like I could puke at any moment, and every second that I don't is a victory.

I've laid off the alcohol for about an hour now, trying to prepare in advance for the hangover I'm going to have in the morning. A love ballad is playing on the speaker, I'm pretty sure it's a Taylor Swift song, but I'm so drunk I can't confirm. Right now I am in Will's arms, swaying together to the music. He's only had one drink tonight, I bet he saw the state of me and thought, *no thank you.*

"You're so comfortable," I mumble against his firm chest, the rapid beat of his heart punching me in the cheek. "You're comfier than my pillow."

Will kisses the top of my head, not responding to my drunken ramblings as he slowly dances with me. I feel his hands tighten around me, like he's suddenly afraid of letting go. I want him to be afraid, I want him to want me as much as

I do him. I want him to love me like I do. I want all of him to be *mine*.

Jeremy is right. I should tell him. Maybe it's the alcohol talking, maybe it's me, I should tell him. How will I get what I want if I don't ask for it? What if Will has the same feelings, and *I'm* the one who's not been clear for their intentions. After all, it was me who asked if we could 'pretend' until we can't anymore. And I can't pretend anymore.

I pull my head off of Will's chest, now feeling like a bag of sand has been used as a hat. I look up at him and drink in the intoxicating features of his face. My favourite feature is his eyes, a sparkling green that I want to paint my bedroom wall. "Will…"

His face changes, like he suddenly remembers something. "I have to go."

My heart stings, like a bee has been let loose and stinging its way through my chest.

"Are you going to be okay with Jeremy?"

I nod, of course. Jeremy has been keeping an eye on me this entire time, with our friend radar, especially when I'm drunk he never lets me out of his sight.

I don't get a chance to ask where Will is going, as he kisses me on the cheek and vanishes through the sea of people. He leaves me to stand alone in Jeremy's kitchen.

Did he know what I was going to confess? Does he really not want to hear it so he made a poor excuse to leave? He didn't even *make* an excuse. He just left.

I can't keep putting my heart through this. I can't keep hurting like this. I'm going to tell Will how I feel.

If I'm going to make an ass out of myself by telling him I love him, I'm going to do it in the most ridiculous way possible to soften the blow.

Chapter Thirty-Three

I'm beginning to wonder exactly *when* this became too much. Was it before or after I scattered rose petals on the bed and lit all of the candles in here, enough that it could send his entire house ablaze.

I don't care. Maybe if he focuses on the ridiculousness that is this room it will take away some of the heat when I confess my feelings.

Will gave me a key to his condo after our passionate night in the hot tub on New Year's Eve. He said it was for emergencies, in case I needed a place to hide from Simon. I haven't had to use it, since Simon has vanished from my life. I have never been more grateful for fate playing its part by giving me this key. I can make a bold statement with it, that he will come home to love if he gives me a real chance. I will kiss him on this bed every day until he is sick of me, I will make him feel worth a million dollars with just a look.

Now that I look around, it looks like I vomited love all over the room and it might be too intense. Maybe I should clear away some of the rose petals...

Click.

It's too late now, the front door has just closed which means he is home. A weird mixture of fear and excitement fills my chest, causing my heart to pound in an uncomfortable rhythm.

I run to the bed in my silk lingerie and get myself into a somewhat seductive position. Tucking my feet under my ass, I position my hair so it tumbles in waves down my shoulder. I try to exude a fake confidence, and not focus on how ridiculous I might look to someone looking in.

"Dinner was wonderful, Will."

All of the excitement in my heart vanishes when I hear a female voice. The small ray of hope has now plummeted further into darkness, completely snuffing out the light. My stomach begins to knot and tears threaten my eyes. When I hear footsteps approaching upstairs a sudden jolt of panic fuels my blood. I crawl off of his bed, a few petals sticking to my bear skin as I look around for a place to hide.

Their conversation is getting closer, and I have zero doubt they are on their way to his bedroom.

The wardrobe! I have no other choice than to jump inside and camouflage within his coats. His bathroom is too risky, if she decides she needs to 'freshen up' it would make hiding a pointless act.

I hide in front of his coats, so I can still see through the slits; it should be dark enough in here that they shouldn't catch me.

I was right, when the door to his bedroom swings open, Will isn't alone. They're laughing about something he had said, a smile I once thought was reserved for me. All of the laughter fades when Will takes in the scenery, the rose petals, the candles and the bottle of wine sitting on his bedside table. I can see him trying to put the pieces together, why the room is laid out this way but empty of the perpetrator

He knows this is my doing, unless there are more women in his life that would be willing to do the same.

"Oh, Will!" The woman he's with clasps her hands together and takes in the decor. "I thought this was just a dinner, I had no idea you wanted to seduce me."

It's hard to get a good look at her through the slits, but she is undoubtedly beautiful and well spoken. Her hair is a bright blonde and styled to perfection, she could easily be a glamour model. Her lips are a full crimson red that match her tight dress, revealing every curve and every line of her goddess-like figure. From what I can see, she and Will look good together.

Jealously spikes my body. Not only is she the most attractive woman I have ever seen, but she thinks Will set this up for her. That this whole romantic evening is for the two of them, when it is supposed to be mine.

Her polished fingernails trail up Will's firm chest, a devilish grin on her beautiful lips.

Push her away, I silently plead. *Prove that this is some misunderstanding, please-*

She kisses him, and it takes a lot to repress the hurt gasp that lodges in my throat. I can't rip my gaze away as she presses her body against his and devours his mouth with crimson lipstick.

Don't kiss her back. Please.

But he does.

I painfully watch as Will wraps his hands around her back and holds her close as he kisses her. It should be me in her place, this is meant to be my night with him. The night where I confess…

I can't watch this anymore. I silently sink to the floor and bury my face into my hands, strangling my sobs to be silent.

After what feels like a lifetime of hearing nothing but the sound of wet kisses, and her giggling, Will's voice suddenly says, "Sorry, I just realised that…I'm supposed to be picking my sister up from the airport."

Such a liar. An obvious lie.

"Can we maybe do this another time?"

"Oh," the rejection is clear in her voice. I imagine she is forcing a smile, possibly wiping the lipstick from his mouth. "Of course. I can see myself out."

Then the door closes and after a while I don't move. I stay curled up on the floor of his wardrobe, in a cloud of self loathing.

This is pathetic. Could there be any more of a sorry sight? Hiding in a wardrobe from a man that I am desperately in love with, when our entire "relationship" wasn't real to begin with? I set up this entire atmosphere, this whole night, to confess to him that I'm in love with him, and he clearly doesn't feel a single thing towards me. When my thoughts were consumed by him, was he fucking other girls?

Is that why he left Jeremy's party so abruptly? So he could hook up with her?

"Lucy?"

I snap my head up, the anger now boiling in my blood. I remain silent for a while, perhaps I could crawl further back into this wardrobe and escape to Narnia.

"Lucy, I know you're in here."

There is something about the way he said my name, like there was a tiredness to it. Almost as though he is fed up of me, and this silly little setting I have created for him.

I stand with my fists clenched at my sides. There is no point in hiding now, I can't stay in here forever, no matter how much I want to.

I push open his wardrobe door and find him at the foot of his bed, examining the petals that are laid out. When he turns to find me, fat tears fall down my cheeks.

"Lucy..." if I didn't know any better I'd say he looked guilty. But just like everything else up until now, I must be wrong.

"I've had enough," I turn away from him and dash out of his bedroom. I can't stand around and wait for him to mock me.

I don't even make it to the top of his stairs when he grabs my wrist to halt me from going any further.

I whirl around and snatch my hand back, he releases me without any hesitation. "Do not touch me!" I yell.

"Lucy, listen to me…"

"No!" All of my emotion, all of my pain, sorrow, and unrequited love slips out in that one single word. "This is *over!*"

I can barely see Will through the blur of tears. I have never felt so heartbroken, so betrayed, in my life. What stings even more, is that I'm not even sure if I have any right to feel this way. "I've had enough," my shoulders shake as I sob.

If the word "pathetic" had a visual example in the dictionary it would be a picture of me in this moment. Tears streaking down my red cheeks in a revealing silk lingerie dress.

I turn and hurry down the stairs, grabbing my coat from the hook. He was probably too busy with his new squeeze that he didn't even notice it hanging there.

"I don't want you going out like this," Will's voice is pleading. "Just stay until you calm down. Don't drive while you're like this, please."

It doesn't take a genius to know why, he doesn't want to feel responsible for someone else if they get hurt. Right now, I am so full of rage that I want to hurt him just as much as he has hurt me. "I'm clearly not your problem, Will."

"Lucy. I am begging you to listen to me, let me talk to you."

"Why should I?" I pull on my coat so hard that the sleeves might rip from the seams. "So you can act like you care about me? Fill your ego with your self righteous deeds."

"It's not an act," Will tried to stay calm at the beginning, now he has lost all control over the volume of his voice. "Just calm down so we can talk about this!"

This situation is becoming too much for both of us. The air feels tight, like neither one of use can inhale a cool breath. Just when we are about to find relief in our lungs, a fire ignites in our hearts.

"This is so typical of you," he snarls. "Running away before being given any form of clarity."

"Clarity? What clarity could I possibly need? I saw you with your tongue down that woman's throat in a romantic setting that *I* created."

"Why does it matter?!"

The question sends a static shock over my entire body, from my head to my toes. Why does it matter? The fact he even asked that question squeezed the last drop of hope out of my heart, ringing it dry for any possibility of a happy ending.

"Why are you acting like I have actually cheated on you?" His eyes are on fire. "Did you forget that *you* went on a date with some guy, laughed with me about how bad of a kisser he was?" Will punches a hand through his hair. "Or does that not fit your narrative?"

"My narrative?!" I shriek. "You are *delusional* if you think any of this had any substance to it! That this entire, *stupid*, plan made any sort of sense!"

I arch my back over, completely at a loss for what else to do. This entire situation is a mess, a ridiculous mess that neither of us should have been apart of. Straightening back up, I curled my lip at him. "You know what, I have been trying so hard to make you see that you mean something to me. That you are an important person in my life that I desperately don't want to lose."

"I am not yours to lose, Lucy!"

I don't think either of us are listening to one another. I heard what he said, but it's not fully registering with me right now. We're both speaking wildly, too freely, not thinking about what we are saying. I've had enough of hiding my heart away for the sake of others, for him.

"What even is this?" I whip my hand between the two of us. "I met your father, he believes that we're a real couple. So *why* are we still doing this?"

"You said you wanted to pretend! Pretend until we can't anymore!"

"Well, guess what, Will?" I scream. "I can't pretend anymore!"

"Do you want to know *why* I was here? *Why* I set up your bedroom, wearing this stupid outfit? *Why I am here?!*" I pull my hair away from my face. There is no use in lying anymore. I've already made a complete fool of myself, why not go out with a bang? "I am here because I wanted to tell you that I have fallen ridiculously in love with you. I love you with all of my stupid heart. There isn't a day that passes that I don't wish you were mine. So, no. I can't keep pretending because all of this feels *real* to me."

Will's face falls into something I do not recognise. It is a mixture of shock, understanding and somehow confusion. He opens his mouth to say something but he is silent. Which only adds the killing blow to my heart.

"I came here to tell you that," all of my yelling has tired into a whisper. "I came here to find out if you held any feelings towards me…"

The vision of him kissing that blonde woman flashes in my mind, and I wince.

"Lucy…"

"Well, I got my answer."

"Please…please don't go." If he says something after that I don't hear it, because I slam his door behind me without looking back.

Chapter Thirty-Four

It's been a week since I made a complete ass of myself. I had to drive home wearing silk lingerie underneath my coat. I'm just grateful I didn't get pulled over for speeding, I don't know how I would explain what happened to a police officer. I can hardly explain to myself what had happened.

The last thing I want right now is to be alone, I've been staying with my parents for a week and calling in sick to work to avoid the possibility of running into Will. Rosie seems disappointed every time I call, tells me to get well soon and hangs up.

Mom has been trying to subtly ask what has happened. I topped everything off with one last lie and told her we broke up. I couldn't get to the reason why, the tears that chocked my breath were too much to handle. Instead of pestering, Mom held me close and brought me a giant tub of ice cream that I ate in two sittings.

What did I really expect to come from this? This entire plan was doomed from the start. I haven't got a strong enough heart to fake date someone, I get attached far too easily. Yet, I can't imagine feeling this way about anyone else. How Will made me feel, the way he touched me, how he effortlessly made me laugh when he wasn't being a pain in the ass...how could all of that be fake?

My phone vibrates in my pocket. I have been avoiding looking at my phone, there have been no texts from Will. He hasn't tried to get in touch with me since that night, which adds salt to my already oversized wound. I'm surprised when I see Erik's name flashing on my screen.

"Hello?"

"Hey, Lucy remember me?" There's a playfulness in his tone, which manages to coax a smile out of me. "I'm sorry that I haven't been in touch since our date. Things at work have been crazy!"

"Don't worry," I say. "I've been pretty busy too."

We small talk for a little while. No mention of a second date came up, thank god.

"The reason I am calling is because my company has an opening for a junior graphic designer." Erik said. "If you're interested, email me your portfolio and I'll get you in for an interview."

My heart swells to twice the size. I never thought I would feel emotional about a job interview, it's not a guaranteed position but I am being offered a chance. When so many other places have rejected me, didn't even look at my application, it really made me feel worthless.

Now Erik is willing to give me a chance. Maybe my life is finally turning around.

"I'll text you my email address, along with the other details." Erik said. "Are you interested?"

It's only when he asked that question did I realise I was stunned into silence. "Yes!" It comes out louder, more desperate than I intended but Erik only chuckles down the line. "Thank you, Erik. Thank you so much for this opportunity."

"Don't thank me yet," he said, I can hear him smiling. "You have to wow the people on the hiring committee. That being said, I don't think that will be an issue for you."

* * *

I'm finally getting a chance to take a huge leap in my career. Erik went through most of the details with me over the phone, giving me a taste of what the company is looking for. It seems my skillset, and style would be a perfect fit for this place. It's a publishing company, and they are mostly looking for a junior graphic designer to help put together concepts for book covers. I can't help but be reminded of Will and the cover I designed for his book. I will be using that as an example of previous experience, it should give me an edge. I doubt Will will use the cover I designed for him now, after how I humiliated myself in front of him, why would he want a reminder of that?

It's been two weeks since I've seen him, or heard anything from him. I was dreading the shifts at the flower shop, that he might turn up and fill the air with an awkward fog that I can't escape from.

Will never showed up.

He hasn't tried to call, or text, or anything. I appreciate that he might want to give me space, especially after how angry I was when I left him. I can't help but feel disappointed that he hasn't tried to get in touch. It's just another nail in the coffin that this entire fake relationship meant nothing to him. That all of the moments we shared were confined to that one single moment, and they would become nothing more than a memory.

I meet Erik outside of his office, when he spots me a smile forms on his life. He looks almost relieved, like he wasn't sure whether I would actually show up. Little does he know how much I want this job, how I would fight my way through a burning building just to make it to this interview.

Seeing him in person after so long, I am suddenly reminded of our interesting kiss outside of the flower shop.

How my face felt like it had been licked by a salivating dog, and how he spent more time making out with my chin than my lips.

"You look great," he touches my shoulder.

"Thank you," I take one last look at my appearance through the window, checking there aren't any loose buttons, my pencil skirt hasn't torn against my thighs, and my hair is still in a neat bun behind my head. I look ready to take on this interview, I *feel* ready. I'm not going to sit in that room and doubt my work, I am going to own it because I do *own* it. The work in my portfolio is mine, and I'm going to show it off the way that it deserves, instead of it being overshadowed by my anxiety and doubt.

Before heading inside, I check that my phone is on silent. I don't want anything to interrupt this opportunity. Before I shut it off completely, I see a text from my mom that reads:

Mom: Good luck on your interview! You'll do great! Make sure you stop by the house when you are done xx

I text her back and tell her I will. After I got the call from Erik I returned to my usual life in my boring apartment. I had to make sure my portfolio was up to date and once I was satisfied with the work I am going to present, my thoughts were consumed on the answers I would give. I had to train myself not to doubt my answers, I've waited too long to waste it on insecurity.

With my mom asking to see her after the interview…I don't want to be thinking about after the interview, I don't want to focus on the ending, I need to be fully available in this moment. I am snapped back into my current situation when Erik asks. "Ready?"

I nod, and exhale my anxiety out of my body — at least until the interview is over.

* * *

I keep my shoulders straight, my back held high and my chin elevated to exude confidence. There are three people conducting this interview, Erik included. It's hard to get a read on their opinions of my work, I can't confidently say whether they like it or not. They all have a poker face as they flip through print outs of my previous work.

I answer all questions as fully as possible, not allowing myself to stammer. I need to prove that I am worthy of this job, my work is worth investing in and I explain how eager I am to learn and build upon my already established skillsets.

I'm grateful to have Erik, he seems to be coaching them and encouraging my work. He seems to be an important figure in this company, that his opinion truly matters.

The interview came to a close, and they excused themselves for a few minutes leaving me to go over every single detail of what I had just said. I can't find faults with any of my answers, I did fumble a few times but I tried not to let it get to me. I managed to shake it off and continue with answering their questions.

I'm a bit nervous that they left the room. Usually, once the interview is over I am thanked for coming and then told I will hear from them in one to two weeks (that's if I am successful).

Once they have deliberated they file back into the room and take their seats. I steal a glance at Erik who shoots me a wink, which makes that small light of hope ignite in my chest. I try not to show it on my face, it could just mean that they are going to let me down easy.

The gentleman in the centre, who looks to be in his late forties with a larger build and grey stubble outlining his jaw, leans forward with a tickle of a smile on his mouth. "We don't normally do this," he said, causing my palms to sweat. "However, we are so impressed with your work." He puts a hand over Erik's shoulder and gives him a light shake before returning his attention on me. "This man has a skill at finding raw talent."

Talent.

It shouldn't matter that this stranger sees me as talented, but I am going to shamelessly relish in it. After constant rejection I am proud to impress someone with my hard work.

"We want to offer you the position as a junior graphic designer," his smile widens, along with the others. "We think you will make an excellent addition to our team, and that you can really grow into something exceptional."

My heart is pounding in my ears. Any restraint of maintaining a pokerface has vanished and I am grinning so much that my jaw hurts.

"If you need time to think it over — "

"No," my excitement gets the better of me. "I one hundred percent accept."

"Excellent," they all share a proud look, and I'm fighting so hard not to spill tears of joy.

Finally.

Finally.

My life is turning around. All of the stress and anxiety seems like a waste of time, looking back. If only I could see into the future, reassure myself that everything will work out.

If I could do that, I probably would have saved myself a lot of heartache in the process.

Chapter Thirty-Five

I should be happy, I got the job as a junior graphic designer for a company that fits my skills. My job is to be creative, come up with concepts and pitch ideas with a group of seemingly wonderful people. Yet, I can't shake this hollow feeling in my chest. Something is missing and I hate knowing what it is. I hate that I can't have the one person who my heart craves the most.

Maybe I could meet someone at work? Start again and develop a real relationship where nothing is confusing. Maybe I could give Erik one more chance, maybe that kiss was just a *very* off kiss for him. At least we both would know where we are headed if we decided to pursue a relationship.

That should fill me with hope but it only makes me more sad.

I arrive at my parents house, ready to give them the news that I got the job, only to find that their car isn't on the drive. Which is odd, considering they insisted that I drive down here the moment my interview ended to tell them how it went.

They're normally at home right now, and if they were going out they wouldn't have told me to stop by.

Maybe Mom wanted a spontaneous outing, I wouldn't put it past her.

I put my key in the door only to find that it won't turn to unlock, because it already is. My heart stalls for a moment and I swallow down a lump the size of a golfball. Mom always locks the door when she leaves, she's particularly anal about that.

I decide to head inside, maybe not the best idea if my parents have been kidnapped or robbed.

I look around the hallway and find nothing amiss, no tables knocked over and all of the pictures are still hanging on the wall.

Why do I still get the feeling like I'm not alone?

That's when my eye catches on red and white rose petals on the floor. It doesn't look like someone accidentally dropped them, it forms a trail leading to the closed living room door.

What the hell is going on? I feel like I have walked into some bizarre thriller movie.

I slowly open the door to the living room and my eyes are overwhelmed by the sight of flowers, taking up every single corner of the room. There is everything from roses, to lilies, to sunflower and so much more that I could be here all day trying to find the different varieties. Then I find the person that put all of these here, his green eyes finding mine through all of this noise.

Will.

He's here in my parents living room, but why? And wearing a black three piece suit, like he is the groom at a wedding. If this is some sort of sick joke, a way for him to tell me he is getting married, it will be easy to turn my love into hate. If that is what he is doing, he truly is the biggest asshole to walk this earth.

"What's going on?" I ask as I step further into the room.

Will meets me in the middle, and offers his signature nonchalant shrug.

"How did you do all of this?"

"I asked your mom if I could," he beams a smile, seemingly very proud of himself. "It was the only place I could think of. I would have done it in your apartment but I don't have a key."

I look around, expecting my parents to jump out like some sort of weird surprise party. "Where are my parents?"

"Out. I paid for a romantic evening for the two, dinner and a night in a hotel so we could be alone."

My heart sinks. Is all of this because he wants to sleep with me one last time? Is goodbye sex even a thing?

I must be wearing my emotions on my face, as Will's face holds nothing more than sincerity."Lucy," the way he says my name still sends a shiver down my spine.

All of these flowers can't mask the boiling rage in my blood. "Don't say my name like that, like this isn't some game to you."

"It's not."

"No?" I curl my hands into fists. "So, what is this? A way for you to get in my pants and play with my heart just a little bit more?"

A hurt cascades over his features, and my heart is thrashing against my ribcage so violently it might explode out of me.

"I have been so stupid, and selfish and…well, an asshole."

I will not argue with that.

"When you told me you loved me…I…I can't even begin to tell you how happy I was."

"Could have fooled me!"

A smirk tickles his lips but that soon vanishes. "But it also scared me because I don't deserve the love from a woman who is so beautiful, talented, kind, and…just so perfect in every single way."

"I'm not perfect enough apparently." The vision of him

kissing that other woman, the beautiful blonde that he held in his arms as I whimpered in the wardrobe flashes before my eyes. "Did you get bored of that blonde?"

Will exhales a deep sigh, "Lucy," the way he says my name, like it coats a physical pain over his body makes my legs weak. "That night was a mess. A complete disaster."

I scoff.

"We had dinner to discuss publishing my book through her company," he explains. "She's a publisher who works with indie authors. I went to grab my laptop to show her the cover you had made, I didn't expect her to follow me, and when she saw the room...well, you know what happened."

Yes, I do know what happened, I had to watch as she kissed him and mistook my romantic gesture for his.

"You still kissed her back." Tears blur my vision of him.

"I didn't know what else to do," Will's face is pleading with me, begging me to believe him. "I didn't want to, I wasn't thinking."

Is it fair for me to be this angry at him when I kissed Erik? I wasn't in love with Will then but didn't I technically do the same thing. Perhaps I am being too harsh on him, when I know he already carries a lot of guilt for things that aren't his fault. Who am I to add to that?

"I'm not perfect."

"No," he smiles. "You can be annoying — " I swat his arm which gets a small chuckle out of him, and he reaches for my hands and holds them in between us. "I was just so afraid of disappointing you because..."

Will dips his head, the ends of his black hair veiling his face for a moment before looking deeply into my eyes. I can't look away, I don't want to. Those dazzling emeralds have captivated my attention fully, just like they did the night we met.

"I love you, Lucy."

I don't bother to stop the tears that trickle down my face. I must be dreaming, William Dawson just told me he *loves* me. There was no joke, no 'gotcha' moment. When he said those three words I felt my heart beat in time with his own.

"You have somehow pieced together my broken heart and made it whole again. I can't imagine my life without you now, I tried when you left. These past few weeks have been torture, and I am too selfish to let you go. I will spend the rest of my life showering you with love and happiness that you will get sick of it."

I push out a laugh, and smile wider than I ever have before.

Will brings my hands to his mouth and place a kiss on every fingertip. "I want to have a real relationship with you, I want to then marry you, have babies with you and I...I just want a life with you."

"You really mean it?"

He nods, filling my heart with a warm golden glow. "Yeah," he drops his voice to a hoarse whisper. "I'm crazy about you, Lucy. I love you. But I will understand if you don't want this, if I..."

"Shut up," I reach up and kiss him deeply on his lips. I wrap my arms around his neck and press my entire body against his. Will holds me up and tangles his fingers through my hair. I open my mouth and invite his sweet tongue inside and hum with delight as we kiss like it's our last. But it won't be our last, it is the start of a new life together.

"Did you really buy all of these flowers for me?" I say in between kisses.

"They may or may not have been in the clearance section," he smiles and I can't help but laugh. Will pushes me suddenly at arms length and locks his gaze to mine, mirroring the desire I feel. "Seriously though, I think I spent over a thousand dollars on these so you'd better make sure these stay alive for at least five years."

I look around and notice that there isn't a single surface that doesn't have a vase of flowers, or some sort of arrangement. "My dad will be mad if these flowers are covering the TV by the time he gets back."

"They won't be back until tomorrow." The devilish look on his face makes my knees turn to jelly. Luckily, Will scoops me up into his arms like a hero saving a woman from a burning building in a romance movie, and carries me upstairs to my bedroom. I can't help but giggle when he nearly trips up over his own eager feet to get there.

Will throws me down onto the bed, and starts taking off his blazer and vest.

"Why are you dressed like that?"

"I thought it would be more romantic," he goes to work unbuttoning his shirt, revealing his god-like body beneath. "Why? Would you have preferred that speech given in sweatpants and a band t-shirt?"

"No," I bite my bottom lip, too distracted by his muscled arms, the deep V trailing down his lower hips. He's gorgeous, and he's mine.

Will climbs on top of me and picks up right where we left off downstairs. One hand grips my outer thigh, whilst the other cups around my breast. I grind my hips against him, feeling his firm cock pushed against his trousers. I'm about to rip them off when Will pulls away from me and takes a long look at my attire.

"You look smart," his breath comes out breathless. "Did you decide to change up your wardrobe?"

I shake my head, "No, I actually had a job interview today." The joy that I should have felt leaving the office has finally come into effect. I am grinning and giggling like I am high, but I don't care.

Will looks at me expectantly, waiting for me to deliver the

good news that is written all over my face.

"I am officially a junior graphic designer for a publishing company."

"That's amazing!" He kisses me hard on the mouth. "Congratulations! You deserve it, but I think my mother will be upset to lose her favourite employee."

"You can take that position," I kiss his jaw.

"Ha, she will put herself before me in that regard."

When Will pulls away I'm confused when his face falls into sadness, it's only when I feel him brush away a tear streaking down my cheek I realise why.

"Are you not happy?"

"I'm probably the happiest I have ever felt in my life," yet the tears still fall. "I think…I'm afraid that it's all too good to be true."

Will plants a kiss on my forehead, "Well, no matter what happens you will always have me. I'm afraid you are stuck with me from now on."

"I just have one question." I bring my lips up so they are almost touching his. "Do you want to fuck me with this skirt on…or off?"

That shit-eating-grin is back and it's now mine to kiss and devour. "Defiantly on," he growls.

Will flips me so I am lying on my front, my face buried into the mattress. Raising my hips and bringing me to my knees, his hands smooth the curve of my ass. "Fuck," he groans. "Why haven't you worn a skirt like this before?"

I bite my bottom lip, "I can assure you it's for professional purposes only."

Will growls and lowers my panties down my thighs and tosses them to the ground. The bed dips as Will removes his trousers and boxers, I eagerly wait for him to slip inside of me, fill me like I desperately crave. Only, when he bunches up my skirt I'm not greeted by his thick length but his wet tongue. On my hands and knees, I feel weak at his tentative embrace. My eyes roll in the back of my head when I hear his own grunting and his licks become faster and faster. I can picture him touching himself, only making my core crave him more.

"Please…" I whimper.

"Please, what?" He doesn't remove his mouth from me to ask. "Tell me what you want."

"You," I breathe, gripping the sheets in tight fits. "To fuck me. Now."

Will presses the tip of his cock against my entrance, teasing me with long strokes. I push back, trying to slip myself down on him, but Will squeezes my ass. "Lucy," the way he said my name, with such a delicate thickness makes me swallow back my emotions.

Slipping his hands around my torso, Will positions me so I am sitting on his lap, hovering over the tip of his cock. My cheeks burn with heat, needing him to stop teasing me and slip inside of me already. I swallow hard as he starts to fill me in such a painfully slow way that I want to devour him in one thrust.

"I love you, Lucy." He whispers against my ear. "I love you with everything in my heart."

I place my hand over his knuckles, digging my fingers into his skin until I swallow him whole.

"I knew from the moment I saw you sitting alone at that bar that I was going to be in trouble."

"Will," I breathe, knocking my head back and leaning against his broad shoulder.

He brings up his hips once, giving me just a taste of what to expect. "In that little blue dress, far too sexy and gorgeous to be there without a date."

Another thrust, and a cry of pleasure bursts from my lips.

"I was going to walk away," he bites my ear. "But I was so

drawn to you...I just couldn't walk away. Not from you." Will grabs my chin and pulls me to look at him, a fog of desire coating my gaze. His eyes clear that fog, showing me the path to his heart. "That was the beginning of everything, Lucy. From that night I could never just walk away. We'd always find our way back to one another, always."

"I love you," it comes out as a throaty whisper.

We weren't done talking, it became mixed with the sound of our equal sexual desire as he thrust into me over and over again. Pushing me further and further over the edge, with the sound of my ass slapping against his hips. I whimpered out *I love yous* until I couldn't talk anymore.

We climbed the mountain together and tumbled down into a climax, his arms not moving from my torso as he held me flush against him.

"No more pretending," I muttered.

"It's you and me, Lucy." Will kisses my cheek. "Forever, and real."

Epilogue

Two Years Later…

I couldn't ask for anything better. My career has truly taken off in the past two years, Will and I have a strong and stable relationship and all-in-all the future is looking bright. It's strange to look back on that time in my life, working at the flower shop, the fake dating, and the whole dark cloud of uncertainty that followed me, that I would come out the other side brighter and happier than ever.

I can't picture my life any differently now. The fake dating was such an outlandish and bizarre decision, that Will still cracks jokes about between the two of us. Even Jeremy joins in sometimes, since he was the only other person that knew about our little scheme.

I'm no longer living in the past. My focus is on my future and the endless possibilities that come with it. There are many paths that I can take, and that thought doesn't fill me with dread like it used to. I'm excited about the unknown, because what I do know is that no matter what choices I make I will always have Will by my side.

We have both taken a break from our jobs, Will even promised not to bring his laptop to Spain since I know he would spend all of his time writing the next book in his trilogy. Much to his fans dismay that he's taking a small break, I'm happy to have him to myself.

Work had encouraged me to take a break. I've been pushing myself to get concepts approved, and working on new layouts that they told me I deserve a holiday. And they assured me there will be plenty of work for me when I get back.

Right now, none of that matters. I am walking along the beach with the sound of the waves crashing against the shore. Hand in hand with the love of my life, the man who's name is tattooed on my heart. Accompanying us tonight are the stars, lighting our way light spotlights on a stage that is all our own.

Will abruptly stops and stands in my view. He looks at me like no one else does, with pure and unfiltered love. Those eyes that captivate me drink in every feature, every blemish, every curve with complete admiration. He reaches out and tucks a strand of my chestnut hair behind my ear and lingers his hand over my cheek. His large thumb stroking my skin, leaving heat in his wake. "My Lucy," he whispers.

I'm so proud of the man Will has become. When we officially started dating two years ago, he started going to therapy to help with his guilt and grief over his brother. It was hard for him, and his feelings didn't change over night. Now it's two years later, and he has come to accept what happened that night and that he shouldn't put all of the blame on his shoulders.

"I don't know where I would be right now if I hadn't met you," his eyes never waver from my face. "Probably wasting away in a bar, and feeling nothing but pain." He offers a small smile. "But then you came into my life, and you changed everything."

Tears are surrounding my eyes, a burning lump forming in my throat. I remain silent as he continues to stroke my cheek with his thumb.

"You've put up with so much from me, you've been there for me, and loved me at times I really didn't deserve it."

"Will…"

I gasp when he gets down on one knee, and fishes for a box from his blazer pocket. My world freezes at the sight of him, a moment I truly wasn't expecting on this trip. I always thought it would be obvious when he proposed, that I could see it coming, but I can't - I didn't.

Will kneels in front of me, holding up a closed box to me and I remain frozen in my stance.

"I promise I will spend the rest of my life being there for you, protecting you and loving you. Every single day I will do those things. Lucy, I love you so much that I can't imagine my life without you." Will opens the box, and inside is a beautiful diamond ring and a loud sob escapes from my lips before I can catch it. "Will you marry me?"

I nod, I don't even have to think about it. "Yes," I open up my arms and dive on his chest, kissing him fiercely on the mouth as tears spill down my cheeks. "Yes, yes, yes." I can't stop smiling and crying and kissing him.

Will takes my hand and places the ring on my finger and it feels so right. This ring was supposed to be on my finger, and I wouldn't feel this if it came from anyone else.

From the moment we met it has been Will and I against the world. I can't wait to see what our future brings. All I do know, is that I will be cherishing him, and the love we share, for the rest of my life.

THE END

ACKNOWLEDGEMENTS

I've had so much fun writing this book. Lucy and Will hold a special place in my heart and I hope they do in yours. I want to always thank you, the reader, first in my acknowledgments. I can't tell you how amazing (and scary) it is to write and have people read my work. So thank you for reading, and sharing in my love for these characters and their stories.

Thank you for all of my followers on BookTok (shameless plug but follow me on TikTok: @ellie'sbookcase). Thank you for all of the support, love and advice whenever I need it. I feel truly blessed to be apart of such a community.

I also want to thank my partner, Kyle. Again. There won't be a book that I write where you are not thanked or acknowledged...unless you annoy me near publication date. Seriously, as always I can't thank you enough for the endless amount of support and love you show towards me and my work. Thank you for always letting me interrupt you games, or whatever it is you are doing, to listen to my work whenever I need opinions.

I would also like to thank Emily Wittig Designs for the beautiful cover artwork! I couldn't be happier with it! Give her a follow on her social media and check out the beautiful covers she creates.

ABOUT THE AUTHOR

As you may have guessed E.M.Mavis spends any and all of her free time writing. If she is not writing, she will be hiding away from the world and escaping into books of romance or fantasy. For hobbies outside of reading, E.M.Mavis enjoys playing video games like Final Fantasy (with an ever-growing collection of merchandise to prove it) and Overwatch.

E.M.Mavis knew she wanted to become an author ever since she was in school, where she would bring a notepad and pencil to class and handwrite stories.

She currently lives in England with her boyfriend, Kyle and two pet rats.

Printed in Great Britain
by Amazon

84805835R00159